A Taste Of Seduction

A SECOND CHANCE REGENCY ROMANCE

THE DISGRACED LORDS
BOOK FIVE

BRONWEN EVANS

A Taste of Seduction
A Disgraced Lords Novel
By Bronwen Evans

Blurb - A Taste of Seduction

The flames of desire fuel a torrid reunion as bestselling author Bronwen Evans returns with another captivating novel of the Disgraced Lords. See why Jen McLaughlin raves, "Bronwen's historical romances always make the top of my reading list!"

Lady Evangeline Stuart chose to wed a tyrant with a title, or so society believes. That was five years ago   five long years she could have spent with her first and only love: Lord Hadley Fullerton, the second son of the Duke of Claymore. Now Evangeline is a widow, and her soul cries out for Hadley. But when they see each other at last, everything has changed. The passion in his eyes has been corrupted by betrayal. Somehow Evangeline must regain Hadley's trust—without revealing the secret that would spoil the seduction.

Hadley is determined not to be distracted by Evangeline. He and the other Libertine Scholars are in pursuit of an enemy who has been striking at them from the shadows, and Evangeline's mere presence could be dangerous. But with one smile, one touch, one taste of Evangeline's lips, Hadley's resolve is overpowered by much more pleasant memories. As the two enter into a discreet affair, Hadley vows to give her his body, never his heart. That she will have to earn.

Prologue

SURREY, ENGLAND, 1811

The shade of the weeping willows protected her from the heat of the afternoon sun, but nothing could cool Evangeline's blood. She fondled the note Stowe had given her half an hour ago. She'd never regretted saving the young stable boy from his brute of a father two years ago. Stowe worshiped her and was the key to keeping her relationship with Hadley a secret from her mother.

She reread the missive Hadley had sent her. He wanted to see her—urgently—so she'd saddled Rosten, her dapple-gray gelding, and galloped straight to their usual meeting place.

"Urgently" could mean only one thing: he had news on their planned elopement.

Her nerves on edge, her body strung as taut as a bow, she had to use all her mental strength to sit patiently waiting for her love in their favorite spot under the willow tree in the paddock behind his stable.

Lord Hadley Fullerton, the second son of the Duke of Claymore, was prepared to defy Evangeline's mother, and his own family if need be, to make her his wife. Her heart burst with joy.

How had she got so lucky?

She'd met Hadley three years ago, when she was a young girl of sixteen. He'd been staying at his hunting lodge, which bordered her family's crumbling estate. She hadn't understood at the time, but the morning she stumbled upon him he'd been out drinking in the local tavern, as any young man of twenty-two would have been, and he'd ridden straight into a low-hanging branch, knocking himself off his horse. He'd fallen into a drunken sleep right where he'd landed on the path.

Evangeline had almost ridden over him. However, when she rolled him over, she'd thought him the most handsome man she'd ever clapped eyes upon, and when he'd woken up to find her cradling his head in her lap, he'd asked if she was an angel. That was the exact moment she'd fallen in love.

They had stayed in contact, writing to each other and seeing each other whenever he visited his hunting lodge, which was every month once she'd turned nineteen, a little over eight months ago. A neighbor, Sir Clifford, had held a small ball on her birthday, which her mother had allowed her to attend, and when Hadley danced with her, she'd known he was the one. Over the past eight months their relationship had strengthened and developed into something more grown-up.

Very grown-up. Sensual awareness flickered over her body. When Hadley kissed her she wanted to melt. Melt into him. She wanted to be claimed by him so badly, but like the gentleman he was, he refused to compromise her and was content to wait until they wed.

Finally, she heard footsteps approaching, and she ran her hand over her hair, pinched her cheeks, and tugged the bodice of her gown lower. More than determined that she would not wait any longer to be made love to, she needed to look like a temptress. If the elopement was organized, then she wanted the first time Hadley made love to her to be here, beneath their tree, on the estate that would be their home, rather than in some coaching inn at Gretna Green.

The branches were swept aside and Hadley walked toward

her. Her heart thrilled at the sight of him, while her thighs clenched in heightened anticipation. What would he feel like on top of her, in her. . . . She waved her hand in front of her face, trying to quell her lustful hunger.

Upon seeing her, he lengthened his stride. He moved with a combination of polished elegance and raw virility that saw her body respond as if it had a mind of its own. Heat and moisture gathered at her womanly core, while his handsomeness stole her breath.

His smile turned sensual, as if he could read her thoughts and had already agreed that they no longer needed to wait.

He stopped before her, and she had to crane her neck to look up the long, muscled length of him. His light brown hair appeared darker in the shade, as did his blue eyes, which were an even deeper blue than normal, almost black-blue, full of heat and desire. He was endowed with a masculine beauty that startled at first glance. It was likely women would deny him nothing; God knew she couldn't.

But it wasn't his striking looks or his family's status that drew her to him. She could probably have married a title if she'd wanted to, and certainly a peer with more money. It was the man who had won her heart. He quite simply was the sweetest, most honorable, kindest, and cleverest man she'd ever met. He'd cared not a fig about her lack of dowry or her family's dire financial straits. He loved her exactly as she was: a little bit wild, mostly unconventional, and quite outspoken.

Despite her mother's doing her utmost to keep her locked away, parading her only when rich gentlemen came to call, she had found love on her terms, in the arms of a handsome man who would cherish her—even though she was the penniless daughter of an almost bankrupt deceased earl.

She finally looked into his eyes. His gaze was fixed intently on her, the flare of heat turning his eyes the deepest of blues. She wished he'd say something, anything, but most of all she wished he'd tell her that the plan they had devised would work.

Finally he gave a slow smile that made her flush deepen. "I have my brother's blessing. He'll stand by our elopement and welcome you into our family."

Her mouth dried as she felt the tears of joy well. The Duke of Claymore accepted her. "I knew I'd love your brother."

"He even agreed to loan me the money for my vines. He recognizes that he owes me for all the times I took the beatings from Father when it should have been him."

She winced recalling the stories Hadley had told her about his father's brutality. Why were men so cruel? Both Stowe's father and Hadley's father had seemed to take pleasure in hurting their children. She would never understand how any person could hurt a child, not to mention their own.

Hadley continued. "It will take a few years before the grapes produce enough high-quality wine to earn well, but when they do, we will never have to worry about money again. We won't be wealthy, but you won't want for most things." He looked at her as if she were his whole world. "I can't believe you've given up the chance to take the *ton* by storm. You could marry a man who could clothe you in silks, house you in a castle, and give you the biggest sapphires to match your eyes."

"I don't want a big house, loads of jewels, or the most fashionable gowns—well, maybe a bit of fashion," she said jokingly. He smiled at her honesty. She reached out her hand and entwined her fingers with his. She pulled him down to sit next to her. "All I have dreamed of for the past three years is being your wife, your lover, and the mother of your children—our children."

"You will be."

She nodded, excitement building. "My mother would never openly object to our marriage if the Duke of Claymore gives us his blessing."

"I'll do everything I can to try to help your younger brother keep the estate afloat until he's old enough to sort out your family's financial woes. Your mother will have to live very frugally, but she won't be thrown out on the street."

She flung her arms around his neck and kissed him with all her heart. "Thank you. I feel a weight is lifted knowing I'm not abandoning my brother to the poorhouse. I almost felt obliged to marry one of Mother's men. Since it was Mother's gambling that saw us ruined, I will ensure that you hold the purse strings, so that there is an estate for Edward to run."

"In three days we will elope to Gretna Green. I've organized to borrow Augustus's coach, and once we are married, my friend Lord Arend Aubury has loaned us his hunting lodge near York for a short honeymoon."

She steeled herself against the hollowness in her chest. This was not how she envisaged her wedding, but if she ended up married to the man sitting next to her, she didn't really care how that occurred. She was the daughter of an earl, yet she had to sneak away as if in disgrace to wed the second son of a duke, all because of her mother's greed. If her mother had her way, she'd be sold off to the highest bidder.

At her quietness, he said, "You are not having second thoughts? You do love me?"

She cupped his face in her hands. She loved Hadley so much it was an ache inside her. Yet she could not help but think of Edward and the lean years ahead for him. "I hope Edward can forgive me."

"When he's old enough he'll understand. He loves you. He wouldn't want you to be unhappy."

She lay down in the cool moss, pulling Hadley with her. "Nothing would make me happier than becoming your wife. Well, maybe one thing . . . make love to me, here, now."

How was a man to deny such a sensual offer? His body burned to be buried deep within Evangeline. All his life he'd strived to be a better man. A man better than his brutal, scandal-ridden, and probably pox-riddled father; unlike his departed father, Hadley held his honor in high regard.

He'd sworn he'd claim her only when they married. He'd spent three years getting to know Evangeline, but the last eight months had been torture. She'd matured into a beautiful, sensual woman, but damn it all, he was nothing like his father, and he could wait a few days more and do this properly—when she was his wife.

"I can't wait to make you my wife, but then and only then will I make love to you. I don't want anyone to accuse me of being dishonorable. We will be the subjects of gossip as it is, for eloping."

His heart swelled with pride. This beautiful young woman had put her life, her heart, into his hands. He'd cherish her for the rest of his life.

An eager Evangeline pressed her soft curves against him. "Why must we wait?"

He inwardly smiled, his erection lengthening as she rubbed against him. "I want to do this right. I want your first time to be special—in a bed, with your husband." Since he was twenty-five, it was up to him to be the sensible one.

"I don't need a bed, only you. I have plans to marry only you."

Her gaiety was infectious. Her laughter soothed his soul and sent tingles down his spine. He drew in a sharp breath as her fingers found his erection. She molded her palm to his length and rubbed. Over the last few months he had taught her too well.

He'd loved introducing her to passion. She gave herself freely and unreservedly. Her desire matched his own, and it was only through his determination and will of iron that he had not taken her maidenhood already. They had done everything but.

"Please," she whispered in his ear. "I want to end this magical day with you inside me. To be claimed and loved by you. It won't be long until we escape to freedom, and then we will marry. I can't wait even that long."

Her hand had worked its way through the placket of his trousers, and he gasped as her clever fingers wrapped round him. He drew back and looked into her eyes. They were brimming with love—and desire.

"You tempt me so much," he declared, and meant every word.

How many nights had he twisted and turned in a fever, dreaming of lying above her, sliding deep within her, and claiming her forevermore. "I've waited over three years—I can wait another few days. Let me do the honorable thing."

"Honor be damned. I want the first time I lie with you to be here, in our special place, in your garden—our garden. I suspect that once we elope we will have to consummate the marriage at Gretna Green. I want to have the memory of you deep inside me, here, where we intend to live happily ever after. Please don't deny me that."

Evangeline looked at him earnestly, and he understood her point. Every time they walked in their grounds, when their children and their grandchildren played here, they would remember this special spot and how they had marked their house, this land, with love.

With no further doubts he took her lips in a kiss meant to convey his desire to please her, to love her—always.

They lay together under the willow tree at the end of the rose garden. No servants were about because he'd informed them to stay away. He didn't want anyone to see Evangeline visit. They had been sneaking visits, and while he knew his staff were loyal, he had to be careful, especially as her mother would try to stop them from eloping.

She wanted Evangeline to marry into wealth in order to save the estate for her younger brother, Edward. Hadley swallowed down his jealousy. She had the beauty, wit, and pedigree to do just that, yet she loved him.

She'd chosen him.

He had no idea what sums of money Evangeline's family required. Money, or more specifically lack of it, was the bane of his existence. If he had more money, he'd give her a dream wedding with the whole of the *ton* at her feet.

What scared him was that, even without a dowry, she was beautiful enough to interest any man. She could have any man she wanted, even a duke. He still couldn't believe she wanted him. His conscience nagged him because she was still quite young. She hadn't had a season, either, so she had not had a chance to meet other men. Her mother couldn't afford a season, so instead she got invited to as many house parties as possible, so that she could shop her daughter through the pool of moneyed sharks. The urgency to elope vibrated through every bone in his body because he knew sharks didn't waste time before biting.

He couldn't help wondering if, in the future, she would think she'd made a mistake settling for him.

Her lips pressing at his throat made him refocus on the pleasure at hand. If he took her now, she'd have no choice but to wed him. He cursed his selfishness and rebuked the idea. It would have to be her choice.

"If I make love to you, you will have no option but to marry me."

Her frown was instant. "Whom else would I marry?"

He sighed and pulled her against him. "You've not even had a season. If your family could afford it, you would take the *ton* by storm and you could have your pick of suitors. You could become a duchess or countess or—"

"I'd rather become Lady Hadley Fullerton."

"How do you know, if you haven't met anyone else?"

He felt her shudder. "My mother has introduced me to many men." She snuggled against his chest, her hand pressing over his heart. "I just know I'll never love anyone as much as I love you. You're in my soul."

They lay under their tree, hugging each other tightly, as his body argued with his mind. They should wait, he knew. But when she murmured against his chest, "I love you," over and over, his will deserted him.

She gave a cry of protest as he pulled back, but her smile returned when he began removing his jacket. He made quick work of discarding the garment. Evangeline quickly sat up and presented her back to him, urging him to help with her dress.

His hands shook as he slipped each hook undone. Today he

would claim his heart's desire. He'd never been so happy, and he wanted to remember this feeling forever.

The heat meant she had not worn a corset. He had seen her naked before, many times, but as she lay spread out before him, a tempting treat, covered only by her thin shift, his throat choked with emotion.

This moment was sacred.

He could barely move, so overcome was he with love for her.

She shyly smiled at him before pulling her shift up and over her head. She wore no undergarments except stockings, and Hadley could barely control his hungry response to the goddess before him.

Her auburn hair fell in waves around creamy shoulders, hiding her long slender neck. Already a few twigs and leaves had become tangled in it; he'd have to remember to pick them out later. But his eyes were drawn to her pert breasts with hard, darkened nipples begging to be suckled. She had a narrow waist, flaring out at her bonny hips. He couldn't wait to grip them as he slid deep within her. Her stomach was slightly rounded, and the thatch of copper-colored hair between her milky thighs sent his blood thundering round his body, racing to his throbbing cock.

"You're a vision. Beautiful beyond words."

She crooked her little finger at him and he rolled toward her, moving between her spread thighs, totally enthralled. He could no longer deny that he didn't want to wait for their marriage either. He needed her.

Desperately.

"I want you naked too," she whispered as her hands tugged his shirt out of his breeches. Before he could suck in a much-needed breath, she had his shirt off. When her fingers fumbled with his breeches he had to halt her questing hands. He'd never last if she kept touching him. His body was ready to explode; the reality of finally making love to her sent his desire spiraling toward the point of no return. He needed to ensure she found her pleasure first so that the loss of her maidenhead would not hurt.

He pulled her hand to his lips and kissed it. "Don't be in such a hurry. I want you to remember this day, as I know I will, forever."

"I will. I'll never forget this moment. It's engraved on my memory." She looked into his eyes and said, "I love you so much."

He stood and looked down upon a vision soon to be seared in his brain. Creamy skin rested on the mossy ground, with enticing stockings cloaking her legs. He divested himself of his breeches and with trembling limbs crouched at her feet, soaking in her naked beauty.

He ran his hands up and over her stockings until he reached the silken skin of her thighs. His fingers stroked softly until on a small sigh her legs parted, allowing him a view of heaven.

He crawled further between her legs to position himself directly in front of where his mouth longed to taste. He'd feasted on her before and loved her taste, like the sweetest nectar. Her thighs parted further and her hips lifted slightly as if begging for his kiss.

He closed his eyes and breathed deep before lowering his head to touch her with his eager tongue.

The world around him disappeared as he lost himself in her, loving her with his mouth until she was writhing on the ground in need, her hips lifting to press her center closer, demanding more from him. He used his fingers in conjunction with his tongue, and soon he sensed her climax nearing. Her body tightened, her thighs pressed tightly against his head, and as he gave one final suck on her hard little nub, she screamed his name.

With arms that could barely hold him because he was trembling with need, he moved to cover her body, pushing his hips between her thighs, and while she was still shuddering from her release he began to ease inside her.

Dreams are for those who reach for the sky, and as her tight sheath clamped around him, he felt like he was in heaven.

Chapter One

L ONDON, ENGLAND, 1816
        The door slammed shut behind him, the sound
        echoing in the quiet street. Standing on the top step,
Hadley loosened his cravat to make it easier to swallow over the
lump in his throat. He gazed along the row of fashionable but
smallish townhouses. They all looked the same, but he wondered
if the people who lived inside were as empty of life as the house
behind him.

A sighed escaped as he looked down his body. All dressed up
and nowhere to go. No one was waiting for him. Missing him.
Wanting him .

Philomena had wanted him.

The first woman he'd let close since Evangeline had decided
that a title and money were more important than love.

It was never easy sounding the death knell on an arrangement
with another mistress. He liked Philomena. She was easy. Easy to
talk to, very easy to look at, and very easy to desire. Not a friend
per se, but neither was she simply a mistress. Was there an in-
between?

He kicked at a loose cobblestone.

As Hadley sauntered down the steps to the street, he tried to summon hurt or disappointment, but he'd only be fooling himself. All he felt was hollowness.

He had hoped Philomena might be a tad upset that their arrangement had to end, but she knew she could find another protector at the snap of her little fingers. She was beautiful, if not a little vapid, but her innate sensuality drew men like a moth seeking a flame. He'd often wondered why she had lowered herself to becoming the mistress of a mere second son, albeit the second son of a duke. It certainly wasn't for the money. She could have earned more elsewhere.

Perhaps that was why she'd been special to him. She had *wanted* to be his mistress. She had chosen to be his mistress.

She'd chosen him.

It hadn't been solely about the coin he could provide.

To her credit, she hadn't cried, screamed, or carried on when he informed her that their time was at an end. Not after he'd explained why. At month's end his brother, the Duke of Claymore, would announce Hadley's engagement to Lady Claire Hampton. Hadley had promised his brother that he would start his new life as honorably as was possible with an arranged marriage.

Goddamn his brother.

Two years ago it had seemed so easy to agree with his brother's request that he marry Claire. Now the time was drawing near, he wished he could take his promise back, but he'd given his word. If a man went back on his word, how could he be trusted? A cold sweat made his shirt stick to his skin. His time was running out.

Hadley had more to worry about than an unwanted arranged marriage. A villainess as evil as any man, De Palma had to be stopped before she hurt any more of his friends or even himself. She had started a war with the Libertine Scholars in revenge for something their fathers had done to her many years ago.

He could not marry Claire and expose her to De Palma's evil either. The Libertine Scholars had three weeks to unmask their foe, or Claire might become a target as well.

After what had happened to Marisa, Maitland Spencer's wife . . . he wouldn't wish her fate on any woman, not even Claire.

At the corner of the street he looked back at the quaint townhouse with deep regret. He'd been fond of Philomena and their time together.

Christ, he needed a drink. He pulled out his pocket watch.

Shortly he was expected for dinner at the townhouse of his fellow Libertine Scholar the Earl of Markham, Christian Trent, but he couldn't face all the happily married couples without fortifying himself first.

A drink at White's was required. He could hail a hack, but it was a fine afternoon, if a tad cool, and perhaps a walk would help him release his frustrations.

It took him more than half an hour to walk to White's. Upon arrival, he spied a fellow Libertine Scholar, Arend Aubury, Baron de Labourd, sitting at their favorite table. Arend was the only other unmarried Libertine Scholar, and the two tended to spend more time together these days.

Arend saw him and waved one of the servants over, asking for another glass. There was a bottle of France's finest brandy on the table.

As he took his seat, Arend commented, "You look as if you could do with a drink."

Hadley grimaced and took the proffered glass from his friend. "It's been one of those days when I wished I'd simply stayed in bed."

"But not the bed of your now ex-mistress, it would seem," Arend replied with a raised eyebrow.

Hadley turned in his chair and looked around the room. Men were staring and joking, and it was obvious they were talking about him. "It would appear news travels quicker than a man can walk."

"Care to share why you brought your arrangement with the lovely Philomena to an end so suddenly?"

"Why? Are you interested in employing her?"

Arend shook his head. "I have to make Lady Isobel fall in love with me, and it's not a good idea to have a mistress on the side. Besides, I would never encroach on one of my fellow Libertine Scholars' women—paid or otherwise."

Hadley nodded once. "You seem so sure that Isobel is involved with De Palma. It's yet to be proved."

Arend lowered his voice. "You and I both know De Palma is her stepmother, Countess Victoria Northumberland. We just have to prove it."

Hadley looked around the room and sighed, not wishing to discuss their enemy further until they were with the rest of the Libertine Scholars. They were joining them for dinner to discuss what they had found out about De Palma. "My engagement will be announced in three weeks."

Arend looked surprised, something that didn't often occur. "Oh," he said with a nod. "There is no other way?"

"I don't see me finding a pot of gold at the bottom of a rainbow. Augustus needs the money he lent me for the winery repaid. He's been waiting five years. Besides, one woman is as good as any other for a wife." Hadley tried to ignore the stares and the men heading to the White's wager book. "I say, is everyone betting on the reason Philomena and I have parted ways?"

"Yes."

"What reason has the best odds?"

Arend laughed. "Unfortunately, the one I wagered on."

"And that is?"

"The return of Lady Evangeline Stuart, nee Althrope, to London."

Hadley felt the floor shake beneath his feet, and it was not an earthquake. He downed his brandy in one large gulp, the burning in his throat stinging his eyes. "Bloody hell," he choked out. "Her husband has brought her to London." For five years he'd been dreading this news.

Evangeline Althrope, now Evangeline Stuart, had been the love of his life.

Everything about her suddenly assaulted his memory. The mere mention of her name undid him.

Forbidden memories rushed into his head. He recalled her sleek limbs wrapped round him. Her uninhibited cries of passion as her exquisite body arched against his. He could almost feel her luxurious hair, auburn silk flowing like flames over flawless creamy skin. Her taste as he'd sampled all she had to give. Her laughter and her smile could bring him to his knees. But it had always been her eyes, filled with intelligence, that drew him. Their light blue color would darken with incredible sensuality.

She was branded on his soul, her memory sharp with a clarity that still seared.

Arend's glass halted halfway to his mouth, which now hung open. "You haven't heard?"

Hadley looked back at Arend blankly.

"She's widowed and just out of mourning. Plus, she has been asking after you, setting tongues wagging and sending men to the betting books."

The ground rushed toward him, and if he hadn't been sitting down, he'd have folded in a heap on the floor. Evangeline was here, in London, and a widow. Anger burned in his gut, raw and powerful. He felt his fists clench. "I hope you didn't wager on her and I forming an attachment."

"Silly, me. I should have known better." Arend ran a hand through his hair. "I thought I had inside knowledge. Sebastian is positive you are still in love with her."

Breath fled Hadley, and a wave of dizziness almost caused him to drop his glass. Those words, "still in love," echoed in his head over and over, like an unforgotten song. He had loved her. "Had" being the operative word.

She'd married another.

But she was now free.

Then, as if Thor's hammer came hurtling from the gods straight to his chest, the blow invisibly knocking him to hell, he remembered.

She'd chosen money, a title, and a safe life over him.

Over their love.

Just over five years ago, he'd received Evangeline's note. A note written in her own hand, telling him she was marrying Viscount Stuart. It had been painfully obvious that he'd been the only one in love.

She'd used him, taken what she wanted, and then married a man with enough money to save her brother's estate and then some. She had a title and lived in a castle, a real-life fairy tale.

He looked at Arend. "You made a foolish bet. I would not change anything in my life for that woman. In fact, I'm more determined than ever to marry Claire now."

Yet given the savage pain lancing through him, he'd be foolish to imagine that he'd recovered from her shattering betrayal. Did a man ever recover from his first love?

Especially a love that was betrayed.

Arend must have picked up the hate in his voice, because he leaned back in his seat and put up his hands in a defensive stance. "Well, the lady doesn't seem to understand that notion. She's been asking after you, trying to ascertain if you are engaged or married. That definitely appears to be a woman on a mission." He laughed. "It would appear the beautiful Lady Evangeline is not aware of how you feel."

Nor aware he was expected to marry another.

Arend looked at him closely. "Even if you are not interested in Lady Evangeline, are you sure about marriage to Lady Claire? There is still time to change your mind. Claire is oblivious to the plan your brother and her brother concocted. No one needs to get hurt."

He shrugged. "When Augustus suggested aligning our family with the Marquis of Corby, I saw no reason not to. I do not care whom I marry. It's simpler and easier if feelings are not involved. Besides, I felt sorry for the young lady. She's almost a spinster."

He'd never marry for love. Having had his heart destroyed once before, he wasn't about to put himself through that again.

However, his brother had agreed to wait until his thirtieth year before he should propose to Claire. Being unaware of her brother's plan, Hadley had hoped that in this time she might find someone else to marry. He could feel himself being boxed into a corner, and even though he'd promised never to love again, his pending marriage seemed somewhat callous in comparison to the love matches his fellow Libertine Scholars had made.

"I admire your practicality. If it was anyone other than you spouting those words, I'd believe you. But you, my friend, are a romantic at heart. That's why you're still torn up over a woman who left you five years ago. I also see the way you look at the other Libertine Scholars and their marital bliss."

Hadley downed his drink in one gulp, determined to ignore Arend's perceptive comments.

His friend leaned across the table and whispered, "You agreed to this stupid match while your heart was broken. There is no shame in changing your mind; nothing has been formally agreed or announced." He sat back. "Even if it had, blast it to Hades, you don't have to fall on your sword."

It was while my heart was shredded, actually, he wanted to yell at Arend.

Arend kept bloody talking. "Don't marry a woman because you're hurt. Get even and move on. You need love. Find a woman who can love you for who you are, and never let her go. That would be the best revenge. You won't be happy with anything less."

"What's to say I won't grow to love Claire?"

Arend choked on his drink. "Really? I'm not shallow enough to decry her lack of looks, but she's as dull as dishwater, and not overly bright. The long winter days and nights will be torture. I suspect you're the type of man who'd honor his marriage vows too, no mistresses for you. Sometimes I wonder how we are such good friends, as you are far too nice for me." He eyed Hadley shrewdly. "You do realize you'll have to sleep with her. Children and all that." At Hadley's angry look, he added, "I can just imagine her lying there and thinking of England."

Suddenly the prospect of wedding Claire felt as if a noose were being tightened around his neck. The he remembered how he'd given his heart to Evangeline and she'd simply stomped on it. He could not go through that pain ever again.

His illusions were few. He knew women flocked to him because he was the son of a duke and wealthy enough in his own right. He hated how mercenary women were, Evangeline being the worst of all. So for the past five years, after his heart turned to stone, he had indulged in all manner of pleasures, sampling women as he sampled his wines.

"Claire may not have beauty or brains, but that suits me just fine. She's unlikely to take other lovers, so I shall know any children are mine, and she'll be even less demanding of my time or emotions."

"Unlike Lady Evangeline, who I hear is a renowned beauty, and quite brilliant. I suspect she won't be a widow for long."

Hurt burned deep and fast at the idea of her marrying again. He painfully remembered that she could blind any man with her beauty and wit. These men didn't know what he knew—that she was a deceptive, cunning vixen, interested only in money and title.

Beautiful? Yes, he expected she was probably more beautiful than she'd been at nineteen. As soon as he'd laid eyes on the auburn beauty, he'd known his desire for her would get him into all sorts of trouble. The need to have her, to make her his, meant only one thing—marriage, but that had not stopped his pursuit.

He'd wanted to possess her, to give her his heart, his body, and his name. No other woman before or since had touched his heart —or crushed it—as Evangeline had.

Unbeknownst to him at the time, she'd lied as easily as she'd breathed.

"Well, if you see *Lady* Evangeline, perhaps you can inform her I have no interest in pursuing any type of relationship with her." He raised his glass. "In fact, you can tell her I'm soon to wed."

"That could be a mistake. The beautiful young widow is now very wealthy. Her husband left her a large portion of his wealth." Arend's words stung. "Money and beauty, a combination to lust after. Marry her for her money. That would teach her a lesson. Rather Evangeline than Claire—long, lonely winter nights, remember?" Arend shrugged as he said the words.

"You obviously don't know the lady" was Hadley's sarcastic reply. He wasn't petty enough to want to see Evangeline on a miserly widow's stipend, but it appeared her marriage had exceeded her expectations, for she'd got the money and title she craved. "She must be extremely happy, for that is why she married her viscount."

"I see." Arend refilled his glass, pouring the brandy all the way to the top. "It's as I have always suspected. A woman is madly in love as long as a purse is full. Love is only tested when the coffers run dry. Her viscount had a fatter purse."

Hadley thought of the other four fellow Libertine Scholars, all happily married. "Tell that to Christian, Sebastian, Grayson, and now bloody Maitland. I tell you, it's as if the French have put something in the brandy. Men are succumbing to the shackles of matrimony far too often of late."

Arend gave a mock shudder and raised his glass. "Here's to bachelorhood, brief as yours may now be."

Marriage to Claire. For a brief moment, Hadley wondered if Evangeline regretted her choice. He shook his head. She had her money and title; that was all she had wanted. What was there for her to regret?

If she thought she could have her title and now also have him, she was very wrong. He'd rather marry a leprous whore—or marry Claire—than succumb to her allure again.

Once he'd drunk the contents of his glass he slammed it on the table. "Come, we should be on our way. We have"— he looked around the room before lowering his voice—"lists to compare, away from prying eyes and eager ears."

The two men took their leave of White's and made their way

to Christian's townhouse. On the carriage ride, the discussion turned to the fight at Gentleman Jack's next week and whom to wager on. An unknown Spaniard had recently arrived, and Arend favored the man. Hadley would be unwise to wager against anyone Arend took an interest in. Arend had the uncanny knack of spotting a fighter's ability, *and* he'd been to see the Spaniard practice.

Besides, it might be a way to make money quickly, something he could use right now.

Even the sporting talk could not completely banish Evangeline from his mind. Under his breath he cursed her anew. Right now it would be ideal to chase away the memory of her touch and taste in an excess of sensual indulgence. However, in three weeks he was about to propose to Lady Claire. Claire had no idea the proposal was coming; he had talked her brother into letting him make an offer directly to her, so that she would have no idea it had been arranged by his brother and her brother. If she heard he still had a mistress, she might not believe him sincere. He wanted her to believe he had chosen her of his own free will. At least one of them should be happy about this marriage. Her life would be irrevocably changed too. He did not want to hurt her.

As the two men had expected, when they were ushered into the Earl of Markham's drawing room, the family setting hummed with loving couples and children. For one fleeting moment a pang of regret consumed him, until he remembered why he was going to marry Claire: to ensure that his heart remained protected.

Hadley hid a smile at the quick flash of horror that passed over Arend's face as little Henry, Sebastian's ward, grabbed Arend's trouser leg with jam-covered fingers. But to Hadley's amazement, Arend swung the little boy up into his arms and pretended to drop him, swiftly catching him before he could fall far. Henry's squeals had the women giggling and the men putting their fingers in their ears.

Lady Portia, Grayson Devlin's obviously pregnant wife, relieved Arend of Henry, while the boy's nurse collected Christian's son and ushered all the children from the room. Once the door had closed on the departing servants and children, they could talk openly.

The women present—Lady Portia; Lady Beatrice, who was the wife of Sebastian Hawkestone, Marquess of Coldhurst; Lady Marisa, who was the new Duchess of Lyttleton, and her younger sister, Lady Helen; and finally Lady Serena, Christian's wife and their hostess, were sitting grinning like Cheshire cats with bellies full of milk. The hairs on Hadley's neck prickled. They appeared to be looking at him, which was not a good thing.

"Good evening, ladies. It's always delightful to be in the company of such beauties." With that Hadley bowed to each and pressed a kiss to his hostess's knuckles.

These women were more than simply stunning beauties. They were intelligent, brave, and loyal to a fault. He doubted any of them would break her husband's heart. They would put their men first.

"And might I say you are looking very handsome tonight too, my lord."

"Oh, God, Serena, leave the man alone. He's only just got here."

Hadley looked across at Christian, who was still scowling at his wife, and the hairs on the back of his neck were now standing on end. The ladies were definitely up to something.

He chose a seat as far from the ladies as he could, and found himself sitting next to Grayson on a chair that was definitely not made for a man. He felt as if it would break beneath him if he made one wrong move. He must have looked like a ninny.

Serena's smile indicated she knew he was retreating. It also seemed to scream *You cannot thwart us.* Thwart them at what? He longed to know, or did he? These women were a force to reckon with. He'd seen them win the hearts of men who were confirmed rakes and then bravely take on their enemy, all with style and wit and determination.

Arend, who'd also greeted the ladies in his fancy French way, had taken a seat next to Serena on the settee. He stretched his arms along the top of the furniture and said, "As we have a guest coming to dinner, I suggest we discuss our investigations before Lady Isobel arrives."

Serena sent Hadley a cheeky smile. "*Guests*, Arend. Isobel is bringing a friend."

The way she looked at Hadley, he wished he could squirm in his chair, but he was too afraid to move lest it collapsed.

Why did his cravat suddenly feel too tight?

Arend sent her a quizzing look but merely continued, "I have only two names left on my list: the Earl of Northumberland and the Earl of Wentworth."

Last month the Libertine Scholars had learned that the woman who was set upon destroying them had worked as a high-priced courtesan in Paris. Apparently she had caught the fancy of an English earl, left the life of prostitution in France, hidden her tracks well, and with her earl returned to England as a woman of quality he'd met on the continent. They had no idea if she was still with the earl or if he had married her, but they thought she'd hardly leave the successful business she'd built up in Paris for anything less than marriage, and they had no other leads.

They had drawn up a list of more than a hundred English earls and then had whittled it down to sixty who had wives in their mid-twenties, the age they thought their enemy now was. Over the past month, the men had been investigating all the names on the list and had cleared all but seventeen.

The discussion was loud and emotional. The other five Libertine Scholars shared the names on their lists. The women chimed in with comments, and with their help a further five earls were struck off the list when Beatrice commented that their wives had been at finishing school with her.

"That still leaves twelve names," Maitland said. "I was hoping it would be smaller."

Arend leaned sideways and helped himself to the decanter of

brandy on the side table. "My money is still on the Earl of Northumberland's widow, Lady Isobel's stepmother."

"You simply want it to be her because Lady Isobel vexes you so," uttered Sebastian. "You want her to be in league with the villain so you can walk away with a clear conscience."

All five ladies present swung their gaze to Arend. Hadley inwardly laughed. If they suspected the start of a romance, God help Arend. Hadley was pleased not to be the center of their attention for once.

"Clear conscience? I don't have a conscience" was Arend's dry reply. "You tell me, then, why Isobel was kidnapped along with Marisa. It doesn't make sense. There has to be a connection."

Last month Marisa had been drugged and kidnapped by their villainess. They had managed to rescue her only when the carriage they were abducting her in crashed. Unfortunately, Marisa had been very badly wounded, and Maitland had almost lost her. Isobel too had been in the carriage, but she had been kidnapped from a different location.

"Perhaps the villain had other plans for Isobel. Perhaps she was taken to extract revenge on another individual."

Arend scoffed. "Her father is dead, so who would that be?"

"She is his only child. Perhaps it was to wipe his lineage from this earth. Something she has savored doing to my husband." Marisa's quiet but venom-filled words hung in the air. The injuries Marisa had sustained meant she could never have children. Maitland, sitting beside her, took Marisa's hand and pressed it to his lips. "But I still have you," he declared softly.

Hadley turned away from the private moment so filled with love and devotion. Once he'd thought he shared this with Evangeline, but he'd been a fool. Love was not to be for him. Sometimes that thought made him envy what these men had found with their wives.

Portia played with a string of pearls round her neck. "I think it's time we women took the lead. Now that we have a smaller list, we should be investigating the *wives*, not our husbands."

Hadley returned his gaze to the ladies as Beatrice spoke.

"I agree, Portia. This needs a woman's touch. If the supposedly happily married Libertine Scholars start asking questions about other men's wives, who knows what gossip will ensue." Beatrice continued smoothly, "And we don't wish our villainess to understand just how close we may be."

The men all started talking at once. The husbands proclaiming how dangerous it was to let the women become so involved, while Arend argued that it made perfect sense.

Hadley understood both sides. After everything that had happened, these men would lay down their lives to protect their women. It was instinctive to guard them from harm, much more than simple male pride. He had always felt a need to protect those weaker than himself. He hated bullying of any form, as he himself had once been its victim, and he had the scars on his buttocks to prove it. He'd been his father's whipping boy, always taking the punishment for his older brother, who was both weaker and smaller in size.

However, Arend's argument that catching the villain quickly would thereby protect everyone was valid.

He remained silent, waiting for a chance to offer his opinion, or to be asked for it.

His chance came after a heated barb from Sebastian. Hadley cleared his throat and spoke rather loudly. "I understand you wish to protect your wives, but there are others who need protection too." He glanced across the room. "Helen, for one. And what about the children?" The men quieted and looked at him. "We are spread too thin to be sure everyone is safe all the time. We have no idea what she plans to do next. I for one don't want to wait to find out." He nodded at Arend. "I believe Arend is correct when he says we are running out of time and that we need to unmask her sooner rather than later. We may find that it is more expedient to let the women—" He held up his hand at the growls already sounding in the men's throats. "To let the well-guarded women do a little investigating of their own."

Portia clapped her hands. "Exactly, Hadley—well said. You know how skilled each of us can be at uncovering secrets. We uncovered all of yours." The twinkle in her eye was all for her husband, Viscount Blackwood.

"And it will be safe if we conduct the inquisitions, so to speak, in one place, with all of the men around us," Marisa added.

Hadley let a smile of appreciation escape. "You have a plan, Duchess?"

"As it happens, I believe I do. We have twelve earls on our list. I propose that we hold four different house parties, one at a time, at each of our country estates, and invite three of the earls on the list, along with other guests, to each one. Then we can observe and question the wives, with the men round us."

Beatrice nodded. "If you look at the list, we can form groups of guests that would not raise any eyebrows when we extend an invitation."

Before anyone could reply, there was a knock on the door and the additional guests were announced.

"Excuse me, my lord," said the butler. "Lady Isobel Thompson, and Lady Evangeline Stuart."

Hadley's head whipped round in the direction of the door as if an invisible rope had tugged it. He barely noticed Isobel's entrance, for his gaze was riveted on the tumble of auburn curls piled in an elegant array on top of her head—a head he thought he would never want to see again. His mouth dried and his heart pounded in his chest.

If he were not under a spell, he would have looked away, but his eyes traveled down, soaking in the beauty of features so fine, so perfect, they made a man think of angels. Eyes the color of a clear summer sky searched the room until they found him. A stranger's smile hovered over her succulent lips, and a look of such longing entered those traitorous eyes that he almost believed the message they tried to convey: *I'm here for you, my love.*

However, he could not bring himself to believe anything

those eyes or lips said. He'd believed once before, and it had left a hole where his heart once rested in his chest.

Summoning the anger that was churning deep in his innards, he broke the spell and turned away, but as he did so, his grip on the edge of the little chair must have been too tight, for in the next second the chair splintered to pieces under him, and he fell with a thud to the floor, landing on his arse.

Chapter Two

A hush settled over the room until Sebastian let out a bark of laughter. Then the ladies dissolved into fits of giggles. Hadley felt his face heat, and he would not look at Evangeline. What made it worse was that Helen raced to his aid, offering her hand. He picked himself up and bent to see the pile of broken wood and torn fabric at his feet.

"Are you hurt?" Helen asked urgently.

"Only my pride." He smiled down at her concerned face. "The chair is only good for kindling now."

"No one cares about the chair as long as you are unhurt," she replied.

Christian came and patted him on the back. "Leave that mess. What on earth made you sit on such a dainty piece of furniture in the first place?"

Hadley glanced over at the women, all laughing behind their hands, and had to admit he must look a fool. He would have laughed too, but having Evangeline present to see him fall was mortifying.

Christian followed his stare and lowered his voice. "I must admit, the ladies can be an intimidating bunch. I swear, inviting

Lady Evangeline was none of my doing. I tried to tell Serena it was a bad idea."

"Very bad idea," Hadley replied.

The rest of the men rose, along with the ladies, who were warmly greeting Evangeline and Isobel as if they were old friends. God damn it, this smelled of Marisa's doing. She'd asked him about Evangeline a few weeks ago, and he hadn't even known she'd been widowed or that she was in London. Nor had Marisa even met Evangeline at that stage. Now it looked as though they were close friends.

Evangeline tended to have that effect on people. *Until she stabbed them in the back,* he thought darkly.

Hadley made his way to Arend's side. "You know Serena is going to expect me to escort Evangeline in to dinner."

"It's looking like they have some plan in mind. Good luck, my friend."

Hadley grabbed Arend's arm. "Let me escort Isobel in to dinner."

"No argument from me. Isobel sets my teeth on edge."

"Oh, and I suspect the ladies will try and seat me near to Evangeline, so you must ensure you are sitting beside her."

Arend glanced across at Serena and then looked at Hadley with pity. "How are we going to stop Serena telling us whom we must escort?"

An arm slipped through Hadley's. "If I may impose, I'd love you to escort me in to dinner, my lord. I'm sure Arend can handle two ladies." Helen smiled up at him reassuringly. "I told my sister this was not a good idea. I knew you would not be pleased with Lady Evangeline in attendance."

Not pleased? Hell would have to freeze over twice before he wanted to spend any time in Evangeline's company.

"Thank you, Helen, for being the sensible young lady you are. I would be honored to escort you in to dinner." Hadley placed his hand over hers where it rested on his arm.

Dinner was called, and before Serena could direct partners,

Helen announced that Hadley was escorting her in, and that Arend would be delighted to escort both Lady Evangeline and Lady Isobel.

With that, Helen allowed him to lead her into the dining room. He took the seat on her left, at the end of the table, so that only Helen sat beside him. Christian would be at the head of the table, on his other side.

It took all of a few minutes for Hadley to understand he'd made an enormously stupid mistake: Evangeline took the chair opposite his.

At least if she had been sitting beside him he wouldn't have had to look at her. *This must be what hell was like,* he fumed.

"Good evening, my lord. After your, ah, accident with your tiny chair, I never got an opportunity to greet you."

Like a man lost in the desert under blazing sun, his tongue seemed to have swelled in his throat.

A smile that would dazzle a blind man spread over her face at his lack of response. "Is this how you greet an old friend?"

"We were never friends." As soon as the bitter words left his mouth he cursed under his breath; he'd been hoping to ignore her, pretend she didn't exist. He didn't want to show how she affected him.

Hurt appeared in her eyes and quickly vanished, replaced with anger.

"I had been hoping to see you privately, but you have not been in town of late."

"I had pressing personal business, and I can assure you, madam, I am not the least bit interested in why you have come to town."

This time there was no hurt, only anger in her eyes. Good; he'd rather have her angry than hurt. And that thought annoyed him. Why should he care if she was hurt? She hadn't cared how much she hurt him all those years ago.

"I thought I was at least entitled to an explanation." Her voice was hard and cold. She'd never sounded like this before. What explanation? He was the one who deserved an explanation. She had money, she was titled, and she was still so beautiful that it hurt to look at her.

"Some things are best left in the past," he added more kindly, trying to make her understand that she was an interlude from years gone by and that he was determined to ensure she stayed in his past.

"I deserve to know why," she insisted.

He had no idea what she was going on about. What did she need to know? She had left him.

Thankfully, Helen chose that moment to put her hand on his arm. "Hadley," she said a voice she'd never used on him before. It was low, seductive, almost lyrical, and his eyebrow rose in surprise. Little Helen was growing up. He tried to think how old she must be now; coming up to eighteen, he thought.

He looked at her as if he had not seen her before. She was a beautiful young woman. Glossy fair hair was intricately dressed with fine pearls. She wore no necklace, but a long curl hung seductively over her shoulder, emphasizing her graceful neck, and drawing a man's eye to her abundant cleavage. Her lovely hazel eyes twinkled with intelligence. She loved to read and had an enquiring mind. He glanced down and with a start noticed bosoms that would spark any red-blooded man's interest. He quickly looked away.

"Hadley," she repeated, "there is a wonderful new exhibit at the British Museum. I was wondering, due to the circumstances we find ourselves in, if I could rely on you to accompany me tomorrow afternoon. Sebastian won't leave Beatrice's side, and it's dangerous for me to go alone." She batted her eyes. She was flirting with him.

Helen had never been so forward before. He supposed it was to defend him against Evangeline, who to his annoyance seemed rather amused by Helen's behavior. But then, why would she be jealous? She had shown him how little regard she held for him by marrying her viscount.

A cold hand wrapped itself around his heart and squeezed.

"I would be honored to escort you, Helen." A tinge of worry made him shift in his chair when he saw the look of pure happiness on Helen's face. This was just an act, wasn't it? Helen even flashed a smug look at Evangeline, who merely inclined her head.

Silence hung in the air, as uncomfortable as his fragile little chair had been.

Finally Arend, who was seated to Evangeline's left, asked, "How long do you intend to stay in London, my lady?"

"Please, call me Evangeline," she told Arend before turning to look at Hadley. "My stay depends on how long it takes me to catch up with old . . . ah, acquaintances. I have some business with one in particular." She finally turned to Arend and added, "I won't be able to leave until I have done so."

Hadley bit his tongue. He wanted to say *Then you will be here for a long time, because I have nothing to say to you,* but that would have seemed childish.

Instead he asked, "And once you have caught up with your acquaintances, will you be returning to Scotland?"

"That depends."

When nothing further was forthcoming, he prodded, "On what?"

"On how our conversation goes."

There, she'd said it. She'd told Hadley Fullerton exactly why she was here. She could not for the life of her understand his coldness toward her. If anyone should be bitter, it was she. She'd spent five years in misery, waiting every day for him to rescue her, but he'd never come.

Love obviously meant something completely different to him. She would have moved heaven and earth to find him if he had suddenly gone missing.

Before condemning him, she would at least give him the opportunity to tell her why—why had he abandoned her to such a horrible fate.

Hadley tried to pretend he didn't understand her meaning,

but it was there in his eyes. His beautiful blue eyes. She had blue eyes too, but hers were light blue, whereas his were deep blue, as deep as an ocean. She used to love how they burned for her when he held her in his arms, when he made love to her, when he swore he couldn't live without her.

It appeared he could live without her very well.

She tried to ease the pain in her chest by drawing in a few quick breaths. She'd been widowed for twelve months, three days, and fifteen hours, yet he still had not had the decency to write to her.

She had hoped he'd explain his behavior of five years ago. How does a man profess such undying love, make love to you as if he can't live unless he has you, and then not even attempt to find you?

Not even when she'd begged him in her letters. She prayed he'd received her letters.

She swallowed back the tears that wanted to fall the minute she'd seen him across the drawing room. Now thirty, he looked the same. The years had been kind to him. He still looked like the handsome twenty-five-year old lord who'd asked for her first dance at her neighbor's country ball. That had been the moment their relationship had become more.

As soon as he'd taken her in his arms for the waltz, she'd known he was the one. He was her future, her life.

Only, her life had not turned out how she had imagined. Far from it.

He didn't reply to her bold statement. So she added, "Nothing to say? How surprising."

Hadley's chair scraped back, and he stood, throwing his napkin onto the table. "Pardon my manners. If you'll excuse us, I'd like a private word with Lady Evangeline."

Christian said, "You may use my study," as he looked accusingly at his wife, as if to say *I warned you.*

Hadley then stood behind her, and she sighed and allowed him to pull out her chair so she could stand. She addressed Serena, the hostess. "Please forgive me. I did not mean to ruin your lovely dinner."

Serena smiled warmly and assured her she had not ruined anything, but Evangeline could barely make out her words over the pounding of her pulse. Forcing a relaxed smile, she preceded Hadley from the room.

Neither of them spoke as he virtually marched her into Christian's study. He closed the door with a deafening thud. With knees trembling she sank onto a high-backed wing chair obviously made for a man, because her feet barely touched the ground unless she moved to sit on the very edge. Her dinner would be getting cold, she worried, then she realized what an odd thought that was. The rise of emotions churning inside her made the idea of continuing to eat dinner unpalatable anyway.

She had thought herself prepared to face Hadley, but she had not been expecting such open hostility or, worse still, indifference.

She'd dreamed of this day every night for more than five years, but never in her dream had she felt so afraid.

Her marriage had been the most terrifying, heartbreaking, and soul-destroying experience of her life. In the space of an hour, not only had she lost the man who owned her heart, but she'd found herself utterly defenseless against her mother's dastardly plan. A tear almost escaped as she recalled how her lady's maid offered to smuggle a note to Hadley. She'd written the note, of course, but he never came.

It was as if he'd washed his hands of her. And was glad of it.

She'd arrived in London three days ago. She'd come to London to finalize her son's inheritance, and to see if Hadley was man enough to tell her to her face that she'd been mistaken. That he had never loved her as he professed.

His rejection, more than her forced marriage, had left her broken, her dreams shattered in fragments of longing and hope.

It was a fragment of hope that had brought her south to London. She wanted Hadley to say the words to her face, to tell her his love had faded, for she didn't believe his indifference. But having now met him, she had her answer.

How foolish to continue to love him all these years when he had obviously never loved her to begin with. He'd been infatuated with her, had lusted after her, perhaps—but not love.

He'd haunted her waking moments and held center stage in her fondest dreams. The memories of his lovemaking—and it was lovemaking; what her husband did to her had taught her that— had sustained her through the nights of terror when Viscount Stuart would come to her bed.

Hadley's touch had always set her soul alight, sending intense, desperate, wild need streaming over her. She ached for his caress, for the indescribable pleasure he had given her.

Why had he deserted her?

The man pacing the room in front of the fire seemed so different, as if a stranger. Being this close to him, seeing him again, remembering his kiss, his touch, his smile, roused an aching inside her for what could have been. Anger was her leash.

Why had he deserted her? She did not deserve that.

It was the tense, hard flash in his eyes that made her want to curl up into a ball and cry. Her hands clenched into fists. Well, he could be as annoyed as the bloody king, for all she cared. It was obvious there was to be no happy ending for her. He clearly cared not a jot. But she would not leave here without answers.

She raised her head and squared her shoulders. Why would he not say something? He simply stood before the fire, his slow appraisal sending prickling heat through her body. His gaze brushed over her bosom, traveling down to take in her waist (which had, to her shame, thickened over the years since the birth of her son), and finally resting on her hips before racing back up to her blushing face.

It was the scrutiny of a man who knew women intimately and didn't care that she understood that fact.

Her nails dug into her palms. She drew in a steadying breath, trying to calm the rage beginning to boil. She did not deserve his scorn.

"You should not have sought me out, Evangeline. I am not the gullible man I was when you last knew me."

Evangeline eyed him coolly. "So it would appear. Nor were you ever this cold, unless your professions of love were all an act."

His head snapped up, and he glared at her. "Cold? You have the nerve to speak of me being cold? Cold is professing love to one man while secretly planning to marry another."

Bolts of lightning flashed in her head. She snapped her head back. "Did you not receive my letters?"

"I received the only one that I needed to receive. The one informing me you had no option other than to marry Viscount Stuart in order to help your family. Duty above love, you said."

She shook her head, and waves of nausea engulfed her stomach. She pressed a hand to her mouth. Finally the bile receded. "I did not write such a letter. I wrote a letter begging you to save me."

He eyed her warily. "No. No more lies. You were kind but clear. The letter said that there were advantages to marrying Viscount Stuart that in your youth you had overlooked."

"That doesn't even sound like me." But his face said it all. He did not believe her.

Oh my God, she thought, *he never received any of my correspondence, or he would not be acting this way.* "You are under an incorrect comprehension, my lord. I was not planning to marry another. I wanted to marry you."

Scorn filled his eyes. "Then pray tell how you ended up married to Viscount Stuart. As I recall a title, money, and standing are every debutante's dream."

Evangeline addressed Hadley with a chilling smile. "You know very well it was not my dream. My dream was you."

"How convenient to profess to have had this dream, now that you have a title and money. How stupid do you think I am?"

"Very stupid," she said under her breath. Either that or he was using this so-called letter as an excuse. Did this letter even exist? She wanted to box his ears. She stood and walked to stand toe to toe with him, even though the top of her head only reached his chest. "You have no idea what the hell you are talking about. For five years I have barely lived—it has been more like merely existing —and if I'd had any choice, I would not have done so voluntarily for money or prestige or title. I doubt I would have even done it for you!" She was shaking so much that the pearl bracelets on her wrist were knocking together audibly.

Hadley's eyes narrowed and his nostrils flared. Before he could say another word she began to tell her sordid story.

"Five years ago I awoke in the bed of Viscount Stuart as he was forcing himself on me." She knew her bottom lip was trembling, and she willed herself not to cry. She had not come to Hadley for pity. She'd come for an explanation. "My mother had sold me to Viscount Stuart. I was told I was legally wed to him, but I have no recollection of the ceremony. I suspect they used a veiled woman in my place to fool the priest. Either that or he was paid to make no objections."

Hadley's eyes did not soften, but his hands lowered from where they rested on his hips.

"I tried to escape several times, but each time I was hunted down and returned to him. I will not tell you what punishment I received." She turned away, not wishing him to see the haunted pain in her eyes.

A hand gripped her wrist, forcing her to turn back to face him. "I received a letter from you, in your handwriting, telling me a different story." When she tried to tug her hand free, he let her go. "You wrote that you could not possibly let your family down. A mere second son was no longer an option you could in all good conscience marry, knowing your family's dire financial situation."

"I did *not* write any such letter."

"I assure you, I still have it, I checked it against the other notes you sent me during our affair, as at first I could not believe the words you wrote." He leaned close. "The handwriting matched."

She took a step back, pain sending her reeling backward. He did not believe her. Five years made such a difference, it would seem.

How could he not believe her? He obviously hadn't known her at all.

"Why would I be here if I had written such a note?"

"I have no idea. That is the only reason I am giving you one moment of my time."

This "moment" was a nightmare—nothing like her dreams, in which he got down on his knees begging for her forgiveness, swearing he'd tried to find her and that he still loved her. Angry tears welled in her eyes.

"I cannot believe you would think me capable of such deception."

"You are a brilliant actress, I'll give you that. However, words on paper do not lie."

"I swear that I never wrote you any letter." At his look of disbelief she added, "I wrote to you after I was kidnapped and forced into matrimony. Aggie, my maid, said she'd send a letter for me."

"The only letter I received was the one detailing why it was impossible for you to wed a penniless second son, even the second son of a duke."

"You obviously didn't know me at all if you were stupid enough to believe those words."

The man she'd once loved looked at her as if she were a stranger.

Evangeline's heart somersaulted violently in her chest. He was as devastatingly handsome as ever, with the same lithe grace, the same lean hardness. Yet when she finally looked closely she saw that time had marked him. There were fine lines at the corners of his eyes, his shoulders were broader beneath his exquisitely tailored gray coat, his thighs looked more powerfully muscled, and his hair had darkened slightly.

Like a hungry scavenging dog, she soaked in his beauty. His

cravat set off the finely chiseled chin, his aristocratic features just as striking now as they had been in the past. His face, with its high cheekbones and noble brow, had always been a beacon for the ladies. He had the devil's own beauty and had always been in demand among the mamas of unwed young ladies, even though he was only a second son.

She still, to this day, wondered how she had caught the interest of such a fine man. Or, as she'd learned to her cost, not such a fine man. To sleep with her, promise her his name, and then leave her to her fate . . .

Perhaps it was lust, not love, and once he'd slept with her, he had been relieved that she'd been forced to marry Viscount Stuart.

It wasn't the five years apart that made them strangers, she thought. Perhaps they had been so infatuated with each other that they had not taken the time to really learn about each other. Had she ever really known him? Or had she been blinded by his looks and the idea of love?

He hammered home his distrust. "You're right. It appeared that I didn't really know you back then, and I don't know you now. How can I ever trust anything you say when you come to me with this convoluted story?"

An ache of sorrow the size of the moon filled her. Once he had looked at her as if his whole world revolved around her. Now all she saw was contempt.

She laughed inwardly at herself. She had expected him to profess that he'd been waiting for her all these years. That he had tried to find her, to rescue her. At the very least he would be filled with guilt and sorrow for abandoning her to her fate.

She'd escaped her dreadful life only because her husband had had the grace to be killed by a highwayman. His title and estate went to their son, but he had left her a very sizeable fortune. She'd been absolutely astounded, as had his servants. The same servants who had not lifted a hand to help her for the five years she'd lived in the wilds of Scotland at Rossack Castle now kowtowed to her. One of the reasons she'd come to London was to escape the people who now did as she bid but who had kept her a virtual prisoner while Dougal was alive. When she returned, *if* she returned, she'd replace them all. . . .

As to the money he'd left her, she liked to think that perhaps her husband had a conscience after all, but it was more likely that he'd hoped it might see him avoid hell because of the wrongs he'd perpetrated against her. No amount of money in the world would atone for what he'd done to her—taken from her. He had stolen her happiness and joy in living. He had stolen Hadley from her, or so she had thought. Seeing him now, she realized he had never been hers in the first place.

She would make him eat his words. "I want to see this letter." She would have her groveling apology. Hadley owed her that at least.

His mouth dropped open and his hands rose to his hips once more. "What good will seeing the letter do?"

Time to turn the tables on him: "How do I know you're not lying simply to cover the fact you were pleased you didn't have to marry me? You wouldn't want me to know you're a coward or a cad."

Anger flared in his eyes and his mouth firmed. "If anyone is a liar here, madam, it is you." Without another word he stormed to the door and threw it open. He called for Christian's butler. "Can you hail a hackney, please?"

She came to stand beside him. "There is no need; my carriage is outside. Please call for my driver."

Hadley's eyes narrowed. She couldn't bear to see the anger marring his beautiful face, so she swept through the door and waited in the entrance hall for her cloak.

She heard him say, "Please let his lordship know that Lady Evangeline and I have been called away."

"Certainly, my lord. Will we expect you back this evening?"

They both said no at the same time.

Unable to look at him a moment longer, she did not wait for him to escort her to her town coach. She was just about to step up into the carriage when a strong hand gripped her arm to steady her. Heat burned through her clothes at his touch. She closed her eyes at the familiarity, the feel of Hadley beside her, the vibrant heat of his body, the sweet sensations of his touch, as the erotic memories came flooding back. It had been so long since a man touched her with tenderness. . . .

As she'd thought when she saw him across the room earlier this evening, she still loved him—and hated him in equal measure.

She didn't know if she would ever forgive him for putting her through this and not believing in her—in their love.

She hated that she still wanted him, had longed for his love these past five years. What did that make her, weak? She wasn't weak. She'd survived.

Some things could never be forgiven.

Once he'd handed her into the carriage his touch was gone, and coldness took its place once more. He followed into the carriage and took the seat opposite her.

Their eyes suddenly locked in the dim streetlight filtering in through the carriage window. She knew from the look on his face that he was remembering the last carriage ride they had shared.

On their last journey together, he had pulled her into his arms, reaching down to caress her, stroke her, arouse her. The memory of his lean, elegant hands fondling the swell of her breasts and hiking up her dress to stroke her wetness, fingers seeking her most private place until she moaned his name, made her nipples peak with longing.

For a moment he simply stared at her, his gaze dropping to her breasts, probably noting her reaction.

"Memories are best left in the past, where they no longer have the ability to hurt you," she whispered into the darkness as the coach rumbled off.

That was a truth she knew well, as she tried to forget the misery of the last five years.

Chapter Three

Hadley shifted uneasily in the carriage seat and, finally ashamed of his erection, crossed his legs. His fierce arousal had taken him by surprise. Flashes of memories flooded his mind. He inwardly cursed the hot blood that stirred in his loins. He tried to think of the villainess De Palma instead. Even that didn't work.

He shouldn't have touched Evangeline, when just looking at her stirred a reluctant yet heated response.

She was even more beautiful than he remembered.

He let anger at her feminine wiles consume him. As soon as they had locked eyes in this carriage he'd seen the blank daze of desire reflected back at him, sensed the subtle softening of her body.

He turned away from her, disgusted at the raw need that ran through him from just one memory. Being alone with her in the seclusion of her carriage was still having a profound effect on his body, and he hated the power she wielded.

She was everything he remembered and more. When she'd entered the drawing room earlier this evening his heart had almost stopped. Her auburn hair shone like polished copper; a few long strands flowed over her shoulders, coming to rest on her ample bosom in a teasing array. The sight of her in a cream gown that displayed every luscious curve to perfection aroused his cravings to a painful ache.

His hands curled against his thighs as his body fought with his mind. Even now he wanted to move to sit beside her and touch her silken skin, trace the outline of her luscious lips with his thumb, slide his arms round her, and bury his head between her full breasts.

Hadley swore under his breath, wishing she'd never returned to torment him. He resented how she had remained just as alluring as his dreams remembered; worse still, she had the power to make him feel so much.

He remembered every look, every taste, every touch, and every promise her lying lips had spoken. He had tried to bury them under the avalanche of her betrayal, deep in his heart where she could never hurt him again, but here he was doing her bidding once again. He would have to proceed with caution if he was to remain unscarred from this encounter.

The only thing to give thanks for was that Evangeline appeared to be agitated by his inner strength. He hadn't rolled over and let her beauty turn him into her lap dog once more. She now viewed him with a tad more respect. He almost laughed when he first began to understand that her womanly wiles would no longer work on him. He was immune to her tears, having cried too many over her betrayal.

He would prove to Evangeline that he was a stronger man than before. He would not succumb to her charms again. He would show her the letter and she could be on her way by morning, back to the wilds of Scotland, where she belonged.

Then I'll never have to see you again, he was thinking as he stepped out of the carriage. He turned to help her down, but she dropped her muff. He bent to pick it up, and as he did, a shot rang out and a rush of air passed over his head. A gunshot. Instinctively he reached up and pulled Evangeline down to the ground beside him, rolling her under him as he used the wheel for some kind of protection.

Her driver stood and fired down the street at a man fleeing on horseback. Then there was simply silence.

Hadley sprang to his feet and held out his hand to Evangeline. She didn't take it. He looked down and a curse hurtled from his mouth. Blood was spreading over her cream gown. A slight trickle covered her right shoulder. She'd been hit.

Icy fear gripped him and guilt consumed him as he dropped beside her and pulled her into his arms.

He pushed his fear away and picked her up, quickly carrying her into his family's townhouse, calling for Mrs. Booker, the head housekeeper.

Mrs. Booker immediately took charge, arranging for the doctor to be fetched, and Hadley carried her to his room, on the second floor.

He kept thinking about the last thought he'd had about her: *Then I'll never have to see you again.* He looked down at her pale face as he carried her upstairs, and suddenly he didn't want there to be a world without Evangeline in it. She might have stomped on his heart, but she didn't deserve to die from a gunshot he was pretty certain was meant for him.

Their villainess had decided to strike, and he should have known what she would do. Setting up a second son for disgrace and ruin would be pointless; no one would care. Dead did the job just as well.

Just then Evangeline let out a moan and her eyelids fluttered open. "What happened? Why are you carrying me?" she asked. She let out a small cry when she tried to move in his arms.

"Lie still. You've been shot."

Her eyes widened and her wan cheeks got paler. "Shot? Who? Why?"

"It was meant for me, but when I bent down to collect your muff, the shot must have hit you instead."

"So it's not just me you have angered recently."

He chose to ignore her jibe, not wishing to upset her further. Her eyes were struggling to stay open against the pain, and when he tried to lengthen his stride, her hand gripped his arm where it wrapped around her torso, careful to avoid one plump breast.

No sooner had he laid her on his large bed than Mrs. Booker entered with one of the maids.

"Off with you, my lord. We will see to the lady."

"My name is Lady Evangeline Stuart. You may call me Eva," she said to Mrs. Booker.

Hadley stood near the bed, not sure what to do. The shot couldn't have been too serious, as the blood was beginning to slow and congeal. He hadn't had a chance to examine the wound, but it was near the top of her right shoulder. He hoped it had not broken any bones and that the bullet was not still in there. According to Sebastian, who had been shot in the buttocks last month, it hurt like the devil to get it out.

His hands itched to tug down the shoulder of the gown to see, but Mrs. Booker would have a fit.

"My lord, the doctor will be here soon, and we need to get her ladyship ready to receive him."

He looked at Evangeline, but she merely gave him a tight smile. He nodded and retreated. At the door he added, "Please send the doctor to see me the minute he has finished his examination. I'll be in Augustus's study." Where he intended to drink until the guilt swimming in his veins drowned in alcohol.

He left the door to the study ajar, wanting to hear what was going on. He slumped into a chair by the fire and hugged the decanter of brandy to his body. If he had not brought Evangeline home with him, she would not be lying up there injured; he, however, would likely be dead.

At that exact moment he recognized that the woman who'd once broken his heart had just saved his life. He prayed her injury was not, or did not turn into, anything life-threatening.

That's not the only reason you're upset. All his posturing tonight was bullshit. The idea of Evangeline dying filled him with sorrow. A depth of loss sank into his soul and hurt just as much as the day he'd received the note telling him she was marrying another.

A note spelling out very clearly that his love alone was not enough.

On that thought, he suddenly realized what bringing her to this house admitted. He'd shown her that she still held power over him.

She knew he'd kept her letter—her letters.

What man keeps the letters of a woman who means nothing to him?

He didn't bother pouring the brandy into a glass; he simply drank it straight from the decanter.

"Drinking until you're drunk won't help Evangeline."

He lowered the decanter. He hadn't heard Arend arrive.

"How did you hear what happened?"

"I'd ease up on the drink. You have a guest who needs your help." Arend sank into the chair opposite him. "Evangeline's driver sent a note to Christian's. I came as soon as I heard. What happened?"

He slammed the decanter down on the side table. "That bloody bitch."

"Let's not treat the brandy so callously." Arend held out a glass for him to fill. "I assume you are not talking about Evangeline."

Hadley shook his head. "Bloody De Palma. If I hadn't bent down . . . That shot was meant for me. Shot in the back. The bitch has no honor."

"I thought as much; that's why I came. Time has run out, and we have to stop her. I'm tired of being nice, of being cautious when our enemy grows bolder. I'm sure it's bloody Isobel's stepmother, Victoria. Everything about her fits what we have learned about our enemy. No one we spoke to really knows where she came from, but apparently she's from the depths of Wales."

At Arend's raised eyebrow, he understood what Arend was

indicating. How the hell do you check out a person's background when they come from Wales?

Hadley rested his head on the back of his chair and closed his eyes. What a mess. He drew in a deep breath, willing the blood still pumping fast around his body to slow. He'd almost died today.

"It's good to feel alive, isn't it? Or is it that a woman you swore meant nothing to you has you worried sick?"

He threw what he hoped was an indignant look at Arend. "I almost died. That is what I was thinking. Besides, Evangeline has nothing to do with our enemy's plans for the Libertine Scholars. She is innocent in that, at least."

"According to you, not so innocent. More of a sly, conniving—"

"She's not in the same league as De Palma. Evangeline might be a liar, but she's no killer."

Arend sat looking at him for a moment before saying softly, "So what are we going to do about De Palma? You and I have run out of time. It's obvious she's getting desperate. Shooting you dead in the middle of the street, in London? Society would not stand for that. Every Bow Street Runner would be employed."

Hadley's head began to pound. He understood what Arend was hinting at. The two of them should investigate Victoria, Isobel's stepmother. The other Libertine Scholars could deal with the rest of the list.

"Can we discuss this tomorrow? I need to see to Evangeline first. One bloody problem at a time." He didn't miss the flash of anger passing over Arend's face. "Come back at a decent hour tomorrow and we will work on a strategy. For what it's worth, I agree with you. Lady Victoria is looking a likely candidate."

Arend sighed but rose from his chair. "Fine. I can wait one more night. Watch your back."

"It's you who should be careful. I'm home and I've alerted the staff to take turns guarding the house, and I've sent word to employ an army of Bow Street Runners for here and Evangeline's house. You're welcome to stay the night if you wish."

"You sure you don't want me here simply to stop yourself from doing something stupid with your patient?"

He wished her could knock the smug look off Arend's face, but there might have been a bit of truth in his words.

Arend clapped him on the back. "Breakfast here tomorrow, then."

"Good night, Arend."

"I shall leave you to your nursing. I hope you have a better bedside manner than you showed her earlier tonight. Remember, she was shot because of you."

He rose to walk Arend to the door. "It's not something I'll likely forget. I'm pretty sure she won't let me forget it either."

Before Arend took his leave he said to Hadley, "I hope Lady Evangeline recovers quickly. It would be safer for her to be in her own house."

Hadley swallowed down his fear. "Would she? I'm concerned I have pulled her into this debacle. If De Palma thinks she means something to me . . ."

Arend cursed. "The bitch might use her to lure you out or worse."

He nodded. "That's what I have been mulling over the past half hour. What do I do with Evangeline?"

"She'd be safer here."

She would, but he would not. "She can't move in here without repercussions. Neither Augustus nor I is married."

"It could solve your other problem if she was compromised and you *had* to marry her."

Claire. He'd forgotten he was all but engaged, and that Augustus would be upset if Hadley put that alliance in jeopardy.

"I would have to ask my mother to come back to town to act as chaperone, and can you imagine the gossip? The *ton* believe I left Philomena because of her."

Footsteps sounded above them. Someone was coming down the stairs.

Arend nodded. "I'll send word to Sebastian. His aunt, Lady Alison, might agree to act as chaperone."

"Good idea. See if she can come first thing in the morning. We'll speak more then. Take one of the Runners with you. Good night."

With that, Arend left into the dark night. Hadley prayed he would get home in one piece.

He moved to greet the doctor at the bottom of the stairs. The doctor's face was not showing any signs of being overly concerned. Hadley hoped that was good news.

"We'll talk in the study," he told the doctor, indicating that he should follow.

Once they were seated he offered the doctor a brandy. "There is a chill in the air. It will keep you warm on your way home."

"Thank you, my lord, most thoughtful." The doctor took a sip. "Her ladyship was very lucky. The bullet grazed her shoulder. It took a chunk of skin out, though. I needed to administer a few stitches to stop the bleeding, but it's not life-threatening. I've dressed the wound, but it will need changing regularly to lower the risk of infection."

Hadley let out the breath he'd been holding, his guilt easing slightly. "That is good news."

"The lady is in robust health, and although she'll have a small scar, there should be no further repercussions."

Hadley sat in silence listening to the doctor explain exactly what the bullet had done, anger building at the knowledge that she'd taken a bullet meant for him.

"May I enquire how this happened, my lord? I tried to get her ladyship to call for the Runners, but she refused. She said you would deal with the situation." He took a sip of his brandy. "Shocking that thieves have grown so bold as to shoot a woman in this fine area of London. What is the world coming to? Although I wonder if it was straight thievery."

"What makes you say that?" He didn't want anyone knowing of the Libertine Scholars situation.

He paused before looking strangely at Hadley. "May I be frank, my lord?" When Hadley nodded, he continued. "During my inspection of her ladyship, I noticed a few strange injuries."

"Strange?"

The doctor colored. "I suspect she has been beaten, and not just once. Her arm has been broken at one stage and reset very badly. And there are other scars. I mention this only in case she needs protection. I understand she is now a wealthy widow, and I wonder if she is being targeted by some nefarious rogue. She told me she has lived in Scotland alone these past twelve months. I wonder if she's come to London to get help." The doctor eyed him as if he were Evangeline's knight in shining armor.

If her story was true, he was anything but her hero. Jumbled emotions rollicked within his body. Rage like he'd never known rose, followed by bile. Someone had hurt her, deliberately. The idea that her story could be true made his heart twist in agony.

"Thank you, Doctor, for being frank with me. Have no fear— I will protect her. I have called the Runners, but they are being discreet. Besides, Lord Labourd has asked to organize the hunt for the perpetrator. I have a wounded guest to see to."

The doctor nodded. "Very wise. We cannot have young women being shot at in the respectable streets of London."

"Quite."

"I shall take my leave, but I'll be back to check on the wound. The next few days are where the risk of infection is likely. She should stay resting and not too much movement of that shoulder until the stitches take."

Hadley stood as Thurston, the family butler, arrived to show the doctor out. "I shall try to get her to obey your instructions, but the lady has a mind of her own."

"Don't they all," the doctor said, smiling. He took his leave.

Hadley's gut was churning with unease. He needed to speak urgently with Evangeline about the letter.

Mrs. Booker knocked on the door, and he bid her enter.

"I've sent word to her ladyship's home to alert them to the fact she's been hurt, but that it is nothing to be concerned about. I didn't want anyone worrying."

"Thank you." At the same time he wondered if there was anyone else who would be worrying about her. As the doctor pointed out, she was a beautiful rich widow. Usually such ladies did not lack for company for long.

"She was particularly worried about her son. He will wonder where she is if she is not there in the morning. She takes breakfast with him every day."

The word "son" hit him in his chest so hard, it was as if he'd been trampled by a bull. A big bloody bull. He had not heard she had a son, and all he could think was any son Evangeline had should have been his.

Thank goodness she was not badly wounded. She had a son. A son who'd already lost his father. Guilt would destroy him if the little lad lost his mother too.

As the haze of hurt and disappointment swirled, Mrs. Butler added, "She's asking to see you."

He nodded. "Thank you. I know it's late and you'll need your sleep. I'm sorry to cause such trouble."

"It was not you who shot her. It could have been a lot worse. Praise the Lord no one was killed." She crossed herself as she took her leave.

He was tired, exhausted really, but he owed Evangeline an explanation. He made his way upstairs to her room, guilt and anger mixing to make his mood dark and dangerous.

He knocked softly, hoping she'd drifted into sleep and this conversation could wait until the morning. However, a strong "Enter" was his reply.

As he stepped into the room, two things struck him. One, the only woman he'd ever loved was finally in his bed, where he had always wanted her to be. Two, he still wanted the dream. Still wanted a life with her as his wife, wanted her to love him so much that she put him first rather than money or a title.

He wanted a fantasy.

He had promised to marry Claire.

Claire would never lie to him. She didn't care enough to. She would never break his heart either, as he cared not a jot for her. They would marry. She would do as her family desired, just as he would.

He took the chair next to the bed. She looked pale but still beautiful. Desire was swimming in his blood, mixing with the guilt and the anger. "I'm so sorry you were hurt. It wasn't my intention for you to get mixed up in this mess."

She shrugged. "Your words earlier this evening injured me far more than this silly bullet. The fact that you don't believe me . . . well, it's like you've taken a dagger to my heart."

His mouth fell open. He'd hurt *her*? Did she even begin to understand the depth of pain her sudden marriage to Viscount Stuart had caused him?

He would not argue with her tonight. Her pallor and the slight gleam on her face indicated she was not as comfortable as she indicated.

"Are you going to explain to me why someone is trying to kill you? Don't deny it. If you had not bent down, the shot would have seen you in your grave." She choked on the last two words, and her hands were gripping the sheets, her knuckles white.

"Do not worry yourself. I can take care of myself."

She scoffed at his words. "Like you did tonight. You didn't even have bodyguards with you."

"I had no idea, until tonight, that I was in such grave danger."

"But you knew you were in danger?"

"Speaking of which, are *you* in danger, Evangeline? Is that why you have come to London to seek me out, hoping I'll protect you?"

"Why would you think that? It's you the bullet was for."

He watched her face closely for signs of deceit, but her expression was open. Either she was a brilliant actress or she really did not feel she was in any danger. "The doctor mentioned you had unexplained injuries."

Her face closed immediately and a haunted look entered her eyes. "He should not have spoken to you of them."

He did not miss the word "them," as if there were multiple injuries. "How did you get these injuries?"

A tear tracked down one pale cheek, and his soul wanted to rage against the person who'd hurt her.

"You wouldn't believe me even if I told you, since you have not believed a word I said to you tonight."

He wanted to believe her so badly, but it wasn't just the letter that made her a liar. He had a witness.

"You know I'd protect you regardless of our past. I'd never let anyone hurt a lady."

She relaxed back against the covers, looking forlorn. "I'm not the one in danger, you are. I know the truth."

He wouldn't push her tonight, but he would learn who had hurt her. "What have the ladies told you?"

She didn't even pretend to misunderstand him.

"Marisa may have told me a little of what is going on. Do not blame her—she was trying to explain how she ended up compromised."

Bloody interfering women.

Over the following half hour Hadley explained the situation with the Libertine Scholars and their common enemy, and the latest intelligence they had gathered.

"She's going to kill you." Her words were spoken quietly, and her face appeared even paler, if that was possible. She was genuinely worried for him, and the thought warmed him.

Hadley simply shrugged. "Unlike my fellow Libertine Scholars, who are all first sons, it would appear there is no point ruining a second son. Killing is quicker and sends the appropriate message to the others."

Evangeline looked at the man before her, really looked. She

had never considered how sensitive he was to his second-son status, but he'd mentioned his station in life several times tonight. Had he been this concerned five years ago?

Maybe her supposed betrayal had caused this lack of self-worth. He actually believed she had married another for money and a title.

If he had received a forged letter on top of his insecurities, then it would be understandable for him to think so little of her. She was more determined than ever to see the letter, so that she could prove him wrong. She had a good idea how such a deception might have been achieved. Her mother had forged other people's handwriting before, when the family needed credit.

Right now, however, she was more concerned with the immediate danger Hadley faced.

"What do you plan to do about this situation?"

He would not meet her eyes. "I don't see that it's any of your business."

"This." She pointed to her bandaged shoulder. "This makes it my business."

"I plan to find out who this woman is and stop her before she hurts anyone else I care for."

The great protector. He'd always been his brother's keeper too. Hadley had always been there for anyone weaker or in need of help. When she'd saved Stowe, Hadley been so proud of her for standing up to Stowe's bully of a father.

But he hadn't come to Scotland to rescue her, and now she knew why. He hadn't believed in her.

Her heart seized with worry. He would risk himself to bring De Palma down because he always put others before himself. That was what hurt her the most, because she'd pinned all her hopes on him saving her.

She opened her mouth to speak again, but he held up his hand. "Let's talk no more about this tonight. The doctor advised you to rest. Mrs. Butler has let your household know you will be here for a few days."

"I cannot stay here for—"

He interrupted, "I forgot to mention that I hope Lady Coldhurst, Sebastian's aunt, will be arriving shortly, so your reputation is safe. And if necessary I'll send a missive to my mother. She left town only last week, but if I explain the situation, I'm sure she would return."

"I'm not worried about my reputation. But my son will fret without me."

She watched some deep emotion flicker in Hadley's eyes at the mention of her son.

"Your son is welcome to come and stay too. In fact, it may be safer for him to do so."

Evangeline's throat dried. She could not bring Sealey here, not yet. Not until she gained an understanding of the man Hadley had become. So far she was not terribly impressed. And it would appear he was in danger.

Sealey was a sensitive child and the move to London had unsettled him. He would fret without her. He wasn't yet five and had not had a very pleasant upbringing until Dougal's death. He was only just starting to blossom into a normal little boy. He would get anxious again if she was not home tomorrow when he woke up.

"There is no need. I will be going home before dawn. My house is not far from here. Actually, I believe my townhouse's garden backs onto your family's garden."

She watched a myriad of emotions swarm over Hadley's handsome face: relief, fear, anger, sadness.

Sadness gave her hope. "Why don't you show me this letter I supposedly wrote? I'd like to see it before I leave."

Hadley refocused on her, worry lining his face. "It's too dangerous for you to leave. Bringing you here was a mistake. With all the talk about us, and then I bring you here, to my family home, society will assume a relationship. This could make you and your son a target."

Fear for her son made her pain fade away. "I need to go home," she said, throwing back the covers with her good arm.

He moved forward. "The doctor said—"

"I don't care what he said. My son is alone. I'm all he has."

Hadley saw she meant business because she began to rise from the bed. "I can send for him. You will both be safer here."

"No." She didn't mean the word to come out so harsh.

Hadley's head snapped back in surprise. "Why on earth not?"

"He has recently lost his father, he's come to a strange town and new house, and he is unsettled. I will not move him again." Evangeline was amazed that she came up with such an excuse so quickly; however, it was very close to the truth.

Hadley seemed to think on her words before saying, "I have already organized for Runners to guard your house. You must promise me not to leave the house without their protection."

She cocked her head to one side and looked at him. "Thank you. Plus, I may be able to help you." In a whisper she added, "Marisa mentioned Arend's fixation on Lady Victoria. It may not be unwarranted. I think there might be pertinent information on Victoria in my husband's journals."

Hadley sat forward in his chair. "I beg your pardon?"

"My husband was a vindictive man. He was also good friends with Victoria's husband, and I know the sudden marriage to her upset him. He didn't trust her. He began digging into her past, and the journals may contain the knowledge you seek."

"You could bring the journals here."

She shook her head. There were things in the journals she did not wish Hadley to see: things about her son, and things about how her husband had treated her. She would not share that with him. Ever.

"They are heavy volumes and contain personal material. I really should be the one to go through them. I may even find the evidence I need to prove to you that your assumptions about me are wrong. That I did not marry for a title and money." She was sure Dougal had confessed all in his journals.

She saw the resignation in Hadley's lovely eyes. All he cared about were the journals, not that he'd maligned her all these years.

"It would be faster if both of us went through the journals," he insisted.

She barely hid her anger. "So now that I have something you want, you're prepared to spend time in my presence." He had the grace to drop his gaze from hers. "Until I see this letter, you will not be looking at those journals."

"I could fetch the letter now."

"No. I'm tired and I'm hurt. You can jolly well wait until it suits me. If you'd be so kind as to fetch my carriage, I intend to go home."

Hadley had the good sense not to argue with her. He must have realized it would not take much more for her to lose her temper completely. He walked over to the door and opened it to call for Mrs. Butler.

Mrs. Butler entered and helped Evangeline move behind the screen so she could dress.

"May I call on you tomorrow with the letter?"

It was a little unsettling to realize Hadley had stayed while she changed. Gosh, he was like Sealey's puppy with a bone. Part of her wanted to make him wait, but since he *was* in danger, and now she and Sealey might be in danger too, time was not a luxury they could afford.

She came out from behind the screen, tiredness weighing heavily on her sore shoulder. Arguing took too much energy. "Shall we say three in the afternoon? And bring the forged letter."

He wanted to say no, but he needed those journals. He wished he'd never told her that he still had the proof of her betrayal. He was lying to himself. The doubt that crept into his head from the doctor's observation was eating at him. He had to know, firstly, if her tale was true, and secondly, who had hurt her.

Plus, he was at least honorable enough to realize that after being shot she deserved consideration.

More annoying was the fact that briefly seeing her in nothing

but her sheer shift had his body humming—and not from tiredness. His mind couldn't seem to remember why she was the
enemy. Memories of long ago, memories that had taken a long
time to forget, flooded back—vividly.

He stood and walked to the door. "My men will see you safely
home, and I shall call upon you at three."

As he pulled the door closed behind him, he thought he heard
her say, "Then the truth will be revealed," and a sickness invaded
his stomach.

If her story was true, how could he ever live with himself?

Chapter Four

Evangeline had been escorted safely home two hours ago, at five in the morning.

She had agreed to allow guards to be posted in the grounds, with two in the foyer of the house, and he'd sent a missive to the Bow Street Runners requesting ten of their best men to keep the house under surveillance at all times. The Runners had been told that someone took a shot at Lady Evangeline.

This didn't help his second problem.

She had the journals, and she refused to share unless he bared his soul. He shoved his hand into his pocket and fingered the letter, fighting an urge to crumple it in his fist. He was a coward for not wishing to face what he now suspected was the truth—her truth.

What irked him more was that she was now back in his life in a way he could not control. He could not simply ignore her or send her back to the wilds of Scotland.

And she'd found the weapon to wedge herself back into his life without having to prove her innocence. He'd need her either way—because he needed the journals.

He pulled his cravat from around his neck, his throat tightening in anger. She would not let him peruse the journals unless he did her bidding.

Lady Victoria Thompson deserved closer inspection. It would appear Arend's hunch was a good one. What Evangeline had revealed about her husband not trusting Isobel's stepmother confirmed that Arend was wise to focus his attention on her. Victoria had a secret past.

A past she kept hidden.

He glanced at the clock on the mantel. It had just gone seven in the morning, and he expected Arend soon. He needed to bathe and change before then. Wearily he stood and looked longingly at his bed; the impression of where Evangeline had lain was evident. He pressed his face to his pillow, loving the scent of her that lingered there.

He drew back. If her story was true, how could she ever forgive him? Either way, there would be no future with Evangeline.

He *was* marrying Claire.

There was no time to rest or to dwell on what might have been. There was a killer he had to apprehend. He moved to the window to watch the sunrise. His rooms looked out over the back garden—ironically, directly into Evangeline's townhouse. He'd had no idea that her husband owned the townhouse backing onto his family's London home.

He was pleased he hadn't known. It would have been too much to bear, as if Viscount Stuart were mocking him.

He stood watching the house over the garden wall. He wondered whose room was exactly opposite his.

He was about to turn away when a movement at the large windows stopped him. A curtain was drawn back and a child's face pressed against the glass, probably looking out to see what kind of day it was. The sun was beginning to shine, but there were plenty of clouds about.

He couldn't make out the child's face; he thought it was a boy with darkish, curly hair, though it could be a little girl. Hadley's hands curled into fists as he realized this was likely Evangeline's son.

The little boy looked up and saw him staring, and a wee hand waved. Hadley waved back. An adult, probably his nanny, came up behind him and pulled the boy away from the window, and just like that, the boy was gone.

A sense of loss swamped him, and he cursed at his own stupidity. How could a simple wave from a child have his stomach in painful knots?

Because it was Evangeline's child.

Later, as he lay in his tub trying not to dwell on what should have been—his son with Evangeline—doubt began to creep in. What if she had been coerced into marriage? It would mean he had been played, duped, and she had paid the price. Paid it with brutality against her person. He pushed that horrible thought away.

She seemed so sure she could prove her innocence in the matter, and that sent waves of unease through his limbs.

Scotland, the Highlands in particular, were remote. What if the note he received had been a clever forgery and she hadn't been able to get word to him? He swiped a hand over his face, scrubbing at the dark thoughts assailing him.

He could feel the fortress around his heart begin to weaken.

What did she want with him? If her story was true, there was no going back—not from this. However, no official announcement of his nuptials to Claire had been given; he could still back out. Augustus would simply have to front up and marry Claire if he wished to help his friend.

If Evangeline was innocent, her return changed everything. If she forgave him, they could have a chance at a future, at regaining the past.

But, he thought, she had a son who was a viscount. Her life should revolve around her son and protecting his inheritance. She certainly didn't need a man like him in their lives, a man with little wealth or position.

A man who had not protected her.

Perhaps he and Evangeline had missed their chance. It might be better for all concerned if they acted like grown-ups and admitted that their time had passed. It was too late for them. What they'd once shared was over. Five years was a long time.

You remember every minute of your time with her as if it were yesterday.

He lay back and closed his eyes, a sigh escaping at his cowardice. A small voice echoed in his head, saying that it was never too late.

Marriage to Evangeline would be more pleasurable than marriage to Claire.

Her son was a problem in this plan. He didn't know if he could be a father to Viscount Stuart's son. If the boy took after his mother, it would be easier. He didn't even know the boy's name. Jealousy, deep and poisonous, seeped into his blood. It was too painful to face the fact that the boy should have been theirs. The warmth of the bathwater faded as the impact of Evangeline's return hit home. Already she had him tied up in knots when he should be focusing on De Palma.

With another sigh he pushed the issue of Evangeline from his mind. De Palma had tried to kill him last night. All his energy should be focused on staying alive and putting an end to this deranged woman.

Evangeline was a distraction he didn't need right now. If he didn't keep his wits about him, he could end up dead.

If Arend's hunch that Victoria was their villainess was right, was Isobel involved? Arend had said very little recently about Victoria's stepdaughter, yet Hadley knew Arend was spending considerable time with the young woman. Arend would use anyone to find out what he needed to know. Hadley felt a tad sorry for Isobel.

And God help her if she was part of her stepmother's plot.

Harper, his valet, knocked on the bathing room door. "My lord, His Grace is below."

Hadley rose slowly from the tub, exhaustion beckoning. "Augustus is in town? When did he arrive? Never mind. Tell Thurston to show him into the breakfast room while I dress. And ask Cook—"

"Already taken care of. Breakfast is waiting for you. I've taken the liberty of laying out your clothes too."

"Thank you. Inform my brother I'll be down shortly."

He wondered what Augustus wanted. He hoped his brother hadn't got himself into trouble. Arend was due soon. It was very unlike Augustus to drive all night to reach town this early. Usually Augustus led life at a leisurely pace. He didn't put himself out for anyone but himself.

By the time Hadley reached the breakfast room, Augustus was already partaking of a plate of food. He didn't even look up as Hadley helped himself from the sideboard and sat down.

"You know, you really should have been the firstborn."

At Augustus's words he realized he'd sat at the head of the table. He usually did because Augustus rarely came to town. He hadn't asked for this quasi-position, but someone had to be in charge, and Augustus simply wasn't interested.

His Grace took after their mother: fair-haired, small of stature, quiet, and withdrawn. He did look the picture of a self-assured duke, always immaculately dressed in the height of fashion, always refusing to get his hands dirty with any menial task. Rather than hunt or box or fence, he preferred reading, music, and of all things, fashion, like a spoiled fop.

Since their father's death, Hadley had assumed control of the family and estates. If he had not, the family would no doubt be in ruins. Augustus had no head for business or estate planning. Furthermore, he refused to take his seat in the House of Lords, saying politics gave him a headache. He was quite happy for Hadley to do everything.

Hadley saw beneath his brother's façade of an indulgent duke to the heart of a man who wished he were anyone other than the Duke of Claymore. Augustus hated the responsibility, the required decision making, and the attention that came with his title. He'd told Hadley that if he could renounce his title, he would. He'd also sworn to never marry, so that the title would go to Hadley. So far he'd kept to that vow.

Instead Augustus stayed at the estate in Cornwall doing . . . Hadley didn't know what exactly. Augustus was his mother's favorite, and he preferred her company to anyone else's, even Hadley's.

Hadley was very much the image of his late father: tall, broad-shouldered, brown-haired, and, most of all, determined to enjoy life. He thrived on challenges, and was happy to take over the running of the estates from Augustus. At least then he knew his mother, sisters, and Augustus would be comfortable, and the family money would be protected.

The Libertine Scholars called Hadley "the invisible duke." No one besides them and Augustus knew that he basically ran the Claymore estates and family holdings.

Their father had named his firstborn son Augustus, meaning "majestic." But poor Augustus had not lived up to the name in his father's eyes. From an early age their father had made Augustus's life a living hell, always saying he wished Augustus had died as a baby so that Hadley would be his heir. Sometimes it crossed Hadley's mind that their father had purposely treated Augustus in a manner that put his frail life in danger. It was probably Augustus's proudest achievement that he'd managed to outlive their father.

Hadley couldn't remember how old he'd been when he began having to protect Augustus. Originally he'd protected him from their father, taking the birching for any prank gone wrong. Then he protected Augustus from the other children on the estate, and then from the bullies at Eton, who loved picking on the weakest boys. He'd vowed that no one would pick on his brother if he was around.

Looking out for his older brother became their way. Augustus, at thirty-one a year older than Hadley, still expected his brother to drop everything and do anything to help, as well as to generally make Augustus's life easier.

Hadley had protected Augustus all his life, and he would continue to do so as long as he lived. He hated how the strong picked on the weak. That was the one thing he admired about his brother. Now that he was a duke, he could have wreaked vengeance on those who at school had made his life hell. But he didn't. He chose to ignore them and live simply, quietly, and with dignity at his estate, where he was happiest.

Hadley cursed under his breath. He should not have sat at the head of the table. But the fact that Augustus hadn't taken the chair spoke volumes about how he saw himself. His brother might hold the title of duke, but he was only the figurehead.

"It's merely a chair." Hadley's words rang false. Nothing was "merely" where the *ton* was concerned. Augustus didn't make a fuss, and waved his hand to indicate that Hadley should stay seated where he was.

Hadley decided to change the subject. "Is everything all right? Why the rush to town?"

Augustus looked amused. "I didn't rush to town. I came up two days ago. I just didn't stay here," he said, then continued eating.

A duke who chose not to stay in his own house? Hell, Augustus was getting worse. Soon the *ton* would begin to wonder who was head of this family, and that could be awkward. Perhaps De Palma was targeting Hadley not just because he looked like their father but because she knew he was, for all intents and purposes, the head of the Claymore family. Without him all would be lost, or at least would run to a loss. "Perhaps, when you are in town, it would be more appropriate to stay here. It is, after all, your house through entail. Where were you staying?"

"With a friend. I do have some, you know."

His brother was a secretive sod. Hadley's suspicions soared, but he would play his brother's game. "Well, it's good to see you. How are Mother and the girls?"

"They miss you." He paused for a moment, then added, "And they are all looking forward to the announcement of your betrothal, and of course helping Claire plan the wedding."

Hadley put down his knife and fork. "I thought we were telling no one until I spoke to Claire. The bride should not be the last to hear that she is getting married. I have not sanctioned any formal announcement as yet."

"Mother was consistently hounding me about your likelihood of marriage. So I told her why you were not pursuing any young ladies."

"Why isn't she hounding you about *your* wedding?" Hadley countered.

"She is. But you and I both know I do not wish to marry. I'd never force any son of mine into this role. Your son would be more suited to it."

How convenient, Hadley thought as anger sizzled within him. His brother had come to town for one thing only—to ensure he married Claire. Suddenly he was sick of having to constantly be his brother's protector, advisor, manager—he felt more like a father than a brother. "We may have to hold off on the announcement."

He watched Augustus use his napkin to pat his mouth. He didn't speak until the napkin was back on the table, all neatly folded.

"I did wonder if the return of Lady Evangeline—Stuart, it is now, isn't it?—would make you reconsider our agreement." He looked Hadley in the eye. "However, if I recall, she ripped your heart from your chest five years ago. Why would you give her the time of day?"

"There may have been more to her marriage to Viscount Stuart than I thought."

"May? You still don't know?" Augustus sat back in his chair. "Yet she's been in this house, I have heard."

The staff had been gossiping. Not their fault—it was hard to deny a duke.

"Two years ago, when you came to me with this idea that I marry Lady Claire, it seemed sensible at the time. I thought an arranged match a prudent way to find a wife." Hadley didn't add that it seemed ideal to have a wife who could never own or break his heart. "And you wanted to help your friend Richard Hampton, the Marquis of Corby, find a match for a sister who had no dowry and was, let's face it, a definite wallflower. It suited us all."

"It still suits us all," his brother interjected.

Hadley pushed his plate away, his appetite gone. "I'm having doubts. Evangeline may be innocent—"

"You agreed that if Claire was still unmarried when you reached your thirtieth year, you'd propose. I gave you that time, as promised."

He ran a hand over his face. "I did agree, true. But hell, Aug, what if she didn't leave me of her own free will? That changes everything." His hand slammed the table, making the cutlery rattle. "If her story is true, I owe her whatever she desires. I didn't protect her, you see. I couldn't live knowing I'd let her be abducted, kept as a virtual prisoner. Think on it."

Augustus waited for the crockery to stop rattling before saying, "If you renege, it will put me in a very embarrassing position. Corby is my closest friend."

"We can find some other way to help Corby and his sister. I don't understand why Richard is so insistent that I marry Claire. Surely he'd prefer her to marry a duke." In recent months Hadley had more and more come to wonder why the marquis had, in fact, preferred a second son as a husband for his sister, rather than a duke; it did not make sense. At the time he'd made the agreement, however, he had been so heartbroken that he hadn't thought to ask the right questions.

"As I said, he's my friend, and he knows Claire is not duchess material. She would buckle under the role."

Augustus himself would have bloody buckled under the role of duke. In that, Hadley thought wryly, Augustus and Claire would be well suited.

Hadley wasn't about to be forced into a marriage he no longer wanted. Until he knew the truth regarding Evangeline, he would not wed another. If he had a real chance at happiness, then he wanted it—wanted it so badly he could almost taste it.

"I've done more than enough for this family, and for you, over the years. I've protected you, managed the estates for you, and increased our family's wealth. You could at least support me in this. Give me a chance to see if there is something there with Evangeline. It's not going to end your friendship with Richard if I decide to pull out. I'll even help you find an alternative groom. Claire won't be hurt, as she has no idea what we have planned—or at least I hope not."

"Claire doesn't know yet. Just as well, as it turns out." Augustus had the decency to look sheepish. "It's true you have been a very good brother to me. You did protect me from the wrath of Father and others."

Hadley sighed. "Look, nothing is certain yet. I still have to hear Evangeline's version of events. I need time to think. I have to decide what I want, and I also must do what is right. We still have three weeks until we have to make any decision."

Augustus gave him a silent look that Hadley could not interpret. He had always found it hard to read his brother; Augustus always seemed as if he held secrets. And it had always annoyed Hadley that Augustus could shield his thoughts so successfully even though he could not protect himself physically.

Before Augustus could respond, Arend sauntered in.

"Oh, I'm sorry—I didn't wait to be announced, as I didn't know His Grace was in town."

Augustus waved away the unintentional slight. "No apology necessary. It's a pleasure to see you, Arend." He stood up. "I was just leaving. Hadley, we will talk later, yes?"

Hadley merely nodded.

Augustus smiled at the two men before leaving the room.

"What did His Grace want?" Arend asked as he helped himself to a plate of food.

"Who says he wanted anything?"

"He never comes to town unless he has to."

That was true. Augustus had said he'd been staying with a friend; had he really? Or did Augustus not wish him to know he'd rushed up to town? And why was it so important that he marry Claire? Surely the Marquis of Corby could find another suitor. In the *ton* money talked, and Augustus had plenty to help his friend. Why did it have to be Hadley?

"He wanted to talk with me about Claire."

Arend laughed. "I don't understand why Augustus is so set on the match. You could do so much better than a mousy wallflower."

Arend's thoughts mirrored his own. Annoyance dug under his skin. Why *was* Augustus so set on the match?

With a sigh, Hadley changed the subject. "Aren't you here to discuss a plan to unmask Victoria?"

Arend gave a sly smile. "Too little sleep, I see. Or is it Lady Evangeline that's turned you into a grump this morning?"

"I have been up all night. But it's more that I'm sick of people poking their noses into my business."

"Evangeline is a beautiful problem to have, though."

"And a useful one. She thinks her husband may have included information on Victoria in his journals. Apparently he wasn't too happy at her unexpected marriage to his friend Lord Northumberland. He began digging into her background."

"How did the viscount die?"

Hadley's head snapped up like a whip. "He was killed by highwaymen—supposedly."

Excitement lit Arend's eyes. "Eat up. We need to visit Lady Evangeline immediately so that can we see the journals."

"One small problem: she's not very happy with me and won't let me view them. She'll let us know if she finds anything."

"Damn it. That's awkward." Arend gestured with his fork. "Well, you'll just have to grovel and get back in her good graces."

"You can be such a prick at times."

Arend nodded as he chewed. He swallowed before saying, "I will have to try something different, then, while you grow some bottle. I have an idea on how to expose Victoria."

"One day I hope a woman does a job on you. Then we shall see who has bottle and who has not." When Arend said nothing more, he added, "Care to share this plan?"

Arend began outlining what they could do.

Chapter Five

Her shoulder ached, and because Hadley had pulled her to the ground, every limb felt as if a tree had fallen on it. Last night she'd been in more pain than she would admit, especially to Hadley. The guilt etched upon his face was more than she could bear. He blamed himself, yet her injury had been out of his control.

She gave a wan smile. He had tried to protect her. That should mean something. But, as she recalled, Hadley protected everyone.

Why, then, had he not protected her five years ago? Her heart refused to believe it was because he didn't care. She could see how much he cared when she was shot. The look on his face . . .

Her stomach clenched tight, facing the knowledge that if she had not accompanied him home, Hadley would never have bent down at the moment the shot was fired. He'd be dead. Accompanying him home had saved his life.

Her head swam, and she lay back upon her pillow.

Someone wanted to kill him.

Rachel, her lady's maid, had fussed over her when they'd carried her into her room in the early hours of the morning, but she'd managed to sleep for about four hours before Sealey could no longer be kept away.

He'd barged into her room before she could hide the bandages. He'd been frightened by her injury. Losing Dougal had been his introduction to death, and given his young age, the little boy was petrified that he'd lose her too.

She stroked the silky curls on her little boy's head as he slept beside her. She'd finally managed to get him to cuddle down and doze, but even though she was still tired and sore, sleep eluded her.

Her first meeting with Hadley had not gone as she'd expected —or, indeed, hoped. It seemed that five years apart had changed him more than it had changed her. Given his story about receiving a letter purportedly from her, she could understand why.

It wasn't the pain of her gunshot wound that filled her eyes with tears. It was the fact he had believed a piece of paper over everything they'd shared and done. She'd given him her heart, her body, and her soul, but he'd simply taken the words on a piece of paper and forgotten *her*. Forgotten who she was.

Plus, when she'd told him it was a forgery, he'd not believed her. If he'd truly known her, understood her, loved her, he should have believed her.

She wasn't naive enough to think that their relationship could be as it was before. Both of them had been changed by what life had thrown at them, but to call her character into question . . .

When she'd set eyes on him yesterday she knew immediately that though she was mad as hell at him, she still loved him. The heart doesn't always listen to the head.

As their eyes met she'd hoped he would still love her.

His cold, rage-filled stare had been like a dagger to her chest. It had looked more like he hated her. Now she understood why. He blamed her for breaking his heart, and that caused her more pain than any bullet.

Prickles of anger surfaced to chase away the sorrow. Her dead husband was still winning. Dougal had forced her to marry him, lie with him, and live with him. He'd stolen her life of happiness with Hadley, and then through a forged letter ensured that when she became a widow happiness would still be denied her.

"Does it hurt?"

She looked at her son's anxious eyes and smiled away her tears. "A little."

He rose up and kissed her cheek. "All better."

She gave a laugh. She always kissed him when he had a hurt. "Yes, all better."

Every time she looked at Sealey her heart burst with pride, joy, and love. He made everything she'd endured worthwhile.

"Nanny said you were taking me to the park today. I suppose that's off now." His face lost its smile. "How many sleeps will you be indisposed for?"

"I'm not sure. How about we ask Lady Isobel if she'll take you and Nanny instead?"

He jumped out of her arms and started bouncing on the bed. "Really? When can we ask her?"

"If you're a good boy and go with Nanny so Mummy can rest, I'll send a missive to Lady Isobel and see if she'll take you tomorrow. How does that sound?"

Sealey slid down off the bed and started trotting toward the door to her room. Before he could reach for the door latch, the door swung open and Lady Marisa, Lady Beatrice, and Lady Isobel swarmed in.

Marisa was in the lead, and she stopped dead in her tracks as her eyes took in Sealey.

"Oh my God," she whispered, and turned her startled eyes toward Evangeline.

Beatrice bumped into her and peered around Marisa, only to gasp when she looked at the boy standing wide-eyed in the middle of Evangeline's room. The only one not to show surprise was Isobel.

The silence was broken when Sealey squealed, "Lady Isobel," and raced into her outstretched arms.

Isobel had befriended Evangeline after Dougal's death while

she was enduring twelve months of mourning for a man she hated. Isobel's father had been Dougal's close friend and confidant, and when Isobel came to visit for the funeral, Isobel fell in love with Evangeline's little boy. When Isobel met Hadley, after the carriage rescue, she'd understood the truth.

"Sealey! Why, I think you've grown in the week since I last saw you. Look how tall you are."

Sealey beamed up at Isobel.

"Mother says you might take me to Richmond Park to see the deer tomorrow since she is unwell."

"Sealey Hadley Masters, where are your manners? Say hello to the ladies first before you start requesting favors."

He turned on his heel to look back at Marisa and Beatrice, who were still staring at him as if he had two heads.

Sealey gave a small bow. "Good morning, ladies."

The ladies curtsied back, with Marisa saying, "It's a pleasure to meet you, young man. I'd be excited about a trip to see the deer too. They are beautiful, but look out for the stags—they can be fierce."

His eyes widened further. "They are not scary, though?"

Marisa chuckled. "A little. You'll have to hold tightly to Isobel's hand so she won't be too frightened."

His little chest puffed out. "I'll protect you," he said to Isobel, and Evangeline had never been so proud of her son.

Just then the nanny arrived to take him for a walk before lunch in the small park round the corner. Evangeline knew she couldn't risk taking the boy further afield just yet. Not until she'd spoken to Hadley.

"Wendy, when you go for your walk today, please ensure you take the extra men with you." She looked pointedly at Sealey and did not say anything more. Wendy merely nodded and escorted the boy from the room.

The second the door closed, three sets of eyes found hers, and the astonishment on two of the ladies' faces was priceless.

"I'm sorry that we barged in unannounced, but the men

couldn't tell us how badly injured you were. We were out of our minds with worry."

Evangeline merely shook her head at Beatrice and sighed. As they stood staring accusingly, she added, "I suspect my secret is out. I'm hoping you ladies can keep my confidences."

Marisa took her gloves off as she bent to kiss Evangeline's cheek. "I take it you haven't told Hadley that Sealey is his son."

Evangeline shook her head. "I'd planned to do so last night, just after he fell into my arms and professed that he still loved me." She added sarcastically, "That didn't happen."

Beatrice was at the door organizing refreshments with Evangeline's maid, and it was Isobel who sat at the end of her bed and said, "I knew the minute I met Hadley—the day the men rescued Marisa and me—that Sealey was Lord Fullerton's son. But I promised Evangeline I would not say a thing."

"You do realize that Hadley will know as soon as he sees the boy," Beatrice said as she took the chair by the window. "In fact, if any of the men see the boy, your secret is out."

"I want time to think before I do anything. Dougal claimed the boy as his own. Society understands Sealey is the next Viscount Stuart."

"You can't expect Hadley to have sat waiting for you. He must have been shocked to hear your story. If I know him, he'll blame himself for not saving you."

"Did he beg your forgiveness? I'm sure his feelings for you are as strong as ever."

Hadley's feelings were strong, all right. He detested her.

"Why have you never told him?" Marisa asked quietly. "A person deserves to know they have a child."

Beatrice reached for Marisa's hand, and Evangeline understood the reason for Marisa's accusation. She knew Marisa could not have children, the result of an injury received when the villainess who had shot at Hadley last night kidnapped Marisa and Isobel a month ago. She thought of what her life would be without Sealey and completely understood the devastation of Marisa's loss. She therefore forgave Marisa.

"I wrote many, many letters to Hadley from the moment I found myself married to Dougal. I hoped at least one might get through to him. I specifically wrote to him when Sealey was born, but the maid I thought was my friend and confidante was working for Dougal. I now know Hadley never received my letters."

Evangeline hadn't understood the depth of her maid's betrayal until she met with Hadley last night. It was obvious that none of the letters she'd written to Hadley during the first eighteen months of her marriage had been sent to him.

Now she understood why he'd never come for her.

She'd never expected to receive a letter back, as Dougal guarded her well. Still, she had hoped Hadley would come for her, scandal or not. It had never occurred to her that he hadn't received her pleas. Instead, she thought he'd decided that what was done was done—now that she was married, he could not change anything without destroying her reputation.

Through all the months of her pregnancy when he'd not come for her, she'd almost despaired. Only Sealey's birth kept her from going insane.

The moment she'd held her son in her arms, the world changed. The dream of Hadley came second to the life of her son.

Dougal knew the boy was not his. He learned she hadn't been a virgin on her wedding night, and she'd paid dearly for that. When her son was born seven months after her abduction, he treated the boy with little more than restrained contempt, something Sealey noticed as he got older. As Sealey grew she could not deny he was the image of Hadley. She thought she'd have to protect Sealey from Dougal, but to her amazement she didn't have to. Dougal barely tolerated Sealey, but for some reason he was only too eager to claim the boy as his own. His previous wife had died with no issue, and so she assumed Dougal was worried the fault might lie with him. Since she'd never fallen pregnant a second time, it was likely he was right.

So her son was now the next Viscount Stuart. She intended to see that he was a far better man than the previous viscount.

"Are you saying he never got your letters?" Marisa's tone was conciliatory.

She swallowed back the sorrow of the past. "He received only one letter, a letter that was supposedly written by me, telling him I was eloping with Viscount Stuart of my own free will."

Stunned silence greeted her announcement.

"No wonder his reception was so frosty."

She wanted to cry at Isobel's words. " 'Frosty' doesn't begin to describe his reaction. 'Downright hatred' would come close."

"A man would hate only if he'd deeply loved. Therefore, he obviously forgave you once you explained . . ." At Evangeline's raised eyebrow Beatrice uttered, "Oh, dear."

"But you left together," Marisa added.

"I told him I hadn't written any letter to that effect. He swore I had, that he'd compared the handwriting to our previous correspondence. So I asked to see the letter. We had just arrived at his family's townhouse when someone decided to shoot him. If I hadn't dropped my muff . . ."

"He'd be dead." Isobel shuddered. "You saved his life."

The women looked at one another. "None of us are safe." Marisa's hands were clenched in her lap. "I want to catch her so badly."

Beatrice smiled at Evangeline. "At least you'll have Hadley's attention and devotion. You were shot because of him, and if I know him at all, he'll be feeling pretty guilty. Once you explain about Sealey, he'll step up and do the right thing."

Evangeline flopped back onto her pillows. "I don't want him to do the right thing. I've just come out of a loveless marriage, and I'm not about to enter another." She wasn't about to marry a man who didn't know her or want her.

"If he finds out about Sealey, you'll have no choice. He'll

insist."

Evangeline looked at Beatrice as if she'd like to slap her. "He can insist all he likes, but Dougal claimed the boy. Sealey is now Viscount Stuart. In the eyes of the law Hadley has no rights."

"He should be allowed to know his son, just as Sealey should know his real father." Marisa stood and moved to stare out the window, lost in private thoughts.

"I agree. However, I'd like the chance to tell him in my own time. He has much on his mind at the moment, what with a madwoman out to kill him. Plus, if it became known he was Sealey's father, wouldn't that put my son in even greater danger?" She felt the breath seize in her chest. "I will tell him the truth about his son when it suits me, and then of course he can see Sealey as much as he wishes, but I warn you now"—she looked at Marisa—"I will never be forced into another marriage. That would destroy me."

Marisa swung round from the window to face her. "What if he had died last night? He would never have known he even had a son." She gave a sad smile. "Plus, he is about to announce his engagement to Lady Claire Hampton. I'm not supposed to know, but I overhead Arend and Maitland discussing it. She doesn't even know yet. His Grace organized the match with her brother." She appealed to all of them. "You see, don't you? He should know the truth in case he is still considering Lady Claire. Once their engagement is announced he would never renege, even if he longed to. He's too honorable and he'll be left unable to acknowledge Sealey."

Evangeline's heart missed a beat. No wonder he was not enraptured to see her; he was about to marry another. It was all the proof she needed to finally understand that Hadley had, of course, moved on. It also proved how she truly felt about Hadley. Sadness engulfed her, and she had to take deep breaths. It didn't matter if she forgave him or not. They were fated to never be together.

Only now would she admit that she'd lied to herself. Her

purpose in coming to London had not been to berate Hadley. It had been to get what had been stolen from her—her happily-ever-after with a man who loved her. The father of her son.

"He's getting married?"

"It's not what you think. I'm not sure of the details, as I'm not proud to say I was eavesdropping. I think it's a favor to Augustus. I'm pretty sure Hadley is not in love with Claire. He only gave up his mistress yesterday."

A fiancée *and* a mistress? Hadley certainly had not been pining for her.

"I'm not the same young girl I was back then, and so I can hardly expect Hadley to be the same man. It would appear he has moved on and forgotten me."

"Rubbish," Beatrice said. "I saw his face when you walked into the room last night. I'd never seen a look of such longing, and it was followed by a great deal of fear. He wants to hate you but he can't. The first thing we have to do is find this letter you supposedly wrote and prove it a forgery."

"Or," Isobel said, clapping her hands, "we find other proof of your story. Have you been through your husband's papers? Even better, perhaps a staff member will come forward to verify your story."

Evangeline sat up when she saw all the ladies energized on her behalf. "He'd be wary of staff; they need jobs and would therefore likely lie for me. I could go through my husband's papers, as he kept immaculate journals."

"I could help you. I'm sure we'll find something in his journals. Perhaps Lord Stuart recanted all his sins." Enthused, Isobel next asked the question Evangeline was dreading. "What of your mother? She is still alive. Would she help you now?"

Evangeline turned her face away and looked out the window. She hadn't spoken to her mother since her wedding night. She could not bring herself to forgive her. The fact that her mother had sold her made her so angry she was tempted to do violence. She had never been a daughter; she was just property to be bartered. She worried about Edward too. Did their mother control him? Had she gambled away all the money she'd received from selling Evangeline to Dougal?

"I won't go to my mother."

The coldness and firmness in her tone made it clear to those present that they were not to push the issue.

Beatrice shrugged. "So, then, just your husband's papers, journals, and the forged letter."

"Where are his papers?" Marisa asked.

"I have all of his papers and journals with me. I want to employ my own man of business to go through all the estate documents. I don't trust anyone who worked for Dougal. I was hoping one of your husbands might recommend someone I could hire. I have to protect my son's inheritance."

"Maitland would know of a man you could trust."

"Thank you, Marisa."

What a wonderful friend Isobel was. Without her she'd never have met these amazingly generous women.

"That's settled, then," Beatrice said. "I'll send a missive to Portia, and we'll help you search through the journals once you're feeling up to it. I suggest we start there rather than his business papers. Isobel, you will ensure that Sealey is kept entertained yet undiscovered. Hadley will come here. He'll want to ensure you're all right, and of course there is the business of the letter. We can't have him clapping eyes on his son until you've had a chance to learn what's in his heart."

Evangeline threw back the covers, "Oh, goodness. I sent Sealey to the park with his nanny. If any of the men come here just as Sealey and Wendy are returning . . ."

Isobel stood and raced for the door. "I'll go to the park and warn Wendy. We'll come in through the back alley and use the servants' entrance." With that, she disappeared.

Evangeline grimaced with the pain of moving her shoulder. She sank back onto the bed. "Thank you. I'm so lucky you befriended me," she said to the women who remained.

It was Marisa who spoke first. "No woman should have to go through what you did. If we don't help each other, who else will?"

Evangeline smiled at them both. Such strong, capable women. She wished she had met them before being abducted by Dougal. What a difference these women might have made. They would have come looking for her, she was sure. They would have known that her heart belonged to Hadley and that she'd never have run off with another.

Why hadn't Hadley believed in her? She kept pushing that devastating question aside, but at some stage she would need to know the answer if she was to ever move on.

She'd never had close friends. Her mother had kept her isolated once she turned fifteen, the year her father died. Perhaps her mother had even then hatched her plan to use her only daughter to save the estate for Edward.

Beatrice rose. "We'll leave you to rest." As they made their way to the door, she added. "If you're well enough, I'll be back tomorrow with Portia to go through the journals with you."

"Perfect." Evangeline hesitated, but soon decided she had to say something. "Hadley and Arend believe De Palma is Victoria, Isobel's stepmother. I wonder if we shouldn't keep anything we find within the journals secret and share it only with the men. If you noticed, Isobel seemed very keen to be involved in perusing the journals."

Marisa and Beatrice looked at each other, and Marisa cleared her throat. "Isobel was kidnapped with me. She was just as frightened as I was, and could have been as badly hurt as I was. Why would she put herself in that danger? Too, I had my season with her. I cannot believe she is in league with our villainess, and I'm still not convinced her stepmother is involved either."

"However, it wouldn't hurt to be cautious. Perhaps we should keep what we find just between ourselves and our husbands until we have proof Isobel plays no part in this revenge," Beatrice suggested, and Marisa nodded her agreement. "Now, I'll send your lady's maid to you. If I know Hadley, he'll call this afternoon. He's probably chomping at the bit to ensure that your injury is not severe."

"I told him to call at three."

"You'll want to be looking gorgeous. To unsettle a Libertine Scholar calls for a hint of frailness, coupled with a load of sensuality. I'd lose the plain linen nightgown and wear something sinful."

Heat flared in Evangeline's cheeks. "I don't think I own anything sinful. I've never needed to."

Beatrice laughed. "Then I'll send my maid round with some of mine. We look about the same size, or we did before I gave birth. My figure is not what it used to be yet." She patted her stomach. "Sebastian ordered loads of slinky garments before we found out I was with child. I have many that have never been worn. I can't fit them at the moment anyway. I'd rather see them be put to good use."

"I'm not sure I want to entice him. If this woman—Claire—is in love with him and he with her, I don't want to cause her heartache."

Beatrice cocked her head to one side. "Shouldn't Hadley be given the chance to make up his own mind? I doubt he's in love with Claire or she with him. They are never seen together and I've never heard him mention her. A man in love would be by her side constantly, and he certainly would not also have a mistress."

"Then why would he marry her?"

Marisa said, "You'd best ask him that."

"Thank you, I will. You're both very kind."

They both rose to take their leave, kissing her cheek and wishing her luck with Hadley that afternoon.

Once they left she lay back and closed her eyes. She was tired, sore, worried, and—to her dismay—heartbroken. Hadley was to marry. She'd asked about his marital status before instigating a meeting with him, and she'd been told he had a mistress. She had not heard about a woman he wanted to marry.

She needed to prove her innocence and find out just what

Hadley's feelings were. Marisa was right. No matter how she felt about Hadley, Sealey deserved to know his father, but could she marry Hadley for her son's sake? She shook her head. She would if he wanted her, and if she could get him to open his heart and let her back in.

She slept for a couple of hours until Rachel woke her. "Lord Fullerton is asking to see you, and Lady Beatrice's parcel has arrived. Shall I help you change first?" Rachel's smile was devilish.

Evangeline's body went hot and cold at once when she spied what Rachel had unwrapped. The scrap, because it was only a scrap, was scandalous. A scarlet lacy silk nightgown that left virtually nothing to the imagination hung from her hand. "I think it will be his lordship who leaves here with a fever," Rachel said with a giggle.

Evangeline slipped out of bed and made her way to the bathing chamber. "Ensure that Wendy keeps Sealey up in the nursery. He should be napping, but I don't want to risk him coming to find me while Lord Fullerton is here."

While she bathed, Rachel went to deliver her message. Rachel came back to help her dry and dress in the silken lace. By the time she'd finished, her shoulder was on fire. It hurt to sit up straight while Rachel went to work on her hair.

She'd made Hadley wait for half an hour. Finally Rachel helped her back into her bed, plumping up the pillows and strategically placing her in the bed for the best visual display of her abundant assets.

When Rachel went to inform Lord Fullerton that her ladyship was ready to receive him, Evangeline's stomach clenched in tight knots. The knots pulled tighter as she heard his heavy-booted feet walk along the corridor toward her room.

She sat up straighter, unease sliding over her skin. Was she doing the right thing trying to win back a love that might not have been there in the first place? She squared her shoulders and pushed up her bosom.

Only one way to find out.

Modesty made her ensure that the bodice of the lace garment she wore covered at least her nipples, and she pinched her cheeks to add some much-needed color. She was beginning to feel a tad light-headed.

She heard him stop before her door. He knocked, and she called for him to enter.

Hadley strode in as if he were going into battle, but stopped dead in his tracks halfway to her bed. His eyes flared with heat, and his mouth gaped open. She couldn't help the smile that skipped over her lips.

She indicated the chair next to her bed, but his eyes were feasting on her breasts. "Please, take a seat."

One look—that was all it took for his body to betray his mind.

Evangeline lay in bed like a succulent feast. For a man facing his first and only love, it wasn't a good thing for his body to roar to life.

Hadley had given himself a stern talking-to as he walked round the block to Evangeline's house. But now the message to ignore her beauty fled under a burgeoning mixture of want, need, and desire. His mouth began to water at the sight of the luscious mounds of pale flesh barely contained in scarlet lace. Christ, she was injured—he could see the bandage covering the wound in her shoulder—yet he didn't care. He wanted to stride to the bed and bury his head between her breasts while his hands ran over that delicious soft skin to tweak the peaked nipples poking through the negligee.

He heard her speak, but couldn't for the life of him contemplate what she said.

He felt himself harden and blood pounded in his temples. God, she was beautiful, and it struck him that he had made a terrible decision to forgo his mistress just as Evangeline arrived in town. He had nothing but his hand to relieve his need. He was liable to give himself blisters trying to sate the desire this vision ignited. And his memory was too keen. He remembered every luscious detail of her warm body under his.

He finally got his body to obey and raised his eyes to stare at her perfect face. He was just managing to contain himself when he watched her pink, wet tongue slide over her bottom lip. He let out an audible groan, and her smile widened. It was a cat-got-the-cream type of smile.

"Please sit before you fall down. Your tongue is almost hitting my floor."

Heat rose in his face at her mockery. It dampened his desire just enough to let him approach the bed.

"Perhaps you should have worn a robe, but then I suspect this is the exact reaction you were aiming for."

She shrugged her slim shoulders. "I wanted to see if you at least still desired me." She looked at his groin. "It would seem you do."

He couldn't deny it. He was ramrod hard.

He nodded toward her shoulder. "It would appear the wound is not grievous. You look remarkably well." He would keep this conversation polite and short. He needed to see those journals, true, but most of all he longed to learn the truth of Evangeline's disappearance five years ago. Was she playing him or, God forbid, was she telling the truth?

She rolled onto her side and leaned forward, causing one dark nipple to appear over the ruffle of lace at her bodice. He crossed his legs.

"Did you bring the letter?"

He started at her question. "Yes. I also came to see how you are faring."

"You came to appease your guilty conscience" came the tart reply, "and to get your hands on the journals."

It was the truth. He shifted in his chair.

"If anyone should have a guilty conscience, it's you." The words slipped out before he could think. He shouldn't have said it, because he'd begun to suspect he'd made a fatal error five years ago. But it was hard to remember his own name with her magnificent breasts in his face.

A , of anger appeared on her features. "I'm going to prove that the story I told you was true, and when I do, you will be on your knees begging me to forgive you." She lay back on her pillow and turned her face from him. "The man I fell in love with all those years ago would have believed me."

He could barely breathe because her words were true. Why hadn't he believed her? The evidence in front of him had been overwhelming, and his pride had destroyed any chance of rational thought. She'd forsaken him for another! Or so he had thought.

He watched her breasts rise and fall rapidly as she fought to contain her emotions. She sighed and said, "You've seen me, seen that I'm recovering well, so your conscience can breathe freely. If you don't intend to let me prove my innocence, then you may as well leave."

The letter was burning a hole in his jacket pocket, but he was hesitant to bring it forth. If her story was true, then what could he do? If she *had* been abducted, then how on earth could she ever forgive him? It would mean he'd walked away from her without a backward glance, happy to leave her to her fate. "I want the truth too. Much of my future hinges on it."

Her head moved on the pillow as she watched him. Her eyes narrowed. "Then we are in agreement. Show me the letter."

"What of the journals?" Before she could berate him again, he added, "May I remind you that a madwoman is out to kill me and my friends, and probably you? That takes precedence over our situation."

She leaned up on one elbow. "I agree. That is why Beatrice and Marisa will help me. They will look for information on Victoria."

"I think you should let me scour the journals. Time is of the essence—for all of us."

"I thought your visit was to ask after my health—and to let me see the letter, as you promised."

"Then what is this display about? What else is it you want from me?"

She sighed and pulled the bedsheet up to her chin.

"Never mind. I have to go back to Scotland once I've appointed a man of business to sort out my son's estate. It will be a few months before I can return to London for any length of time. Once my son's inheritance is secure, then I will have to decide where I wish to make my home. I don't want it to be awkward should we bump into each other."

She wasn't leaving for good, then?

A home. He didn't want to admit where he called home. When he was in London he lived at his brother's house, the family townhouse, although he was thinking of purchasing a townhouse a few streets over once he married. However, the place he retreated to, where he spent the majority of his time, was the old hunting lodge, Lathero, where Evangeline and he used to meet.

It held his best and worst memories. Over the past five years he had found no joy in his visits because the memories were too painful. Only his vines, his love of making wine, kept him there.

He'd almost sold Lathero when Evangeline left him, but he couldn't bring himself to part with it. Perhaps it was to remind him that he could not always get what he wanted.

He looked into her eyes, and it was as if she could read his thoughts. Her look was filled with shared memories.

He remembered the day she'd given herself to him. It was the day they had planned how and when they would elope. It had been a hot summer afternoon, humid and sultry. Here in her bedroom he could almost smell the grass and flowers that had surrounded them on that fateful day. . . .

Had she already known on that day that she'd marry Viscount Stuart? The thought made him ill, his stomach churning with outrage. Only a day later he'd received her letter informing him she had to help her family and that she would wed Viscount Stuart.

"You are remembering that day under the tree, aren't you?" she whispered.

He held her gaze and watched as tears filled her eyes. When he slowly nodded, she said, "I remember the day like it was yesterday. It was perfect. Making love with you was like touching heaven." At his silence she added accusingly, "Did you not remember anything I said to you that day? How could you think I'd want to marry a man for a title?"

"And money for your family," he snapped back.

Her lips firmed into a thin line, anger flashing in her eyes. "We had discussed how to control Mother's spending and help Edward."

He couldn't hold her stare. Panic gripped him. Once again he thought, what if the story she had told last night was true and he had left her to her fate? God forgive him, for he never would. Bile squirmed like a sea of snakes in the pit of his belly.

Suddenly he had to know the truth.

He pulled the letter from his pocket and handed it to her.

Her hands shook as she opened it and scanned the contents. Her face paled, and he saw her swallow.

"It's a very good forgery. Even I had to look carefully." She leaned closer, pushing the letter under his nose. "But look at the letter *f*. I do not do little loops like hoods on my *f*'s. Do you have any of my other letters to compare?"

If he said yes, he was admitting that he'd kept them all these years, but he was past hiding from the truth, no matter how painful. "I have them all." He saw her start at his honesty. "I brought a few with me."

She watched him pull a bundle of her letters from his other pocket. Hope all but sang in her veins. He'd kept her letters—that must mean something. However, she had to focus on proving her innocence.

She handed the incriminating letter back to him, and watched his face as he carefully studied the evidence. He turned the pages of one of her love letters, peering closely at the letters. Then he started going through each one of the letters, his fingers flicking through them faster and faster.

She saw the exact moment he became convinced of her innocence. His face paled, and drops of sweat marked his forehead. He licked his lips. Then he dove for the chamber pot sitting near the entrance to her dressing room and promptly cast up his accounts. She didn't feel any sympathy for him.

When he finally rose to take his seat once more, the bleak look in his eyes revealed his pain and sorrow. He reached for her hand. "I am so sorry. God forgive me. I—I don't know how to make this right. . . ."

"That's a start." She covered his hand where it held hers tightly. "Why did you not believe me? I loved you—so much," she choked out. "You owe me an explanation at least."

"The letter was delivered by Stowe."

Her heart missed a beat. Stowe was the young stable lad who was devoted to her. When he was only eleven, she had brought him home from the village when she'd caught his father beating him, and given him a job in the stable. The job paid little, as they did not have money, but he had a roof over his head and food in his belly, and he loved horses. So when she'd needed someone to send notes between herself and Hadley, she knew whom to trust.

Her hands began to shake. "Stowe brought you the letter." Understanding began to dawn, and she felt ill. "You therefore thought it was from me."

"Yes. I even asked him, and the boy said you told him to put the letter in my hands."

She bent forward her body, heaving with the pain of betrayal. Not Stowe. She could not believe it.

"Perhaps he was threatened in some way . . ." Hadley's words petered out.

"Oh, God." She turned to him, finally understanding how thoroughly her mother had planned her abduction. "If Mother has hurt Stowe, I'll kill her."

"I read your note," Hadley continued slowly, "and when I

said that it couldn't be true, Stowe swore that the contents were correct. I never considered for a moment how cruel your mother would or could be, or that Stowe would deceive me. He seemed just as upset as I. Now I know why, because he lied." Hadley hung his head, cursing under his breath. "We didn't stand a chance, did we?"

"I guess, against the world, our love was not enough," she whispered. "Now I understand why, even when I told you to your face that I hadn't written the letter, you still didn't believe me. Stowe was our ally. How could you know it was a lie?"

"I *should* have known. I knew you."

"Does anyone ever really know another?" She hadn't realized she'd spoken out loud until he raised his pain-filled eyes to hers.

They sat in silence, the realization of shared, shattered hopes and dreams creating a cavern of hopelessness between them.

The silence stretched on as the light began to fade. It wasn't until a maid entered to stoke the fire in the grate that they both roused from their thoughts.

Hadley rose to take his leave, his face pale and his eyes filled with sorrow.

At last he said, "You must hate me. I hope that one day you can forgive me."

Her heart wanted to reach through her chest and embrace him. "You still don't appear to know me. I could never hate you. It was not you who arranged for me to be abducted. It wasn't you who lied. I know exactly where the blame sits, and it is not with you."

"But I should have known. I *should* have." He threw his hands up. "I should have saved you." He ran a hand through his hair. "Now there are two women I'd like to kill—our villainess and your mother. What do you intend to do about your mother?"

She briefly closed her eyes. "Nothing." At his startled look she explained, "Nothing I do to her will change what happened. What's done is done. I can't take back the last five years. I prefer to pretend she does not exist."

He hesitated as if he wanted to say something, but he merely bowed and made to leave, all talk of the journals forgotten.

"I'll contact you if the ladies and I find anything of note in the journals," she told him.

His hunched his shoulders in shame. "Thank you. That is more than I deserve."

She sighed. "Of course I'll help. I'd never want to see you injured or killed. Besides, it will also protect my son."

He stood looking at her, a range of emotions swirling in his blue eyes. She watched him swallow hard. Finally he nodded and turned to leave. Just as he reached the door she asked quietly, "Do you still paint?"

His hand stayed on the latch. "No."

"Why not? You were very good. You found joy and release on the canvas."

He looked at her over his shoulder, his face a mask of pain. "Five years ago I lost my muse."

"Perhaps you might get your muse back now?"

A shudder ran through him. "Perhaps." On that soft, defeated-sounding word, he departed the room.

Evangeline lay back on her pillows, numb in thought and body. She had got what she'd wanted, his admission that he'd made a dreadful mistake, and yet it hadn't been his fault. He was not to blame. Five years ago the world, or fate—or her mother's gambling—had ensured there would be no happily-ever-after. Could there be now?

A tear slid down her cheek, and she didn't bother wiping it away. What could she do now? The last five years had been all about surviving and finding a way to be free. Well, she was free now, and it filled her with fear.

She had no idea what she wanted to do with her life. She would be twenty-five in three months. Still young. She yearned for more children, a sibling for Sealey, yet the idea of marriage scared her witless.

Could they go back? Could they start again and have that

which had been torn from them both? And then there was Sealey . . .

Hadley was to marry. Why was he going to marry Claire? She had forgotten to ask him, so wrapped up in her victory had she been.

Love warmed the coldness she felt. He'd loved her once, enough to marry a woman with no dowry and an evil, gambling-addicted mother. Could he love her again?

She could play the Sealey card. Hadley would likely do anything to marry her once he learned of his son. Was that fair to either Hadley or Sealey? Once again Hadley's free will would be compromised. She wanted him to choose her—to choose *them*.

Her pride made it impossible to use her son to persuade Hadley to marry her instead of Claire. She wanted to know that he loved her. After she'd had his love before, a life tied to him without that love would be unbearable.

The worst outcome would be if Sealey's parentage became common knowledge before this villainess was caught. Sealey would be in grave danger. Better to wait until the Libertine Scholars captured the evil woman before learning what, if anything, could be between them.

Should she tell him about his son, or shouldn't she? Part of her wanted to rush into Hadley's arms and reveal all, but she was a wiser, more cynical woman now. To err on the side of caution was best, for her son's safety must come first. She would tell Hadley when they caught the enemy, or before he married Claire. The latter, she hoped, would not occur if he still loved her enough.

"Love" was a scary word—easy to spell, easy to define, easy to say, but very difficult to believe. When you found love, you had to have faith that it was reciprocated. She prayed he would love her enough this time to give up Claire.

She closed her eyes and began to doze. The next three weeks would determine the outcome of her life.

For the first time in months she felt she could breathe. She knew he still cared for her, she had her son, and she had hope. Hope that she and Hadley would have their happily-ever-after.

Because she still loved Hadley.

Her shoulder burned, and she understood she had a more serious problem. Hadley could be dead in three weeks if this madwoman was not caught.

Hope was a trinket she'd cling to. The last time, love hadn't won, couldn't have won, against those evil enough to destroy them. She couldn't bear to give her heart and fill herself with hope once again, only to have that hope snatched from her grasp. It would end her.

And Hadley had a woman set on killing him.

Her priority right now was helping her friends find a monster. She hoped the journals held the clues Hadley needed. It would be the only useful thing her husband had ever done for her.

She rang the bell to summon Rachel. She would not be attending any social functions tonight, not with her injury. So she would jolly well put the time to good use.

She drew out one of Dougal's journals and began reading. Like the man, his written words were tedious, droning on and on.

She hoped he was burning in hell.

Hadley walked toward his home, his world in tatters.

She'd been innocent!

His insides crawled as if maggots were eating his soul. He swallowed back a bellow, his fists clenching by his sides. He'd let her down—badly. He'd let her live in hell—yes, she'd called it hell —for five long years, let a man force himself on her, beat her most likely . . .

Bile rose thick and fast in his throat.

His heart broke in his chest, the pain so intense he had to stop walking. All this time they could have been happy.

His heart lurched, pounding madly in his chest. A string of expletives exploded from his lips, directed partly at the world, but more so at himself.

With sudden brutal clarity he understood how thoroughly

he'd underestimated Evangeline's mother. His heart thundered as a wave of anger crashed through his mind. He drew a shuddering breath. One enemy at a time. But he vowed before God he would have his vengeance.

Evangeline had always loved him. Raising a hand to his head, he pummeled himself. Understanding nearly brought him to his knees; she had always loved him, yet he'd left her trapped for five long years. That thought was paralyzing. His was a debt he could never repay. Money was one thing, possessions another, but how did you give someone her life back?

He'd stood back and let evil ruin the only truly wonderful thing he'd ever had in his life. Ruined the woman he'd professed he loved more than life itself.

Instead of trusting in her love, he'd abandoned her to a terrible fate, letting his own insecurities blind him to the truth.

He was so lost in his thoughts that he didn't hear the footsteps behind him. It was the shadow from the gaslight above that alerted him to the danger he was in.

He instinctively turned and twisted to his left just as a knife plunged toward his heart. He deflected the blow, but the dagger sliced his arm. Without thinking, he exploded into action, fueled by his pent-up rage. His fist connected with his attacker's chin, and his knee rose to slam into the man's groin. His assailant went down in a heap at Hadley's feet, out cold.

Hadley stood over him breathing heavily. He had to fight every instinct not to beat the unconscious man to death.

A hackney turned into the street, and he waved it down. He opened the carriage door, picked up his assailant, and threw him onto the floor of the carriage before providing the driver with Arend's address.

He looked forward to being there when the man came to. And he hoped the man would not be reluctant to provide him with the answers he and Arend needed, because by God, he badly wanted to pummel something, or someone.

Chapter Six

"My lord, Lord Fullerton is here."

Hadley heard Arend impatiently say to his butler, "Well, see him in, Jeeves."

"He has, ah, a *person* with him. . . ."

Hadley pushed past the butler and dropped his prisoner at Arend's feet. The man was beginning to stir.

Arend took in the sight of Hadley's thunderous face and smiled. A shiver went down Hadley's back. He'd hate to make an enemy of Arend.

"It's all right, Jeeves. Lord Fullerton has brought me a present." Arend shooed his butler out before closing the door and slowly turning to study the man moaning and drooling on Arend's expensive-looking Persian rug.

At Arend's questioning raised eyebrow, Hadley told him, "He attacked me in my street, a few doors down from Claymore House."

"He must be good to have got that close to you," Arend said as he tugged his cravat off and wound it round Hadley's forearm.

Hadley looked at the spots of blood dripping on Arend's rug. He hadn't even realized he was bleeding.

"Apologies. I'll buy you a new one."

"Think nothing of it. I'm rather taken with the present you've brought me."

Arend turned his dark gaze toward the man whose eyes were slowly opening. He crouched down and checked him for more weapons. He found nothing. He rose and handed Arend the dagger he had taken off the man earlier.

Arend leaned close to the man's ear and let the dagger, glinting in the lamplight, drift toward the man's eye. "Lord Fullerton and I are not in the mood to play games. So, my friend, we shall let you live, and go free, if you tell us who hired you."

The man's eyes rolled back in his head, and it looked for a moment as though he might pass out again.

Arend stood. "Where are my manners? A drink perhaps." He poured some whiskey into a glass and then promptly threw it in the man's face.

The man spluttered and licked the drops off his chin before finally gaining focus. He tried to roll away from Arend, who once again was leaning over him with the knife.

"Now, my man, why don't you tell us why you tried to kill my friend?" Arend pushed the tip of the dagger into the flesh of his neck.

"They said I could earn two hundred pounds."

"Two hundred pounds?" Hadley scoffed. "My life is only worth two hundred pounds?"

"I think you're missing the point," Arend said to Hadley before returning his focus to the man on the floor. "Who said they'd pay you?"

Their captive looked between the two men, fear creeping into his expression. "It was a man, but he wore a mask."

Hadley asked, "Are you sure it was a man if you could not see a face?"

"Aye, I'm sure." Then he added to Hadley, "Nothin' personal. Gotta earn coin."

Hadley stomped across the room and back again. "I'll call for the Runners. He's told us nothing important."

"Hold on," the man broke in. "There *was* a woman with him. A woman, and another gent who wore a cape and hood." He paused briefly. "In fact, the man in the cape could have been a woman too. He was small in stature, even sitting on a horse."

Arend stood up and looked at Hadley. "Describe the woman."

"I couldn't see her very clearly, but she had dark hair, wound on top of her head in some fancy braid. She was slim but with big breasts—her riding jacket was straining at the ties."

Arend slammed one fist into his palm. "Isobel. I knew it. It's Vic—"

"Shh." Hadley looked at the man at his feet. Could they believe anything he said? What if he was telling them lies? Lies he'd been paid to tell them? The information had been shared far too easily. They hadn't had to hurt him at all.

He pulled Arend aside. "He could be lying. He gave up the information too quickly."

Arend, his face a mask of seething rage, tore his eyes away from the man lying on his rug and stared at Hadley. "Then best we dig a little deeper." He moved back toward the man, the dagger glinting in his hand.

An hour later, the rug was definitely ruined, and the man lay moaning softly at their feet. Both Arend and Hadley were now satisfied he was telling the truth. A woman who looked like Isobel *had* been at the meeting where he was offered money to attack Hadley. Another person, who could also have been a woman, had been with her, while it was a man with a mask who had procured his services.

They honored their word, giving the man a stiff whiskey and letting him go. He took off into the night before Arend had closed the door.

They moved to Arend's study while Jeeves organized the removal of the blood-stained rug and Arend washed his hands in a bowl. Then Arend poured them both a drink while Hadley tried to get his emotions under control.

"You were very stoic tonight. I expected you to object to my methods."

Hadley stared at his friend, the emotions of the day choking him. He'd learned this day that he'd let the woman he professed to love be abducted and sold into a form of slavery, and he'd been attacked once more. He'd had enough.

"I'm sick of being a target. I want this to end."

Arend raised his glass to that. "It's proof we need. If Isobel was present, then it can be no other than Victoria."

"It could be a coincidence that the woman looked like Isobel."

"You don't believe that any more than I do. Victoria is our villainess, and Isobel is involved. However, we can't accuse a lady, or ladies, of murder without proof. I hope the journals Evangeline is looking through contain evidence. Alternatively, we need a confession."

At the mention of Evangeline, Hadley's world darkened even further. He was amazed she still wanted to help, given how he'd betrayed her love.

Why hadn't he believed in her? He'd ask himself that question until the day he died.

Arend leaned forward in his chair. "Evangeline *is* going to share what she learns, isn't she? Please tell me you haven't told her to sod off back to Scotland just yet."

Hadley threw the rest of his whiskey down his throat and held out his glass for a refill. He couldn't meet Arend's eyes.

"Christ, Hadley! Did your pride stop you from asking for her help? So, she up and married another. You had a lucky escape, if you ask me. A fickle woman who owns your heart could make your life a misery. If you have to marry, and I know you feel that you do, better to marry Lady Claire to appease Augustus. At least with her you know where you stand."

For one tiny moment Hadley wished he could be like Arend. Arend didn't appear to need anyone, not even the other Libertine Scholars. He'd been close with them at Eton, and then he'd disappeared for several years. No one knew where'd he gone, and he never talked about his time away. He'd been broke, not a penny to his name, when he left, and wealthy beyond measure upon his return. But he'd changed. He was darker, more moody, and the joy seemed to have left his world. Would the truth Hadley had learned today even shock him?

"She didn't marry another voluntarily." He almost wept over the words.

Whiskey spat from Arend's mouth. He looked at Hadley in horror. "My God, do you mean her story is true?"

Hadley closed his eyes and let the guilt and pain sweep his body. "Yes," he said, and proceeded to tell Arend the story of their betrayal at the hands of her mother, his friend's face growing darker as the story unfolded. "Fucking hell." Arend refilled his glass and downed it in one gulp.

They sat in silence for ages. Finally Arend spoke. "Just as well her husband is dead, or I'd have helped you kill him. No one should be forced to . . . Well, I can't say I'm surprised she won't help us."

"That's just it. She *will* help us. She and the ladies will go through the journals. She understands that she and her son are in danger, given society's preoccupation with gossip around our relationship."

Or lack of relationship. He couldn't deny he was still attracted to her. She was as beautiful as ever. When he thought of what could have been, his heart broke.

"She must still be in love with you." Arend's words jarred his soul.

"How could she be? I left her with that man, a man she hated, a man who forced himself on her. She had a son. . . ." He uttered a curse. "When she came to tell me, I turned her away, telling her she lied. And to top it all off, it was because of me that she was shot. She must hate me."

"Love and hate share a very thin line, my friend." Arend cocked his head to one side. "More important is how you feel about her."

"Feel? I feel so much I can barely think of tomorrow."

Arend scoffed. "Don't. Don't torture yourself by endlessly going over 'what if' and 'if only.' Believe me, it will eat at you until the end of your days. Given Stowe's collaboration, you had no reason to believe the letter she wrote was not a forgery."

"Ah, that's where you are wrong. I knew something wasn't right. I did. Deep down inside I knew it wasn't right, but my stupid bloody pride convinced me not to run after her like a lovesick puppy. If only I had—"

"Stop, Hadley. We have two women to destroy now, Victoria and Lady Althrope." Arend propped his boots up on the stone fireguard of the hearth. "It would seem Lady Evangeline has a good life now that her husband is dead. She has her son, money, homes . . . What's done is done and cannot be undone. You've both moved on."

Moved on. Arend had no idea what he was talking about. He'd not moved on. Hadley recalled the moment, two nights ago, when she'd walked into Christian's house. After five long years without her, his body had seized with pain, want, and need. The fortress around his heart burst open with one simple look at her. He instantly remembered the day he'd met her. He'd wanted to make her his. And he still did.

The dream of her as his wife was gone. Surely, after his lack of trust and faith in their love, she would most definitely not wish to trust her heart to him again.

"You're right, of course. We have both moved on. I'm about to announce my engagement at the end of the month, and she is already talking about heading back to Scotland. She's here to appoint a new man of business to help look after her son's inheritance."

"Bullshit. A woman who hates you doesn't scour all of London to find you, get her apology, and then stay to help you catch a villain who's out to kill you. If she hated you, she'd walk away. Don't be such a coward. Face the past and see if you can have a happy future."

All Hadley could think was *Too late.* Arend was right—he'd go crazy if he kept repeating "if only" one more time. The Evangeline who had returned from Scotland was different from the young girl he had known. Of course she would be after everything she'd gone through.

He had to change the subject—his emotions were still too raw for him to talk about what could be. "What are you going to do about Isobel?" Hadley asked.

Arend's eyes darkened even further. "She thinks she's playing me . . . us. I shall turn the tables. A woman in love can be very malleable. I intend to seduce her and make her turn on her stepmother."

"A tad risky, don't you think?" At Arend's grim smile he added, "I hope it doesn't backfire on you. If she is innocent, you could end up married to her."

"If she is innocent, I'd ride naked in the derby," Arend muttered. "I'm sure it was she at that meeting with your attacker. Victoria and Isobel didn't arrive at the opera until intermission. She told me Victoria had to run an errand first."

Hadley sat up in his chair. "You need to consider that Isobel may not be involved in the plot, but was simply taken along because her stepmother is her chaperone."

"Perhaps, but I'll soon find out. The guilty cannot hide things from me."

Hadley looked into Arend's eyes and nodded, though inwardly he wondered. Usually the people who could read others like an open book became blind when feelings entered the equation. Whether Isobel was indeed guilty or not, Arend was consumed with her. And that was not a good sign. Hadley wondered if Arend realized that the young woman, not Victoria, had become his obsession.

Chapter Seven

I t had been three days since Evangeline last saw Hadley. She had not invited him to her house while she was convalescing, even though he wrote her a note every day asking after her health. She couldn't have any of the Libertine Scholars in her house, because should any of them run into Sealey it would ruin everything. In addition, she didn't want to put Sealey in danger by indicating any sort of relationship with Hadley.

Luckily, the men hadn't bothered to push the issue about the journals, because their wives were helping her. So far, the ladies had learned only that Evangeline's mother had in fact set up her abduction by approaching Viscount Stuart, and that it was her mother who'd written the forged note. Evangeline had begun to hope that her mother would die a painful death, and she itched to write to Edward to assure herself he was well.

She pushed all thoughts of journals aside as the carriage drew up outside a very fashionable London townhouse. Tonight she'd joined Marisa, with Maitland acting as escort for them both, to attend Lady Claudia Beaumont's ball. As she ascended the stairs to the ballroom with her arm linked through one of Maitland's, Marisa on his other side, it appeared that every pair of eyes turned her way.

The news of her injury had spread like a leaf caught in a hurricane. She'd been shot outside Lord Fullerton's house. The *ton* was abuzz as to why—why she had been there, and why she had been shot. And by whom? Thieves had been blamed, but as to why she'd been at his house . . . The whispering behind the fans was worse than the stares.

It had been Maitland's suggestion that Hadley also attend the ball, though Evangeline suspected Marisa had been behind it. However, when she spotted him, Hadley didn't look very happy to be here.

As they joined the rest of the Libertine Scholars and their wives, she whispered to Hadley, "Smile, my lord. Anyone would think you hated me."

Hadley started at her words and turned his head to smile at her briefly before resuming his scowl. "Good. If Victoria thinks I have feelings for you, that places you in too much danger. I have already left you in danger once before, and I refuse to do so again."

She felt her face flush with pleasure. "Well, you are a fabulous actor. You look as if you'd like to squash me under your shoe. You look angry, true, but also a little sad."

"Not sad, merely reflective."

She hoped he was thinking exactly what she was—that if not for her mother, they could be standing here with their friends as husband and wife. "Let's make a pact not to keep focusing on the tragedy of the past. I want to be happy again. I'm sure you do too."

He hesitated for a moment. "Can you so easily put aside what was done to you?"

A shudder make her knees knock. "Easily? No." She still had nightmares, and found it hard to get to sleep before two in the morning, still expecting her husband to come to her for his husbandly rights. She couldn't relax until her mind fully understood that he was never coming again, that he could never hurt her again.

A sigh escaped her lips and she fought to keep the smile plastered on her face. "Fate is an evil bitch, isn't it?" she said with a droll laugh. "You still have some groveling to do regarding your treatment of me at our first meeting. Why did you hate me so?"

This was a test of his honesty. Would he share his feelings?

"Your leaving broke my heart, and it's been broken ever since."

Her hands unclenched. He'd admitted he still had strong feelings for her. Shock ripped through her. Without a thought to their audience she reached out and cupped his cheek. "I'm sorry. I assumed I was the only one who had been hurt."

A cough at her shoulder broke the moment, and she stepped back. Marisa whispered in her ear, "If Victoria had any doubt about your feelings for each other before, it's very clear now," and she nodded toward the other side of the ballroom, where Lady Victoria was watching them through assessing eyes.

A flutter of fear slipped across Evangeline's skin, but she told herself not to spend her night watching Victoria. Or Hadley. That would be far too obvious.

Just at that moment Isobel spotted the ladies and began to make her way through the throng toward them, Victoria following in her wake.

She watched Arend's eyes darken and his shoulders stiffen. She nudged him. "If I can read you this easily, Victoria will too. Relax."

Arend immediately lost the angry scowl and bowed over her hand. "Lady Evangeline, would you do me the honor of this dance?"

He didn't wait for her reply but simply swept her into his arms as the waltz began. They moved away just as Isobel and Victoria reached their party.

"My apologies," he murmured as they danced, "but I needed to get myself under control before meeting Victoria or I'm liable to alert her to the fact we have them in our sights."

"'Them'? You can't mean Isobel. She would never be party to

such villainy." She felt his hand tighten around hers, and she pressed on. "I think you do Isobel a disservice. Besides, I hope you are wrong, as she knows about the journals and what they may contain." Isobel also knew about Sealey's parentage, but Evangeline couldn't tell Arend that. She searched his eyes. "What do you know that I do not?"

"Hadley was attacked again." Luckily, Arend was holding her tightly, or she'd have tripped over his feet. "He's fine, as you can see—just a slight cut to his arm. He managed to capture his attacker, who told us that he'd been hired by a man who wore a mask but that a woman who matched Isobel's description was nearby."

Her racing heart began to slow. Isobel? That didn't make sense. "Why would the man hide his face only to let Isobel be seen?"

"I agree, it's very suspect. The other person with Isobel also hid his—or her—identity."

"It's almost as if someone wanted us to know it was Isobel," Evangeline said, and Arend nodded.

They danced for a while without speaking. At last Evangeline looked up at Arend and asked, "Is she attending tonight?"

This time it was Arend whose step slightly wavered. He cleared his throat. "Who?"

"Don't play games with me. I know he is soon to announce his betrothal to Lady Claire."

"He doesn't want to marry her."

A thrill washed over her. "Then why?"

"Because it seemed sensible at the time. Augustus is the Marquis of Corby's best friend, and the two of them needed to find his wallflower sister a husband. Augustus asked, and Hadley agreed that if Claire was still unwed when he reached thirty, he'd marry her."

"Again, why?"

Arend looked down at her for a long moment. "His heart was broken when you married someone else. He knew he'd never love another woman, but he wants children, and that requires a wife. Claire was as good as any other."

"No, I mean, why was it Hadley who had to marry her? Why not Augustus?"

"Lady Claire would never cope as the wife of a duke. So the two of them foisted her off on Hadley, taking advantage of his low point. He should have said no."

Her mouth firmed. "Men are so bloody stupid."

She gazed across the room at the man she had loved—whom she loved now—and wished their lives were as simple as they had been five years ago. Then they had had eyes only for each other, and were prepared to break all the rules and elope. Life, it would appear, was never that simple.

Arend looked at her closely. "You still love him, don't you?"

She did not reply. She couldn't bring herself to say *Of course.* She was nervous that the words weren't true, and frightened that they were. What if he didn't choose her?

It was as if Arend had read her thoughts, for he said, "Then make him see it's not too late to change his mind. There has been no announcement, and Claire doesn't even know the plan." At her blank look he added, "Do you want him to marry Lady Claire?"

"Shouldn't he be allowed to make up his own mind for a change?"

Arend frowned. "Only if he makes the right choice."

"And you think you know the right choice better than he? Isn't that exactly what Augustus was doing, forcing him down one path rather than letting him choose? I want him to choose me because he wants to. Because it's his heart's desire. Not because he thinks he owes me for . . . well, you know."

"I want him to be happy. He's been more animated since you arrived than I've seen him these past five years. He has strong feelings for you. Convince him to forgo Claire—he'll deeply regret it if he doesn't."

The music seemed louder, and she could barely think. "You

know him better than anyone else. I know he's forgiven me, but will he ever forgive himself? He can barely look at me."

Arend twirled them closer to where Hadley was standing, then leaned in and whispered in her ear, "See how he's watching me? He looks like he wants to kill me right now for being overly familiar with you. Imagine how much worse he'll feel if he's married to Claire and must watch you marry another. You're young and beautiful, Evangeline. You deserve happiness too."

She sighed at Arend's words. He was right—if Hadley married Claire, it would make sense for her to eventually marry someone else. She just couldn't imagine giving her heart to anyone else.

The evening dragged like a full fisherman's net. Hadley was excited to see Evangeline again but was concerned about what the night might bring. Victoria was clever, and it was obvious to all that he was besotted with Evangeline. He tried not to watch every step she took, tried to hide how much he hated all the men fawning over the beautiful, wealthy widow.

It also appeared that Augustus was watching them too. Usually he never came to these events. Perhaps if his brother saw how he and Evangeline felt about each other, he'd understand why Hadley had to back out of their agreement.

To make matters worse, Isobel seemed intent on playing Cupid and bringing Evangeline and Hadley together. And her stepmother was paying close attention to Hadley's every interaction with Evangeline.

To his shame, he had declared his interest inadvertently. Marisa told him he was clearly staking a claim with his eyes, and he himself had realized that several rakes who had approached Evangeline had seen him scowl at them and scurried away. It meant only one thing: Evangeline was now a target. Goddamn it all to hell.

He needed to warn her. He saw that she had just finished dancing with Lord Atherton, near the doors to the terrace. He could do with some fresh air away from watchful eyes, and he'd bloody well make sure Atherton didn't take her out onto the terrace, as he was obviously trying to do.

As he drew near, her scent titillated his senses. He loved how her eyes were once again shining and full of laughter. She'd had a haunted look about her on their first meeting, but he'd been too defensive to analyze her body language and notice her pain.

His heart beat faster. The noise of the crowd seemed to diminish, and all he could see and hear was Evangeline. As she turned and spotted him approaching, the welcoming smile she gave him made him feel as if he were walking on air.

For the first time that evening he didn't give a damn that Augustus was watching him as closely as Victoria seemed to be. He wanted to be by Evangeline's side. He wanted the whole world to know she was his.

Without a word he offered her his arm. She immediately took it, and he steered her out onto the terrace and down into the garden. Neither of them spoke as he guided her further into the quiet darkness, behind the shrubbery.

Before she could say a word, he hauled her into his arms and kissed her. It was something he'd wanted to do ever since the day she'd walked back into his life. She didn't fight him but simply pressed closer, her arms rising to wrap tightly around his neck.

His heart was pounding like a drum in his chest, drowning out all thought, all sounds, until every feeling centered on the woman in his arms, warm and supple.

His hands roamed over her abundant curves, and he gave thanks for the fashion of flimsy silk dresses. His hands molded her bottom, and he pulled her closer, letting her feel his need of her.

She sighed into his mouth, and her hands stroked his back down to his buttocks, which she gripped in order to rub herself along the hard length of him.

The sensation caused him to lose all reason. He ceased to care who might stumble across them in the garden—even Victoria.

Slowly the ferociousness of the embrace lessened, and in its place came a surge of gentleness. Her lips softened invitingly under his, and at the tentative touch of her tongue on his own, Hadley felt an emotion akin to triumph. He had her in his arms again, something that had been a dream for five long years. He was careful not to tangle his fingers in her elaborately upswept hair, but really he wanted to let the thick copper tresses cascade over him in a sensual cloak.

Evangeline was making small sounds of pleasure deep in her throat—a sound that he remembered as if it were yesterday and they were still under their willow tree. The flowery scents from the garden around them caused memories of making love to her to flood his brain.

Finally she pulled back just enough to look into his face.

"I have missed you so much," she said as tears began to trickle down her cheeks. "I survived because I thought of you. Because I dreamed of us."

He wiped them away with his thumb, wishing he could erase the last five years for her. "I'm so sorry this happened to you —to us."

She nodded, too choked up to speak.

"If I could, I'd turn back time for you, though I can't. But I remember everything about you as if it was yesterday. I want you so badly. However, wanting you is dangerous—for several reasons."

She stepped out of his embrace, angrily wiping her tears away. "Because of Victoria, or because of Claire?"

He looked up and took a deep breath. Honesty was needed; both of them had been lied to enough already.

"Augustus wants me to marry Lady Claire. However, nothing is set in stone, and I only agreed because—"

"Because you'd lost me."

He looked away into the dark night. He could barely get words past the lump in his throat. "I acceded to the match because you'd broken my heart. If I had known you had been abducted and that you would come back to me, I never would have agreed."

"I understand. What I need to know is what you plan to do moving forward. Will you go through with a marriage to Claire?"

"No. Not if there is a chance that you and I could recapture what we lost. Do you think you could forgive me enough to let me love you once again?"

"There is nothing to forgive, my love. It's a shame we don't have more time to learn how we both feel after all these years. I don't know if I'm in love with the dream of you, a dream I've held on to for so long, or with the honorable man who stands before me."

He pulled her close. "People change. Circumstances and experiences all affect us." So much had happened since she'd been torn from him. He wasn't even sure he was the same man. "Do you still love me?"

"That's a bit unfair. You want me to declare my heart when you are keeping yours hidden."

He pulled her back into his arms. "I know that my world lights up when I see you, that my heart races when I hear your laugh, and that when any other man comes near you I feel a fierce need to mark you as mine." He leaned toward her, his lips nuzzling her neck, her earlobe. He simply needed to taste her.

"If only we had the luxury of sneaking away for a few days with no distractions, to see if it is possible to rekindle what we once shared."

"I think we deserve the chance to see what is still between us. I've already made the decision—even if we cannot go back, I know I cannot marry Lady Claire. I want more for my life. I want happiness."

"God knows we both deserve a chance at happiness."

"We could go to Lathero," he declared.

He felt her breath catch. At last she said, "Aren't you needed here to help capture Victoria?"

"Damn. You make me forget everything when you're here in my arms." He thought hard. "Arend is still working on Isobel. I don't think a few days will make much difference. We have been after Victoria for months as it is."

"It would give us more time to go through all the journals—together. I must warn you, you won't like some of things you read."

Bloody hell, he thought. "If you survived your captivity, then I can survive reading about it."

"I don't want you to feel any further guilt. I know you want to help and protect everyone, and sometimes that just isn't possible."

He felt the anger and guilt build again, but tempered them by inwardly swearing to himself that he'd never let anything happen to her—or her son—ever again.

"What about your son?" he asked.

"Of course I don't want to leave him even for a few days. But I can't help but think he would be safer if you and I are away from him. I'm sure you'll make certain that he is well guarded."

"We could send him to stay with Sebastian and Beatrice. He is a similar age to young Henry."

He felt her stiffen in his arms, but she simply nodded.

Reluctantly he kissed the top of her head and hooked her arm in his. "We should get back. I suspect we have been away from the ballroom too long already."

"I don't care about the gossip except insofar as it provides Victoria with a weapon she may use against us . . . and Sealey. I also saw Augustus looking pretty angry when he watched you dance with me earlier. You'll need to inform him of your change of heart."

"Leave Augustus to me. I'll organize some of the Runners to depart for Lathero tomorrow. We can leave the following day. It would be better if we were not seen leaving together, however. I'll ride, and you take your carriage. Is that enough time for you to make your arrangements?"

She pressed a kiss to his lips. "Yes. I cannot believe I will be staying at Lathero, in your bed—it's a dream come true. But please, promise me one thing?"

"Anything, my darling."

"I have been in one loveless marriage already, and while I know you would never treat me as Dougal did, I can't be with a man who can't fully commit to me. If your feelings for me have changed, if you no longer can give me your heart, then we part as friends."

He had loved her once before, and when he looked at her, when he held her in his arms, it was as if it was five years ago. Not only did he desire her physically, but he wanted her by his side to share his life, to be the mother of his children. No other woman made him want those things or stirred his heart so.

He stopped at the base of the steps leading up to the terrace. "Let's make no promises and have no expectations. All that does is put pressure on us from the start."

She looked at him for a moment and finally nodded. "As you wish." But her tone made him realize he had disappointed her with his answer.

He let her slip into the ballroom behind two other couples who had been taking the air. He remained outside and lit a cheroot. He took a long drag, trying to get his rioting emotions under control. Elation filled him. Evangeline was coming to Lathero. They could at least pretend that the past had not happened.

"If Victoria was unsure of your relationship with Lady Evangeline, she isn't now. You've made a social faux pas, staying in the garden so long."

Arend. Hadley blew out a lungful of smoke, not even acknowledging the comment. Finally he said, "Evangeline and I are going to Lathero. If Victoria follows, we've got proof of her involvement."

"She might not follow personally. She might simply send someone else."

"True," Hadley acknowledged.

"I've been thinking . . . ," Arend began.

"That could be dangerous," Hadley tossed out with a laugh, but Arend ignored him.

"What if we let slip that we know it's Victoria behind our troubles? It might force her into making a mistake."

Hadley stubbed the cheroot out under his shoe. "It would also make her very dangerous. A cornered bull charges."

Arend nodded. "But if she loses control, she won't be thinking carefully or rationally, and she may well make a mistake. At any rate, we need to try something." He slapped the railing of the terrace. "The others are still not convinced it's her, and that wastes time."

"Christian will demand proof before we target her. Publicly confronting her is risky. And you're not known for subtlety. What do you propose?"

Arend swung to face him. "I intend to converse with her. Here. Tonight."

"Are you going to ask the others about this approach first?"

"They would likely say no, so I shall tell them afterward. Do you have a problem with that?"

"They will not be pleased. You *will* have to tell them what you have done, because it puts each of them in even more danger. However, I agree that we should try something."

As the two men entered the ballroom, Arend nudged him in the ribs and nodded to their right. Hadley looked in the direction he was indicating and saw Victoria across the room. She was looking directly at them with an expression that could only be called smug.

"Christ, she already knows we know," muttered Arend. "Bloody Isobel."

"That's not fair. We've not confirmed that she is in league with her stepmother."

"How else would Victoria have any idea that we know about her, unless . . . *Salaud!* What did we say in front of the man we interrogated? We let him leave. He might have gone straight back to Victoria."

"I can't recall," Hadley muttered. "We might have mentioned Isobel's name, if not hers."

Arend's scowl deepened. He looked directly at Victoria and raised his glass to her in a mock salute. To Hadley he said in a low voice, "Get Evangeline out of London. Go and work out if there is anything between you that is worth fighting for." At Hadley's stunned look, Arend added, "Life is short. Make sure you bend it to your will so you have no regrets when it ends. I'll ensure Victoria is kept busy here. I intend to up the pressure on her."

"And how do you plan to do that?"

"You don't want to know," Arend said, and slipped away into the crowd, heading in Victoria's direction.

Chapter Eight

The door to Claymore House opened just as Hadley reached the top step. It was surprising to see Thurston still up at this late hour, the lamps still blazing in the entryway behind him. Most unusual at three in the morning.

Bugger, he thought. It could only mean Augustus had waited up for him.

Thurston's words confirmed it. "His Grace asks if you would join him in his study."

Hadley knew it was not an invitation but an order.

He handed his hat and gloves to the tired-looking butler. "Has he been waiting long?"

"No, my lord."

"And his mood?"

"That is not for me to say."

"Of course." Hadley sighed, wishing he'd already bought his own London residence. But it had seemed pointless to do so given that Augustus and the rest of the family rarely came to town. He wished he could leave Augustus to run the family and estates and simply settle at Lathero. Thanks to Maitland's financial expertise, he'd developed his small winery at Lathero, and he loved working with the grapes. There was something about rolling up his sleeves and working with nature. Often in London he longed for the Surrey Hills and his vines. He employed a good vintner to create the wine, of course, but he took pride in helping him shape the final product. The vines were now producing quality grapes, and they'd developed an excellent sparkling wine to rival anything the French could make.

Maitland and Christian both believed in and applauded his plan to make sparkling wine. He'd gotten the idea from Charles Hamilton, also based in Surrey, who'd had great luck in producing sparkling wine that could compete with French champagne. Given the heavy duty placed on the French products, the Surrey made wine was becoming more popular, and Hadley needed to spend more time on that venture. But he hadn't counted on how much of his time and energy he'd need to devote to propping up his brother and managing the family's financial matters. He could put his hand on his heart and categorically say he'd never envied Augustus his role as Duke of Claymore. It just annoyed him that Augustus never performed the role.

He stopped outside Augustus's study and composed himself before knocking on the door and entering.

Augustus was half asleep in the chair by the fire. He looked tired. Hadley hesitated, wondering if he shouldn't simply withdraw, but at that moment Augustus stretched and saw him.

"At last. I wondered if you would come home at all. Then I remembered you'd given me your word that you have parted ways with your mistress. And I doubt Lady Evangeline would condone your staying at her house, given that her son is in residence."

Hadley sank into the chair next to him. "It's late. What do you want?"

"I'd like to continue our conversation from the other morning. I don't think we came to an agreement."

"True. But why is a discussion of Lady Claire so urgent that you stayed up so late to talk to me?"

"Because of Lady Evangeline Stuart."

Anger spiked in Hadley's gut. "I no longer wish to marry

Lady Claire, and it has nothing to do with Evangeline. Well, that is not true—it has something to do with her. She showed me that I no longer wish to settle. I want a marriage based on love, like my fellow Libertine Scholars. If that upsets you, I'm sorry. But *you* could always marry Claire."

Augustus's eyes narrowed. Hadley guessed that he too wanted more in a wife than a woman such as Lady Claire could give.

"It was not I who gave my word that I would marry her. Two years ago you appeared quite pleased with the match."

Hadley squirmed in his chair. Augustus was right—he *had* agreed to the match. "At that time I didn't know the truth about Evangeline's abduction." He leaned forward in his chair, almost pleading. "I have a chance at happiness, a real chance. If I promise to continue to run the estates, would that make a difference?"

His brother's face twisted in agony. "You don't understand. I hoped it wouldn't come to this. I need you to marry Claire."

Hadley stared long and hard at his brother. "I don't understand. Why is it so important that I marry her?"

His brother sighed and looked away, staring at the flames in the fireplace and fiddling with the Claymore ring he wore on his little finger. The silence lengthened until Hadley's pulse began to pound. Christ, what had happened? He watched his brother swallow several times.

When Augustus started speaking, his tone was filled with bitterness and fear. "I'm being blackmailed."

Hadley's mouth gaped. "I beg your pardon? That can't be. I can't think of anything you have done in your life that could see you put in this position. Father . . . he's another story." Hadley sat forward. "My God, it's not something that Father did, is it?"

"No. It is not about Father." Augustus beat his chest. "It is my mistake."

"Then what, for God's sake?" He could see Augustus was shaking. "Come, it can't be as bad as anything Father did," he offered with a laugh, which petered out when he saw Augustus's face.

"I can't bear this—you'll hate me. Please don't make me tell you."

Hadley hated seeing his brother on the verge of breaking down. Gently he said, "If you don't tell me, I can't help you."

"The only help I need—and the need is urgent—is for you to marry Lady Claire as agreed."

"I can't do that. No, I *won't* do that. So you had best tell me what the hell is going on."

Augustus's face paled even further. "Bloody love. It has a lot to answer for."

Suddenly it all became clear. "Is it the Marquis of Corby who is blackmailing you? What on earth with? I thought he was your friend!"

Augustus jumped to his feet and began to pace the room, his hands curled into fists. "He heard of Evangeline's return, and he suspected you would withdraw from our agreement to marry his sister. He has a weapon against me, and if you do not go along as planned, he will use it."

"If he's blackmailing you, why on earth would he not insist that *you* marry Claire? Why must it be me?" None of this was making sense.

Augustus spun about to face Hadley. "Because he knows I never intend to have children and that the dukedom will fall to you."

Hadley shook his head, not sure he had heard correctly. "Why would you not marry?"

"I've told you before. I do not wish to father children."

"That is just something you say." Again Hadley was momentarily speechless. "I know I am not stupid, but this is making my eyes cross, so can you please explain? I don't wish to be the next duke. I know what that role entails. I want a much simpler life."

"We can't always get what we want." He flopped back into his chair. "I can't explain further. All you need to know is that you or your son will be the next Duke of Claymore, and that is why Corby insists on you marrying Claire."

He could tell he'd pushed Augustus as far as was wise, but it rankled that he was being asked to give up his freedom without knowing if there was any other way he might be able to help his brother. "Who's to say the marquis won't continue to blackmail you?"

Augustus dropped his head into his hands. "I don't know that he won't. But there is nothing more he needs from me, and nothing more I have to give."

Hadley didn't know what to say. At last he uttered, "I think I deserve a bit more if I am to make the sacrifice for this blackmail." Internally he vowed that he would not make such a sacrifice, not if he could bloody help it. There was no way a weasel like Corby was going to blackmail his brother and ruin Hadley's chance at happiness. He and Evangeline deserved more.

His brother hesitated, as if on the brink of confession. "My situation is dire. It could destroy the family totally. Think of our sisters. If it became known . . ."

"If what became known? Please, tell me. You're asking a lot of me."

"You agreed to the betrothal before."

"As I said, that was years ago. And now that Evangeline—"

"She left you to marry another."

Why should he have to explain himself? "Evangeline's marriage was not what it seemed."

Augustus shrugged. "I've heard that she was abducted."

"Heard? From whom?"

"Lord Markham and His Grace paid me a visit the day I returned to town. They suggested that I—how did they put it?—start acting like a duke and stop leaving everything to you. They said you should be free to pursue Evangeline if you so wished. They explained what had happened to her."

A warm glow infused him, while at the same time his pride stung. "They should not have done that." He could fight his own battles.

"I agree. This is family business. My business. My life," Augustus muttered. He looked up at Hadley. "The return of a woman you may have loved five years ago . . . I'm sorry, but this is far more important." At Hadley's look he added, "I can't tell you—it's too mortifying."

"You expect me to give up the life I've always dreamed of, yet you won't provide me with a good reason? That's not fair."

"Since when has life ever been fair? You of all people should know that. Do you still love her?"

Did he? She appeared to be the same warm, beautiful woman he'd fallen in love with. But what if her ordeal had changed her? He knew he'd changed. He'd become colder, bitter . . . He longed for the chance to see if they could recapture the love they'd once shared. Yes, he longed for a home and family of his own, which was why he'd agreed when Augustus approached him with the plan to marry Claire. But what he really wanted to make that dream of his own family come true was a woman who would love him unconditionally. It was an ache that had only grown with time. Hadley remained silent.

"I see," Augustus said at last.

He was scared to try again—he had to admit that, at least to himself. It was as if Evangeline had cut off one of his limbs, and now she was trying to make it grow back. What if he could not find what they'd once shared? Or what if she decided that he was not what she really wanted? If she walked away a second time, the rejection would kill him and he would have upset the plans he'd agreed to with his brother for nothing.

Augustus sighed, a sound of despair. "Then I must tell you. Corby set a honey trap and caught me in bed with . . ." Augustus closed his eyes, and to Hadley's horror a tear slid down his brother's face. "Don't make me say this."

Being caught in bed with a woman was not blackmail material, Hadley thought. Then a revelation struck Hadley with the force of a lightning bolt. *How could he not have known?*

Hadley had not even known of his brother's tastes until this moment—that was how well Augustus had hidden it—had had to hide it. Now he understood his brother's fear.

He gripped the edge of the chair, anger filling every inch of his gut. That such a harmless man as Augustus would be put in this position, just because his predilections were not for the female form. . . . But what Augustus had done was punishable by death. The family would be disgraced, their lands and title would be stripped from them, and their sisters would be tainted as having bad blood.

Was that why Augustus didn't want children—because he thought they would be like him? His heart bled for his brother. What must it be like not to be able to love openly?

"I can see the disgust in your eyes." Augustus's voice was full of sadness and resignation.

Hadley rose and crouched at his brother's feet. "Not disgust for you! No, never. What I feel is anger and hatred for bloody Corby. How could a so-called friend do this to you? I'll kill him."

"You're not disgusted?"

Hadley hugged his brother. "Man or woman, we cannot choose whom we love." With a small laugh he added, "Believe me, I've tried to forget one woman for years, hating that I still wanted her back after what I thought she'd done to me."

He pulled back and looked directly in his brother's eyes. "I'm proud to be your brother. I always will be, and I think I respect you even more given the fear you must live with every day."

Augustus wiped his face with his hands. "I . . . thank you."

Hadley retook his seat. "Still, we're in a bit of a pickle."

"I'm sorry. When I heard of Evangeline's situation, I thought you'd likely want to rekindle your relationship. And so did Corby. That is why he's now blackmailing me. He has a maid who will come forward to say she witnessed me . . . with a man. I'm sure she's been paid, but even so . . . I can't see any way out of this."

One solution flew into Hadley's mind: Corby six feet under. "You do realize you'll have this problem all your life. Every man you're with could blackmail you."

"I've met someone. There won't be any other men."

Hadley tried to think who his lover might be. It must be someone on the estate, as Augustus was very reluctant to come to town these days. He was happy for Augustus but also fearful.

"Still, wouldn't it be better to marry so that you can deny any allegations? You are a duke, after all. They would have to have irrefutable proof."

His brother shifted uneasily in the chair. "What of my children?"

Hadley understood what Augustus was worried about. "You mean will they be like you?"

"Yes. I wouldn't wish my condition on any man, let alone my son."

Hadley thought long and hard about how to answer this. He had no idea if this sort of predilection was passed by blood. He'd never heard of anyone else in his ancestry being like Augustus, but he also realized that had there been someone like that, it would likely have been hushed up. "Well, you didn't turn out like our father. He more than loved women. And I hope I'm also nothing like Father. Perhaps we don't all take after our fathers."

"I'm not sure I can risk it. This affliction should die with me."

"The same blood flows in my veins. And I love women."

Augustus's silence spoke volumes. There would be no convincing his brother to marry Claire, and he doubted Corby would agree either.

Just when Evangeline and the life he'd always wanted was within his grasp, he now had his brother's life and his family's very safety and existence to contend with—*and* the villainess who was out to kill him.

He would not allow his brother to be humiliated and be sent to jail—or perhaps even sentenced to hang. Either he had to find a way to keep Corby quiet or he'd have to marry Claire.

"I'm sorry," Augustus said, deep sorrow in his voice. "I'm sorry that Evangeline is free and you are not. I'm sorry God made me this way. If Corby allows, I will marry Claire."

"You don't hold much hope of that?" At Augustus's shake of the head, he added, "Well, we will deal with Corby when we have to. Evangeline and I are still not sure what we both want. She may not want to marry me." That thought hurt a lot.

Besides, he still did not know how *he* felt about Evangeline's return. He desired her, yes, but he'd buried his love for her under a mountain of hurt and disillusion. He was finding it difficult to let his feelings develop, afraid that something else would happen—that she would realize what a diamond of the first water she was and decide that she did not wish to be with a man such as he.

"Rumor is she came to London for you."

"Only to find out why I did not save her. I still don't understand why she does not hate me." As a rich, beautiful widow, she could now marry any man she wanted. Why would she settle for him? Before he could consider walking away from his obligations to Claire and Augustus and his family, he had to be sure, not only of how he felt about her but also that she loved him enough to overlook how little he'd bring to any relationship.

"A woman who wants answers is either out for revenge or in love. I don't believe it is revenge, so it must be love."

Hadley bit back an impolite retort. "Your talk is premature. Evangeline and I are not even sure if we wish to rekindle our past relationship. Anyway, if the Libertine Scholars do not stop this madwoman who has tried to kill me twice now, it may be a moot problem. You do understand that Evangeline was shot because of me. I should be dead. In addition, I was attacked a few nights ago in this very street. I have a knife wound on my arm to prove it."

Augustus's face paled. "I did not realize the situation had become so serious. We should move the wedding up in case anything should happen to you."

His brother's words were like a slap in the face. Was Augustus really more concerned with ensuring that he was wed before he might be killed, rather than with the fact that he was targeted for death?

"Then who would protect you from Corby and run your bloody estate?" The words came out of Hadley's mouth harshly.

"I'm sorry, I'm sorry," Augustus said immediately. "It's just that I can't think of anything but everyone finding out that I . . . If you are dead, I don't know what Corby will do."

Hadley sighed. "I am taking Evangeline to Lathero. Partly it is to keep her safe, and me along with her. And partly, perhaps, it is an effort to lure out our enemy. But mostly it's to see what is left between us. Before you object, Evangeline is now a target, and I will not let her be hurt on my behalf. There would be no honor in that."

What worried him, though, was that if Victoria truly wanted Evangeline dead, he might not be able to stop her. The Libertine Scholars were running out of time. *He* was running out of time.

"We need to hold Corby off until I can think of a way out of this mess," Hadley said decisively. "We agreed to announce the engagement at the end of the season. You may tell Corby I'll honor that agreement." If matters worked out between him and Evangeline, he wouldn't mind reneging on his promise, given that Corby had demonstrated that he had the honor of an alley cat. He would find a way to stop Lord Corby and protect Augustus while giving himself a chance of a life with Evangeline.

"Thank you. I'm so sorry to put you in this position. If we defeat Corby, I swear I'll learn how to run the estates." Augustus rose tiredly from his chair. "I'm going to bed, and I'll be returning to Hardstone Hall in the morning."

Hadley rose to his feet and shook his brother's hand. "Once I find the Libertine Scholars' enemy, I will seek a way to ensure that Corby keeps his mouth shut. If I find one, I won't marry Claire. Agreed?"

"Agreed. It is more than I deserve." As Augustus reached the door he hesitated. At last he said, "Please don't tell anyone about me. Even your friends, and especially not Evangeline. I couldn't bear for them to know. Promise me."

That was going to be difficult, Hadley knew. He would have

to enlist the Libertine Scholars' help with Corby, and as for Evangeline . . . How could he keep this a secret? He might have to marry Claire, and if he did, he wanted her to know why. "You never told me what proof Corby has."

"Corby says that a maid spied through a keyhole and saw me with a young gentleman. I do not know if that is true, but in any case Corby knows of my condition, though I have no idea how he learned about it. I swear I'll be more discreet in future."

Hadley felt a great wave of sadness for his brother. Augustus was not free to love whom he wished, and suddenly Hadley understood how heartbreaking that must be. To have to live in fear, watching every smile, every touch . . .

"I swear I'll not tell a soul unless you approve. I will always do everything I can to protect you and the family." As he had done all his life.

"I don't know why you're being so honorable. I have left everything to you all my life. I am a grown man now, and still I need you to save me."

"Perhaps it's time to learn to stand up for yourself."

"Perhaps so."

"I'll always be there to support you."

"I know that." Augustus stepped into the corridor. "I hope all goes well between Evangeline and you at Lathero," he said, looking back at his brother. "And if it does, we will find a way to stop Corby, even if I have to kill him myself." At Hadley's startled expression, Augustus gave a sad chuckle. "That's me trying to stand on my own two feet."

"Let's hope it won't come to that," Hadley said, his words genuine. As he watched his brother slowly close the door, his heart hurt for Augustus. Only a couple of hours ago a life with Evangeline had seemed within his grasp if he wanted it. But there was a madwoman out to kill him, and now his brother's blackmailer had to be stopped, or else he would have to marry Claire.

What was it Augustus had said? Life truly *wasn't* fair.

Part of him was champing at the bit to get Evangeline alone at

Lathero, but now he wasn't sure what to do. Unless Corby could be stopped, wasn't he simply getting her hopes up for nothing? And while he'd thought that another reason for bringing her to Lathero was to avoid having her remain a target in London, he now had to wonder whether, by leaving town, Evangeline wasn't walking directly *into* danger rather than away from it.

Hadley rubbed his face. Exhaustion saw him wanting his bed, but now he had to talk to Arend. He hated doing this, but as he set off into the night, he could see no other way to both help his brother and leave him free to pursue Evangeline. The Libertine Scholars would have to help him find something on the Marquis of Corby.

And fast.

Chapter Nine

Evangeline was astounded at how happy Sealey was when they took him to Lord Coldhurst's house. Henry and her son were inseparable from the moment they met, indicating that Sealey needed other children round him. He was lonely.

The only reason she had been reluctant to leave London—well, the main reason—was her son. Sealey was her everything. She knew the men would never let anything happen to her boy, and that he was safest of all in Sebastian's house with the other children.

Sebastian, of course, had been amazed when he first saw Sealey, but soon that amazement had changed to anger at Evangeline, though Beatrice had successfully pleaded with him to keep it in check. Nevertheless, the fierce words he had said to her as she was leaving—"You tell him before he marries Claire or I will"—reverberated in her ears as the carriage began its journey to Lathero. She did hope that soon she'd be able to share her amazing secret with the man she still loved. Hadley would be overjoyed, she was sure. They had talked about having a family. A very large family.

A warm glow infused her body, starting at her toes. Finally

they would have their chance to work toward happiness, and she wasn't about to let Victoria ruin that.

Yesterday, as Evangeline had been packing, Marisa had been in her room reading the journals, and she'd struck gold. She'd found a passage implicating Isobel's stepmother.

Evangeline had packed that journal in her hand luggage, which was safely on the seat opposite her, and she was buzzing to share it with Hadley. Marisa had copied the page verbatim and would soon be sharing it with the rest of the Libertine Scholars. Shortly they would have the proof they needed to ensure Victoria's defeat.

At the same time, Evangeline worried about Isobel. What would happen to her? The social disgrace would ruin her chances of a good match. And Evangeline was concerned about the game Arend was playing with her friend. Should she warn her to be wary? When she got back to London, she decided, she would speak with Isobel about Arend.

Soon her thoughts returned to Hadley, though, and what this time together at Lathero might mean for their future. She was eager to have a chance to rekindle their love affair. No, it was a chance to start again. To build something stronger. A future.

To keep scandal from ensuing, she had left London on her own, informing everyone that she was visiting a sick friend. The carriage had headed northwest out of town before turning south toward Surrey.

Hadley had left last night. There was a risk that their disappearance from London at the same time would cause gossip, but to her it was a risk worth taking. The Libertine Scholars had Runners watching Victoria, and Evangeline's carriage was well guarded.

She made the trip slowly, taking it in easy stages, stopping frequently to change horses. She spent one night in a comfortable coaching inn that Hadley had recommended. She wore her widow's weeds and veil to hide her identity.

As they drew closer to her destination the countryside became more and more familiar, and her thoughts turned black. Her childhood home was only a few miles from Lathero, and the thought of confronting her mother was very appealing.

She sighed, abandoning the thought. It was an indication of how much she'd grown that she realized nothing she could legally do would give her back the five years her mother and Dougal had stolen from her. She had to let the anger go or it would eat her from the inside out. She didn't want to waste her life seeking revenge, as Victoria was doing. She had a son to live for, and now, potentially, a life with Sealey's father.

Rachel was traveling with her, and it was her exclamation that pulled Evangeline out of her morbid thoughts.

"I somehow imagined Lord Fullerton's lodge was small. It's magnificent."

Evangeline smiled and let her eyes take in the familiar sweeping expanse of lawn running up to the well-appointed garden marking the entrance to the lodge. The circular drive with the Aphrodite fountain was bubbling, the sun glinting off the water, framing the majestic four-story lodge of Bath yellowed limestone.

Lathero had never looked so alive and thriving. It had been a very long five years since she'd been here. Her hand flew to her mouth to stifle a happy sob. She'd never imagined she'd be back here, or that she would see Hadley again, or that she would be able to be enfolded in his warm embrace—that she would feel safe. She decided there and then that she would not allow the bad memories of the past to encroach on her time here. This was their sunshine place. This was a step into her future. And when she looked at Lathero's beautiful setting, she prayed that one day it would be a home she could share with Sealey and his father.

Joy lifted her as she saw Torbet standing on the top step. As the carriage drew up he came down to help her alight, and he defied convention by drawing her into a hug. He was the closest thing Hadley had to a father, given how his own father had treated him as a punching bag, and her heart swelled with emotion at his gesture.

"Welcome, Lady Evangeline. It's wonderful to see you again. I'm sorry that I did not assist you when—"

She gave a gentle shake of her head. "That time is past. There is nothing for you to apologize for. I don't want to spoil this reunion with regrets or undeserved guilt, so we will no longer mention my . . . my time away."

The butler stood straighter, the years almost seeming to drop away. "As you wish." He swept his arm out to indicate another section of the estate. "We did not know when you would arrive. His lordship is in the field behind the stable, with his vines."

She looked up at him. "Vines?"

"He has become quite enthused with winemaking. But I will leave him to tell you his story."

As she stepped over the threshold, her body began to tremble. This was really happening. Her senses exploded with the familiar sights and sounds and smells of the house. The entrance's wooden floor was so highly polished she could almost see her face in it, and the staff were lined up along the Persian rug in the hall as if to greet the lady of the house. She was touched by the honor Torbet was extending to her.

She'd just finished the introductions and seen that Rachel was shown where her luggage was to go and what room she'd been given—a suite next to Hadley's—when she happened to glance through the doorway into the garden room, a smaller, less formal room overlooking the rose garden. It had been her favorite room years ago. On a fine day the doors opened wide onto a terrace, and the fragrant scent from the roses would drift in as she sat watching Hadley paint. His easel would be set up near the doors where the light was best, and she would watch his face, a picture of concentration, as his brush worshiped the canvas. He was very talented.

The doors to the garden were closed, so it wasn't the roses that attracted her immediate attention. Instead she found her eyes drawn to a massive portrait hanging above the large fireplace. The painting was exquisite. You could almost see the willow's branches waving in the breeze. The woman sitting under the tree was her, yet wasn't her.

Evangeline had not seen this painting before, so it must have been painted after she had been abducted. The other clue was the way Hadley had portrayed her. She looked quite beautiful, her hair falling in waves around her bare shoulders, her profile exquisite, until you looked closer. Her eyes were cold and hard, her smile pure evil. The coldness and artifice made this woman, the woman who looked exactly like her, a stranger.

Evangeline drew in a deep breath. Someone in pain had painted the image; it was obvious in every stroke of the brush. He'd been so hurt, surely as hurt as she had been. She had to keep remembering that she wasn't the only victim.

Torbet came to stand beside her as she gazed at the painting.

"He painted for months after you left. I think expressing his bitterness and hurt on canvas was cathartic for him. Unfortunately, as soon as he finished this he never painted again."

"That is indeed a shame. He loved painting, and he was very good."

Torbet nodded. "Perhaps now that you have returned he'll start painting again."

She looked once more at the portrait before her. "I hope so." And she truly did. Painting had always soothed Hadley and filled his life. Torbet was the one who had seen his talent and nurtured it.

Taking leave of the butler, she made her way through the rose gardens, down past their special willow tree, and out the back gate to the small hilly fields behind the stable, where the land sloped down toward a stream.

She put her hand up to shield her eyes from the sun and drank in the beauty of the vineyard in front of her. She noted a few men working among the vines, yet only one man drew her eye . . . the man who stood in the middle of the farthest row, bent over working.

His coat was off, he wore no waistcoat, and his shirtsleeves were rolled up, revealing tanned arms. If not for the cut of his trousers and the innate presence about his person, he could have simply been another farm laborer.

As she watched, one of the men called to Hadley, indicating he was not doing something correctly. Hadley made his way to the worker's side, allowing him to demonstrate—it looked like they were tying the vines to twine hung between the posts.

He didn't notice her arrival, and she moved under one of the many willows lining the stream, into the deep shadows of the overhanging branches. The shade cooled the heat she felt at the knowledge that tonight she would be in the embrace of those strong tanned arms once again.

The men patiently showed Hadley how to prune the vines and tie them down. He worked alongside them, and when they handed him the pail of water, he drank from the ladle with the rest of them.

This was what she had always admired and loved about Hadley. He was the son of a duke, yet he treated everyone with equal politeness, grace, and importance. No doubt his upbringing, watching his father behave worse than the lowest cad and brute, was at the heart of his ability to cross the barriers of the class system. He had always had an affinity for those less fortunate. That was probably why, when they'd met, he hadn't minded that her family was poor, even though a second son, especially a second son of a duke, usually looked for a financially advantageous match. She now understood how much he must have loved her to be willing to run away to Gretna Green. Did he love her still?

A feeling that he was being watched made him look toward the tree line. For a moment he thought an enemy was present, and given that his life had been threatened twice already, he looked hurriedly round. Out in the open he was a target.

Still, something in his brain indicated that whoever was watching him was not a threat. It took but moments for him to determine who was gazing his way and understand why he had reacted so. His body recognized her even from this distance, and his heart now thundered in his chest. He looked at the sun, realizing it was later than he'd thought. He let a smile wash over him. She'd arrived.

He called to Jack, his head vintner, and said, "Let's call it a day, gentlemen."

He loved that Evangeline was sitting quietly watching him. Did she feel the past dropping away as he did? Having her back at Lathero heightened his senses.

Then he remembered Augustus, and his heart plummeted to his feet. She was not going to like the conversation they would have to have.

He'd debated long and hard about telling her Augustus's story, but he'd sworn to his brother that he would tell no one, meaning that until he had sorted out the situation his tongue was tied. He could only offer her these three days. He wasn't at liberty to offer her more. If he could, he would.

With his heart weighing heavily in his chest, he strode toward her, wanting this conversation over with as quickly as possible. He hoped she loved him enough to stay anyway, but he would understand if she couldn't.

When he reached the willows she ran into his arms, and for one tiny moment, everything felt right with the world. She hugged him as if her life depended on it, and his resolve weakened. Perhaps he should say nothing right away, let her think they had a future together. Then what? Destroy her world if he could not find a way to stop Corby? As he looked into her eyes, filled with so much love and hope, he couldn't do it. It would hurt whenever he told her; best to get it done now.

As if she sensed him holding back, she stepped out of his arms and looked at him with a cute puzzled frown. He took her hand and led her toward their special tree.

Once she was comfortably seated she said, "Something is wrong."

He sank down to sit beside her and cupped her chin in his palm. "You are so beautiful." He bent and placed a soft kiss to her lips but pulled back when she tried to deepen the kiss. Again she looked at him in confusion.

"You agreeing to come to Lathero means more than I can ever express in words."

"I feel exactly the same about being here. I have to keep pinching myself to make myself believe I'm . . . with you."

"When you made the suggestion that we spend time together here, to get to know each other again, I knew in my soul I didn't really need any time. You've owned my heart since the moment I woke up with you cradling my head on that little country lane." He inwardly cursed at the unfairness of it all. "However, since we made the arrangement to come here, I've learned that I may indeed have to marry Lady Claire." Her hand flew to her mouth to stifle a cry. "I will spend the next two weeks doing everything in my power to ensure I don't have to, but you deserve the truth. For too long we were in the dark. If I don't, ah, take care of a situation, I will have no alternative but to marry Claire."

Her eyes searched his face. "If this is about money, if your family needs money, I have money. Plenty of it."

He raised her hand to his lips and pressed a kiss on her knuckles. "I wish it were about money, but it's not. Our estates are thriving. And before you ask, I cannot divulge the situation I am facing. I made a vow of secrecy, and I have to honor that."

"You cannot share it with me? After everything we have been through, you still do not trust me? How is it that you are prepared to throw our chance away but you cannot explain why?" Her eyes began to fill with tears.

His heart tore. "I absolutely trust you, but it is not my secret to tell. Besides, telling you won't make our situation any easier. You won't be able to fix the problem. I have Arend working on a solution, but it may not come in time."

The happiness shining in her eyes disappeared like the flame of a blown-out candle.

"I'm not saying this to hurt you," he went on. "When I found out what they did to you, that you hadn't left me of your own free will, I grabbed with everything I am at the hope that perhaps we could have the life together we've always wanted."

She pulled her hand from his. "Don't do this. Don't tell me what we could have, then take it away from me. That is not fair. Don't be cruel."

He tried to take her into his arms, but she pushed him away.

He sat back, his gaze fixed on her. "I just wanted to explain that I am not doing this lightly. You will always own my heart. But honor forces me to—"

"Honor. Sometimes I despise honor." Her breasts were rising and falling with emotion. "Sorry, that was my disappointment speaking. I love that you are a man of honor."

"It literally is a matter of life and death. Not mine," he added upon seeing the panic on her face.

"Then whose? Augustus's?"

He did not speak, but she must have seen something in his expression, because she went on, "It's your brother again. That is not fair. You already face a threat from Victoria."

Victoria. She said the name as if she was certain. His body stilled. "You found proof?"

She nodded. "Yes. I have the journal with me. I didn't deem it safe to leave it behind. Marisa has copied the page to share it with the others." She looked out over the vines. "I suppose that now, given the journal and your secret, you want to head back to London."

"That depends on you." Her eyes met his, and he was pleased to see a spark there. "I have no right to ask this of you, but I'm praying you'll agree." She moved closer, almost as if she was willing him to say the words. "Will you share my home, my life, my bed for the next three days, even if I cannot make any promises? Needless to say, I hope we can have our happily-ever-after, but if we can't, I'm selfish enough to want this time with you."

Her mouth had dropped open with surprise, and he saw a flash of emotion cross her face. "You ask a lot of me. For me to have what I have longed for and waited for, and then to have to give it up . . . I'm not sure my heart would stand losing you a second time. I need to think. Can I let you know at dinner?"

He tried to hide his disappointment. "Of course."

They sat staring at each other, the tension between them palpable. The last time they'd sat together under this tree had been to plan their elopement. Afterward he'd made love to her all afternoon, and the sweet memories had him wanting to wail at the injustice of his situation. However, his brother's life and his family's standing were at stake, and he would not have those on his conscience just so that he could obtain his own happiness.

He rose and gave her his hand. "Let us return to the house. Dinner is being served early, as Cook thought you might be tired after your long journey. Is your room satisfactory?"

She took his hand and stood. But then she slipped her hand out of his and turned toward the house, sorrow evident in her stance. "I don't know. I haven't seen it yet. I came straight outside to find you."

Her words stabbed at his heart. He wanted to be with her. Wanted to learn about the woman she'd become. It was a credit to her resilience that she had not become a bitter shell of a human being. He wondered what had fortified her all those years, while she was being held captive by a man she loathed. He'd have likely gone mad.

If she stayed, he would have the opportunity to explore, savor, possess, and finally connect with her, more deeply than he'd connected with her in the past. Back then he'd not really under-stood how deep love could go. Real love consumed the soul.

She'd endured more than most women, yet she had retained the essence of who she was. That took strength. She'd been brave enough to confront him about why he had not come for her. And it had taken courage to face the answer.

Now he prayed she had the courage and fortitude to stay. To at least give them both a moment in time that truly belonged to only them.

To say Evangeline was disappointed was a gross understatement. She seethed. This was so unfair. She'd really thought this was going to be their time. That for once no one and nothing would stand in the way of her and Hadley's happiness.

Hands screwed into fists, she sat looking out the window of the drawing room. The moon mocked her; it was full, and the moonbeams were too bright for a night that should be dark and brooding, to match her mood.

Hadley had left it up to her to make the decision to stay or to go.

Her choice.

At least Hadley had been honest with her. He had to marry Claire. A debt of honor . . . a matter of life and death. What the hell did that mean? Bloody Augustus. Hadley had always been his brother's keeper. If it wasn't about money, then what on earth could it be? Worse still, why could he not confide in her? She bit her lip, agitation washing over her in waves.

Her head swam with noise. *Stay. No, go before your heart is, to pieces.* For once she did not know her path.

They could be lovers for the next few days, and then . . . and then they would be what? Friends? Could she move on with her life and watch him marry Claire after sharing his home, his bed? It would become Claire's home, and she would be the one sharing Hadley's bed. Her heart felt like it was being attacked by a dagger, each slash cutting deeper.

It would not only be she who suffered because of Hadley's honor. Soon everyone would notice how much Sealey looked like Hadley, and she refused to make her son the center of gossip if Hadley would not be available to support him. She would have to return to Scotland.

She thought about Sebastian's words: *You tell him before he marries Claire or I will.* But if Hadley's marriage to Claire was a matter of life and death, then telling Hadley about Sealey would rip him apart. What good would come of it? In the eyes of the law, Sealey was Viscount Stuart.

The pain Hadley carried—visible in his eyes, around his mouth, and in the tension in his body—indicated that this was not something he was doing lightly. And the pain she had seen in that painting told her that Hadley had loved her deeply. If Hadley had to marry Claire, he was doing so because he really thought there was no other course to follow.

No, she decided, she would not add to his burden by telling him about Sealey now. She'd tell him after he married Claire.

A tear slid down her face. All her dreams were in ruins, and she felt powerless to do anything about it. She'd been powerless for five years, held captive by a man who didn't love her. Dougal hadn't seen her as a person; he simply wanted children from her. Now she'd found a man who loved her, but he wasn't free. Their roles were suddenly reversed. He was trapped and she was free.

Yet perhaps, she thought suddenly, this time she could save him. Perhaps she could find a way. . . .

So what was she to do regarding his offer to stay at Lathero for the next three days?

She already knew. She'd known the moment Hadley had offered her the choice. She would take whatever Hadley had to offer. Three days of pleasure. Three days of pretending they had forever. During their time together, she'd pray that some divine answer to their situation would reveal itself.

She'd lost Hadley once before, and she'd be damned if she'd lose him again.

Hadley stood in the doorway to his drawing room watching her. Her face was controlled, giving no clue to her decision. He'd hated hurting her earlier, but he wouldn't take her to his bed on a lie. His promise to Augustus meant he couldn't share the reason he might have to marry Claire, and he would not pretend that he could guarantee a happy ending for them after their time here. Yet Lathero had always been the place where their love was freely given and shared.

Would she remember that fact?

After several moments he walked slowly toward her, wondering what he would do if she said she would not stay. Could he bring himself to let her go?

She looked at him, and the tears in her eyes made his heart stop. All he wanted to do was pull her into his arms and say he was so sorry for letting her down again. For not being able to give her what she truly wanted—him. An irritating, irrational sense of failure over not being able to put her first ate at his insides until he wanted to scream.

He stopped by the chair where she sat with hands clenched.

Raising her head, she looked at him and calmly said, "I want to stay with you for as long as I am able."

He looked into eyes that were the lightest of blue, and he almost wept with relief. She had chosen him, and he was not oblivious to the cost of her choice. She might never be his wife, but she was willing to risk her heart by being his lover.

She'd chosen him.

Finally he understood. She did love him. Deeply.

He took her hand, uncurled the tightened fingers, and placed a kiss on her palm. "Are you sure? I don't want you regretting any moment we spend here."

Her answer was a smile that could light up the world. "I may be uncertain about many things, but not this." With her expression one of pure joy, she lifted her free hand, cupped the nape of his neck, drawing him down, and kissed him.

Desire roared through him, and he pulled her to her feet and took over the kiss.

Thankful she'd accepted his offer of days of pleasure, and with a sense of urgency, he knew this was his opportunity to imprint everything about her on his mind, body, and soul, so that if he had to, he could live the rest of his life with only the memory of her. How she filled his senses—her taste, her scent, her softness, and her beauty.

He kissed her again, and it was as if the past five years had suddenly dropped away. He found it so easy to feed her demand and satisfy his hunger, his need, his desire for her. Here she would be his, only his, and he wanted to lock her away and never let her leave. He pushed the agony of parting from his mind; he would pay a terrible price for these few days, but he didn't care. This moment was worth a lifetime of knowing what he had lost five years ago and how he'd had to give her up a second time.

Instead, he decided to focus on the pleasure, on the woman whose softness was in his arms. Her lips were a delight, luscious, pliant, and welcoming. He took ages to savor them, while exploring the delectable curves under his questing hands.

His tongue stroked hers, remembering just how she liked it, and he was rewarded with one of her sensual moans.

God, he was all she remembered. Only with him had she ever felt this whirlpool of desire. With him she was free to indulge all her senses and to find joy in being with a man—this man.

Oh, how she'd missed his touch, his taste, his smell . . .

Never with Dougal had she ever experienced that telltale surge in want, the tug on her senses and on her heart until she gave everything of herself.

Evangeline became lost in his kiss, and she never wanted to be found. His lips moved over hers, and she remembered how glorious his loving was. All that she had missed during the past five years almost overwhelmed her. On a suppressed shudder of anticipation, she parted her lips. A shiver in her soul exploded when his tongue stroked hers.

She couldn't miss his persuasive command. There was no other word for the way he owned the kiss; it was a claiming.

And she reveled in it. He was all sensual heat, masculine strength, and male hardness, rigid and demanding against her stomach. She loved it when he angled his head over hers, snaring her senses and drawing them into a world where they were all that existed, into a world where heat and desire speed toward a hurricane of primitive wanting, coupled with a need that seemed the size of the moon.

The heated mating of their mouths soon wasn't enough. The mingling of breaths, the evocative, provocative, tangling of their tongues saw them racing toward combustion.

She wanted to slow down and savor every moment, but when his arm slid about her waist, drawing her closer, a flash of desire hit where her curves met his muscled heat, and she forget the need to go slow.

The blatant strength of him surrounded her. She knew he would protect her, whatever was to come, and his touch reassured her, gave her comfort after the years of living in hell, promised that he would cherish this time together. To cherish her.

Her hand stroked down his chest and she could feel the steel of him, feel his heart galloping, feel the increasing tension that screamed of his rising desire for her.

He swept her into his arms and carried her upstairs to his room. As he laid her on his bed, he whispered, "I've been waiting what seems a lifetime to have you in my bed." He lay down beside her so that they were facing each other, the rampant desire still there but that by the fact they had all night. No one would interrupt them here.

They had never made love in his room, only under the tree, preferring to wait to make love in his bed until they were wed and she was his wife. Now she might never be his wife.

Her smile faded, and the look on his face changed as he saw the emotion pass over her face. He must be remembering too. "I let insane jealousy stop me from seeing the truth. I'm so sorry I didn't come for you back then. If I had, our lives would be very different now. I would have happily lived in scandalous sin with you until Dougal died."

"You had no reason not to trust the words on the page, or to think that Stowe would betray us."

Pain ripped across his face. "I should have believed in our love.

I was a fool to underestimate your mother's need for money. I let your mother sell you when I should have protected you."

"If you had known I'd been abducted, you would have come after me. I'm sure of it."

"Would I?" He gave a bitter laugh. "I wonder if my pain blinded me to the truth. After I received the note I was concerned only with surviving my wounds. Yet my wounds pale into insignificance now that I know what you must have endured." His voice was ragged.

Evangeline cupped his face, and she pressed a kiss to his lips. She blinked back tears because she wanted none shed in this room or in his bed. This would be their new special place. During her imprisonment in Scotland she'd thought she might die from a broken heart, but Sealey had sustained her. Hadley had had no one.

"No more recriminations. Only words of love, desire, and need."

She'd endured in her husband's bed, but she'd never forgotten the true ecstasy of being loved by Hadley. "You were the only man to teach me about love, about passion. Care to show me what I have missed all these years?"

He squeezed his eyes shut. "I'm scared that when I open my eyes this will be but a dream. I can't believe you have forgiven me."

"There is nothing to forgive. Open your eyes. I'm still here. For as long as you want me."

The look of pain reflected in Hadley's eyes when he opened them made her heart ache. She wrapped her arms about his neck and snuggled closer. "Make love to me."

He shuddered against her as he pulled her tight into his embrace. She felt safe. Loved. All she could think was how fervently she wanted Hadley, how much she needed him to exorcise her dark memories. Already the terrible loneliness of the past years was fading.

His mouth found hers and gently sought entrance. All it took was a sigh into his mouth for his kiss to grow desperate, as if he needed her to save his soul.

Her questing hands began to undress him, and when she broke from his kiss to press her lips to his bare chest, he gathered himself and began to unhook her dress.

"You unman me," he whispered.

"I hope not. I'm expecting wonderful things," she teased, trying to lighten the mood.

Praise God. He really didn't deserve her. She kissed him tenderly, letting her warm mouth linger against his as she undid the buttons on his breeches. He drank in her kiss, soaking in her forgiveness. He used his hands to free her auburn tresses and watched them tumble like waves of sunset over her shoulders and the breasts he'd bared. God, she was so beautiful.

He tried to stop the shudder of fear that hit him. He worried that his punishment for deserting her five years ago would be to give her up now. If he had to marry Claire instead of having this vibrant, caring, gorgeous woman by his side for the rest of his life, he would long for her for the rest of his life.

As if sensing his mental withdrawal, she urged him to lie back as she finished undressing him and then herself.

Once they were both naked she kissed his entire body slowly, letting her soft tresses sweep his body in a sensual caress as she moved lower. He was already heavily aroused, and the erotic image of her leaning over him, her full breasts hanging tantalizingly over his chest, caused him to harden even further. When Evangeline's tongue licked the tip of his erection he almost rose off the bed.

He lost track of how long her mouth tortured him. He grew light-headed as she attended to him, licking, stroking, and remembering every inch of him. She paid special attention with her tongue to his nipples before delivering a feather-light kiss to his stomach. His muscles clenched in a mixture of tenderness and wrenching desire.

He'd never wanted or needed her more.

When her luscious lips slid down his shaft, his hands tangled in her hair. Hadley whispered her name over and over as she loved him with her mouth. She ran her tongue up and down his rampant erection, intermittently taking him deep into her mouth, suckling him. His eyes squeezed shut. He wouldn't last long if he watched this delicious sight.

Soon the coiling tension became too much to bear and he pulled her up and rolled her under him. He wanted to be inside her when he came, and he wanted her to have the most intense orgasm of her life. He wanted to banish the horrid memories of Viscount Stuart.

She was breathing as heavily as he was. Her breasts pressed into his chest, her nipples hard.

He rose above her, the muscles of his arms standing out as they supported his weight. He wanted a moment to soak in the vision of her. "I never thought you'd ever be in this bed with me like this. I will cherish being here with you, cherish this memory, until I die."

A tear leaked from the corner of her eye. "Just love me. Banish the terrible memories for good."

He needed no further encouragement. Pushing her thighs wide, he slowly entered her tight, wet sheath, never taking his eyes from hers. Only when he was seated deep within her body did he let his eyelids close. He held still, savoring this moment.

Finally his body urged him to move. He went slowly, willing his own needs away, wanting to drive Evangeline's desire skyward. Their joining was heaven, and soon her response made his body throb with sensation. He could feel the rampant need rushing through her into him. His desperate longing caused his heart to ache. She would always be his and only his, no matter what the future held.

The tenderness of their lovemaking gave way to a firestorm of need. In the throes of passion they moved as if one, drinking in each other's cries, shuddering with each thrust, and reaching the pinnacle together, cresting on shattering swells of release that seemed to last forever.

As the waves lessened he realized they were clutching each other tightly, as if scared this moment would be stolen from them. He would never let that happen. She would haunt his heart, his soul, and his life always.

"I never thought I'd be capable of hurting a woman, but I want to kill your mother for what she did, to you—to us."

She hugged him tighter, but he moved off to lie next to her. He lay staring up at the ceiling for a long while.

Her voice soft, she said, "What good would that do? It won't change the past, and it would simply see you destroyed. No one would believe she had anything to do with it. My mother is safe behind the walls of society. No one would consider my marriage to Viscount Stuart as anything but sensible and lucky."

"There is nothing in his journals?" He could not bring himself to say the man's name. Just thinking about Viscount Stuart made his anger grow.

She turned her head and looked away. "I haven't looked. I couldn't bear to learn that my younger brother was party to her evil plan."

He sought her hand and linked his fingers through hers. He understood what it felt like to want to protect one's siblings.

He said nothing more, but silently vowed he'd make her mother pay.

A serene peace settled in her heart. He loved her, and she didn't need a marriage to tell her that she owned his heart. She exhaled softly on a sigh. No matter what happened, she would always have this special connection with him. No one could ever destroy that again.

She felt cleansed somehow, as if the five years she'd endured with Dougal no longer defined her. Her heart felt light. She was finally free of the past.

It was the future that concerned her. It was her turn to free

Hadley—free him from whatever was forcing him to go against his heart and marry Claire.

The men were searching for Victoria. Well, she would search for the reason Hadley was trapped. Why he felt forced to marry Claire. She knew who had answers—Augustus. Everything Hadley did was for his family. She would start there.

She felt his fingers trace the silver scars peppering her stomach and breasts. "My body is not quite what you remembered," she said with embarrassment. Perhaps he didn't find her as attractive as before.

"They are part of you, and you are beautiful," he said, and placed a kiss on her stomach.

"Are you sure? My breasts are no longer those of a young girl. I did not wish to use a wet nurse. My belly is marked with these lines, and my waist is a bit thicker. And . . ." She hesitated, but she knew he would eventually see them if he hadn't already felt them. "I have scars on my back."

Hadley gently rolled her onto her side, and the curses that left his mouth when he saw her back made her want to cry. She had known this conversation was coming, but she didn't want this time with him tainted by the past.

She changed the subject, rolling back over to face him and pulling the sheet down his body. "Age doesn't seem to have marked you. You are just as gorgeous—in fact, you have only gotten more handsome, more masculine." Her hands traced the muscles rippling over his stomach, down one powerful thigh, and back up. As she did, she brushed manhood, and she enjoyed watching it begin to harden. His arms were solid muscle, and his shoulders screamed strength. He was a living, breathing vision of a Roman god.

"I have my vines to thank for the muscles. I love working on the land. If I didn't have to look after the family, I'd spend all my time here."

They lay on their sides face-to-face, quietly exploring the changes in each other's bodies. Their conversation turned to memories of their original courtship, his painting, and her love of riding. They talked for hours before it became clear that the only elephant in the room was her time with Viscount Stuart.

She knew he wanted to ask about the scars on her back, but when he ventured a question, she merely shook her head and said, "Not tonight." Their first night together was not the time or place to grieve over her story.

Finally he ran his fingers over her stretch marks. "These are from the birth of your son." She nodded. "Tell me about him. He should have been our son, and the fact that he is not hurts more than you'll ever know. But I know I will love him because he is part of you."

"His name is Sealey. I picked Sealey as his name because it means 'happy.' He made me happy at a time when my life was so miserable." The strongest longing to tell him that he was a father filled her, but she would only cause him heartache. Once he was free, then she would share in the joy of Sealey being his son. "He kept me sane. He became my world. I love him and will protect him with my last breath. He will always come first."

"How old is Sealey?"

This was difficult to answer; would he guess? "He is four." Well, Sealey was four, but Hadley did not yet need to know that he would be five next month. If he did, he might do the math and . . .

"Is he a good boy?"

Her smile widened; she couldn't help it. "He is an angel until he wants something he's not allowed. Then he becomes a devious little monster," she laughed. "I usually can deny him nothing. I'm worried he'll become a precocious, spoiled brat."

"You'd never let that happen. I'm almost jealous." He hesitated. "I *am* jealous. He gets to spend his life with you."

"Hopefully you will too. I have faith that Arend and you will find a way to beat both Victoria and whoever is forcing your hand regarding Lady Claire."

He merely gave a weak smile. "Speaking of Victoria, what evidence did you find?"

"Nothing that proves she is out to destroy the Libertine Scholars, but the ladies are still looking. I have found evidence that she was the woman known as Fleur de Lily, the French brothel owner. Lord Northumberland confessed to my husband that she blackmailed him into marriage."

He pulled her into his embrace. "That will please Arend. He can say to the others 'I told you so.' Identifying the enemy also makes it easier to protect ourselves."

She stifled a yawn. It had been an emotional day. An emotional week. Her shoulder had largely healed, and now, lying here in Hadley's arms, she felt that the scars of the past were beginning to fade too.

"You're tired. Sleep. I'll be here in the morning, I promise."

She snuggled deeper into the quilt, and with the warmth of Hadley's arms round her, she drifted into a restful sleep.

Hadley couldn't sleep. The scars on Evangeline's back had spurred a boiling rage that threatened to consume him. The man he wanted to kill for laying his hands on her was already dead. Instead his desire for revenge focused on her mother. And, of course, he felt guilt—the scars would be a constant reminder of how completely he'd failed to protect her. Even if he married Claire, he swore to himself, he would not again fail in his goal of protecting her.

He couldn't quite believe that she had forgiven him. If it were he who had had to endure captivity, he would not have been so forgiving. Watching her sleep, he wondered at her generosity of spirit. Her love of life and her ability to see beauty in everything around her were merely part of the things that attracted him.

She was still beautiful, but her generosity of spirit drew him more. He admired how strong she was not to have turned into a bitter woman.

He, on the other hand, had turned bitter. He'd stopped enjoying life and begun simply going through the motions.

He slipped his arm out from under her, rose from the bed, lit a lamp, and walked to his armoire. He pulled a small canvas and charcoals from the bottom. Lifting a chair and placing it near the bed, he sank into it and, heedless of his nakedness, began sketching her.

He'd not drawn in years, but the feel of the charcoal in his hand, the swish when it scraped across the canvas, made him realize that the artist's eye he'd thought he'd lost was back. He sketched her over and over until the sky began to lighten. Only then did he put away his tools and climb back in bed beside her.

He would now have a sketch of this night to cherish. If he married Claire, when his existence with her became unbearable, he could look at this and remember the most perfect night of his life.

The very next morning, their hopes of having at least a few days to themselves were shattered. Evangeline wanted to tear up the missive that had arrived earlier from Christian, informing them that Arend had gone missing, that Victoria had fled, and that Hadley was needed back in London.

She stretched like a sleek cat, sore in private places but for all the right reasons for a change. He'd awakened her near dawn and then proceeded to show her how much he loved her until they had both fallen into an exhausted sleep. No wonder she hadn't heard Torbet knock in order to deliver the missive. She'd woken again to a string of curses and saw that Hadley was dressing in a hurry; it was then that he'd told her about the letter.

She pried open a reluctant eyelid and saw the sun was blazing. She groaned and pulled the pillow over her head.

A few minutes later, she reluctantly rose and dressed. She looked out the window to see Hadley talking to the stable boy who had brought his horse around.

She went down and met him at the front entrance. "I would wish that you need not go, but I know you must. We are all in danger until she is captured."

"Will you wait for me here?"

"Do you know how long you will be?"

He shook his head.

"Then let us return to London." She glanced back at the house. "I've had the most magical night here, but it wasn't the location—it was because I was with you. I will join you in London. Wherever you are is the most wonderful place in the world."

He pulled her into his embrace and kissed her soundly. "On your way home, please make sure you have the men guarding you at all times. Victoria is at large and cornered. She'll be dangerous."

As she watched him ride off, she made her plans. She would meet him in London, but only after she'd had a trip to Hardstone. She'd use this opportunity to face Hadley's family and learn what on earth was going on. While he hunted for Victoria, she'd hunt for whoever had a hold over him. There was no way he was marrying Claire. She and Sealey had too much to lose.

She asked Torbet to arrange her carriage and luggage. Then she wrote two notes. One was to Beatrice, telling her she'd be back in a few days, and asking her to inform Hadley that she'd gone to Hardstone. The other was to Hardstone, to let Augustus know to expect her.

Chapter Ten

Hadley made London as night fell, frustration growing with every long stride from his trusty stead. He rode directly to Christian's house and fairly flew out of the saddle and up the front steps. He entered Christian's study to find his friend sitting alone, a bottle of whiskey open on the table.

Hadley approached slowly, his heart still pounding. "You have found him?"

"No. He bloody well should have told us what he was up to regarding his investigation of Victoria. Perhaps he would not be missing if he had."

Hadley ran a weary hand over his face. "I knew."

Christian's eyebrows rose. "Care to tell me why you two decided not to share his plans?"

Hadley flopped into a chair. "We did not think you would condone his actions. The women, your wives, seem to think Isobel is innocent, and so by association they thought Victoria must be innocent as well. Only when they had read the journals did they realize Arend was right—it *is* Victoria. By then he'd already confronted Victoria, and . . ."

A glass slammed on the desk. "And now he is missing. For all we know, dead."

Hadley flinched. "He's too clever to die, and too mean to boot."

Christian shook his head. "I don't know what to do. I have no idea where he is, and then you disappeared and I thought . . ."

Hadley jerked his head up. "You thought I was taken too? I've been at Lathero."

"So I have heard. With Lady Evangeline. Serena tells me you two are courting."

Christian filled Hadley's glass with whiskey. After he'd gulped some of the fiery brew he admitted, "Not exactly. I may still have to marry Claire."

Christian sighed and pushed back his chair. "It's as my wife said, then. Marrying Claire would be a huge mistake because you don't love her. From what I have seen and heard, I'd say you still love Evangeline."

Hadley didn't even hesitate. "I do, But life isn't always fair."

"Then I suggest you fix whatever it is that keeps you from following your heart. Life is short, my friend, and can be very lonely."

"If we are through discussing my private affairs, what are we going to do about Arend and Victoria?"

Christian rose and walked around his desk to perch on the corner. "Go home. Get some sleep. You look like you're about to drop. I need you fighting fit tomorrow."

"But—"

"We will all meet here first thing tomorrow morning to plan our next move. Racing off without a solid plan won't do Arend any good and may put more of us in danger."

"When was he last seen?"

"Two nights ago at Lady Seaton's ball."

That was after Hadley had left for Lathero. "Were Victoria and Isobel there?"

Christian nodded.

Hadley was worried. "He wouldn't have been stupid enough to try to capture her on his own, would he?" At Christian's smirk, he rolled his eyes. "Silly me. Of course he would. Damn him. I should not have gone to Lathero."

"Arend doesn't need you protecting him every hour of the day. He should have had patience and waited for us."

True.

Christian held the study door open for Hadley. "Go home. Sleep. And come back tomorrow prepared to leave London at a moment's notice. I have Runners looking into his disappearance. So far nothing, but tomorrow is another day."

As Hadley mounted his horse for the ride home, he thought about calling at Evangeline's. She should be arriving soon. However, he didn't want to draw any attention to their liaison until the situation with Claire was sorted.

So it was a surprise to arrive home to find a note from Beatrice informing him that Evangeline had gone to Hardstone.

He should be angry with her, but he wasn't. It meant everything to him that Evangeline wanted to try to help him. He wondered what Augustus would do. Would he tell her the truth? If so, would she understand why he had to help his brother? Perhaps she'd be appalled. Somehow he doubted that. She had a big heart and would feel his brother's pain at having to hide who he really was. Hadley knew he could be overprotective when it came to his brother, but from an early age he had always hated how their father picked on Augustus.

Had their father seen the type of man Augustus would be? Was that why he'd picked on Augustus mercilessly? Perhaps their father had thought to beat the predilection out of him. If so, it hadn't worked. But then, Hadley had taken most of the beatings on his brother's behalf.

And now it seemed as if Hadley would have to agree to marry Claire to help save his brother's life. He tried to picture how his life would be. He would be running his brother's estates as he did now, only he'd have a wife whom he felt absolutely nothing for. He'd have nothing but duty to keep him company. His heart would always belong to Evangeline.

As he slipped between cold sheets he prayed not only that they would find Victoria but also that they would find a solution to Augustus's problem.

Evangeline left Lathero shortly after Hadley and arrived in Kent late at night to find that they were expecting her. She'd never visited Hardstone before and she couldn't see much of the estate in the dark, but if the vast grounds outside matched the inside of the grand house, then she was sure it was beautiful beyond words.

It was too late to grill Augustus tonight or to meet Hadley's sisters and mother. What would they think of her visit? Did they know of her past relationship with Hadley and that he had wanted to marry her? She retired to her room with those questions swirling in her mind.

Too weary and restless to sleep, Evangeline lay in bed remembering how she'd felt last night in Hadley's arms. She'd been scared that it would not be like it was before. That all she'd suffered in Dougal's bed might have changed how she thought about and enjoyed sex. Her face heated. She'd enjoyed it even more than she could have imagined. Hadley was a wonderful lover. Patient, thorough, giving, and more. She understood that making love was infinitely different from having sex or being forced to have sex. What she felt for Hadley when he was in her, loving her, was indescribably beautiful.

She rolled onto her side and stared into the darkened room. Augustus's problem must be very serious for Hadley to give up on the idea of a life with her. No one would persuade her that Hadley didn't love her, not after last night and what they'd shared. With those thoughts warming her, she finally drifted off to sleep, vowing to help Hadley's brother and free Hadley from any obligation.

The next morning she found her nerves stretched taut as she prepared to meet Hadley's family. What must his mother think of her unscheduled arrival?

She'd been invited to join the family for breakfast, and as she made her way down the sweeping staircase she heard friendly voices and laughter coming from the breakfast room. She hesitated at the door, swept a hand over her hair and down her dress, took a deep breath, and then entered.

The conversation died instantly as four pairs of eyes swept over her.

Finally Hadley's mother said, "Good morning, my dear. Please take a seat. Clive, would you dish some breakfast up for our guest and a fresh cup of tea?"

"Tea would be lovely, thank you," Evangeline said as she took the seat indicated, next to one of Hadley's sisters, the younger girl —Lady Cynthia, if she recalled correctly.

She felt a smidgen of relief that the girls were present; that meant the questions could not be of a personal nature.

"I do apologize for dropping in on you uninvited, but I was visiting nearby, and as I was close, I thought I'd take the opportunity to seek advice from His Grace."

Augustus didn't look surprised at her arrival, but Her Grace appeared perplexed.

"How odd—I cannot image what His Grace could help you with. But it's delightful to finally meet you," she said with a warm smile. "My younger son mentioned you often many years ago, and Augustus tells me that you are recently widowed and have returned to London. Have you seen my son Hadley?"

"Indeed, Your Grace. I saw Lord Fullerton at Lady Beaumont's ball."

"Was he pleased to see you?"

Hadley's sisters were watching her closely.

"Mother, I'm sure that's an inappropriate question for our guest," Augustus said. "Lady Evangeline, I would be happy to indulge you as soon as you have finished breakfast. I'm sure you would like to return to London as soon as possible."

Was that a polite question or a request that she leave? She decided to play dumb. "Thank you, Your Grace. I won't take up much of your time, and yes, I'd like to return to London as soon as possible."

"To your son, I assume. What is his name?"

At Her Grace's question her heart stilled. Hadley's mother was better informed than she'd thought, though Evangeline was sure Her Grace had no idea she was a grandmother. The guilt settled heavy on her heart. Sealey should know his grandmother. "His name is Sealey, and he's a good little boy." *And he looks exactly like your son.*

"Your firstborn was a boy? Your late husband must have been pleased."

She could not bring herself to reply, so she took a sip of tea.

Polite conversation flowed as she ate breakfast. The girls wanted to know about the latest fashions and whether she had met the Prince Regent at any of the balls. She envied them their comradeship. She would have loved a sibling close in age. Perhaps a sister would have helped her all those years ago.

Soon she could delay her conversation with Augustus no longer. At his raised eyebrow, she nodded, and he rose and helped her with her chair.

"It was a pleasure to meet you," she told Hadley's mother. "I am just sorry it is such a rushed visit."

Her Grace exclaimed, "You must come again, and bring your son. The house could do with little children running round." With those words she looked pointedly at Augustus. "Both my boys appear to be slow in producing my grandchildren. I hope one of them will marry, and soon." Her smile widened. "Give my love to Hadley when you see him."

Evangeline blushed furiously and stammered an affirmative reply before following Augustus from the room. They walked in silence until they reached his office. She noticed Augustus fiddling with his cuffs.

As they entered his study, a young man was gathering up papers from a second desk. He looked close to her in age, perhaps twenty-five years old, and he was dressed all in black with a white shirt. His face lit up when he saw Augustus, but the smile vanished when he saw Evangeline.

"That's all, Mr. Vickers. We shall continue my correspondence once Lady Evangeline departs."

After the other man left, Augustus gestured to a chair. "Please, take a seat. What can I do for you?"

She drew in a deep breath, leaned forward in her chair, and said, "It's not what you can do for me but what you can do for Hadley. You know he does not wish to marry Lady Claire, and I know you understand why he will go through with it. I assume he is protecting this family, as he always has."

Augustus had the grace to look ashamed. "He has not told you, then?"

"I know he is not marrying Lady Claire because he wants to. He is doing it because he has to. His words, not mine. If you loved your brother, you'd want to see him happy."

"Life seems so simple to you."

"I can't believe you just said that to me." Her voice rose. "I was kidnapped, torn from the man I loved, and sold into virtual slavery. I of all people know life is not simple. Life can be hard, painful, and unfair."

"I'm sorry, I spoke without thinking. I know my brother loves you, but I don't know what else to do. I'm as trapped as you were."

She pressed her hands to her cheeks. "I'm probably the only one who can understand what that feels like, and I would give anything to help you. Why don't you tell me what is going on? I'm sure we can think of a way to free both you and Hadley."

"I know my brother once loved you and that you broke his heart. I also know it was because your mother sold you. That does not mean I can trust you with personal, *private* family matters. We are strangers, are we not?"

"I am hoping that if I can help you, I'll eventually be your sister-in-law. If I share a secret with you, perhaps you'll trust me."

When Augustus said nothing, she braced herself. Either this was going to work or it would make the situation much worse. "My son, Sealey Hadley Masters, Viscount Stuart, is not Lord

Stuart's son." She waited, but still Augustus did not speak. "He is Hadley's son, and if you don't believe me, you will as soon as you meet him. He looks exactly like Hadley."

"Does Hadley know?"

She shook her head. "How could I tell him? He would be torn between this family secret and his son. Instead, I've come to try to help us all."

He spoke quietly. "If I reveal the truth to you, I'm putting my life in your hands."

So it *was* Augustus Hadley was protecting. She held out her hands. "These may be small hands, but when given in assistance they will not betray you. I know what betrayal tastes like."

He assessed her intently before finally nodding. "I'm being blackmailed by the Marquis of Corby." He then proceeded to tell her his sad story.

Her heart began to pound in her chest. Now she understood why this was a matter of life and death. Augustus's behavior put not only himself in danger but the family too.

She wasn't sure how she felt about His Grace and what people would call his "perversions." She studied him. All she saw was a man, a man who for some reason found other men attractive. With a sentence of death hanging over his head, she supposed it was not a perversion he would choose lightly. What would she do if her son developed into such a man? Would she love him any less? Of course not. Just as Hadley still loved his brother.

It was not for her to judge. She would help them escape this situation.

"Surely they would not take a maid's word over a duke's?"

He gave a bitter laugh. "Oh, I'm sure he will produce a string of servants and God knows who else to say they saw me with a man." Augustus stood and began to pace before the fireplace. "He has wanted our families aligned for years. He was pestering me to marry one of my sisters to him, but I refused to sign any such agreement. I wanted her to have a choice in her husband. I didn't understand how ruthless he would be."

"But why Hadley? Why not force you to marry Claire?"

"Tainted blood. The plan is for me to remain unmarried and the title to pass to Hadley, or Hadley's son."

Her hands curled in her lap. Hadley would make a fabulous duke, but he'd not want his brother to suffer. "I'm sorry."

He shrugged. "Don't be. I've never particularly wanted children. I like my life as it is."

How could he? He had to hide who he really was. The risks he took . . . His life and his family were all in danger. "I would have thought taking a wife would protect you from innuendo and rumor."

His eyes flickered to the office area next to his study, where young Mr. Vickers had gone. At that moment she realized he'd found his heart's desire.

She cleared his throat. "So we need to discredit the witnesses." She bit her lip and looked at the rug beneath her feet, willing an idea to come forward.

"At least they don't know the name of the man I was with. *I* don't even know his name."

Her head snapped up at Augustus's words. "That's it." She gave a smile. "You weren't with a man—you were with me."

"I don't understand."

"I met you dressed as a man because we were having a torrid affair and I'd snuck away from my husband in disguise, not wishing to be recognized. The witnesses merely saw me still in my disguise. Then it is my word, and yours, against that of a few servants. My husband's dead; there is no way anyone would know I've been exclusively in the wilds of Scotland these past five years."

Augustus looked shocked. "But that could ruin you. If you marry Hadley, they will think I'm handing him my seconds." When she shrugged, he asked, "You'd do that for me?"

She shook her head, excitement making her breathy. "No. I'd do it for Hadley and myself. To have a life with Hadley. The fact that it helps you is a bonus." She rose and leaned forward, her hands on the desk. "I won't let anyone steal my happiness from me again. Shall we pay a visit to the Marquis of Corby?"

Augustus smiled back. "Excellent idea, my dear. I believe he's in London presently. Care for some company as you head back to town?"

She stood up, joy almost making her dizzy, and said, "I'd be delighted."

The meeting in Christian's drawing room was as cheerful as a wake. There was still no word from the Runners regarding Arend's location, or Victoria's. The ladies had visited Isobel to see if she knew her stepmother's whereabouts, but she didn't. Isobel had been distressed to learn that Victoria was probably the villainess. The women still did not believe that Isobel was in league with her stepmother, but the men had refused to allow her to attend this meeting.

"Lord Stuart was very thorough. The journals clearly detail Victoria's history, but only beginning with her time in Paris. He hadn't dug further into her past. She arrived in Paris almost nine years ago, not long after the incident at Serena's father's house."

"She made a name for herself as an exceptional madam. Her house, the Fleur de Lily, was the most powerful in Paris, and the most sought-after. The establishment catered to every carnal taste."

"Arend would know more," Grayson put in. "He told me Angelo worked in that establishment before he opened the Top Hat." Until Victoria had killed him in order to prevent him from revealing her identity and providing evidence against her, Angelo had run the Top Hat, the most exclusive molly house in London.

Hadley spoke up. "I can't understand why Lord Stuart gathered this information. What was he hoping to achieve?"

"He believed Victoria killed her husband."

Silence descended over the group at Marisa's words.

"He was gathering evidence against her. He'd had men investigating Northumberland's death. Did you know he died in a fire at his mistress's cottage on his estate? They both perished in the fire. A burned body is a great way to conceal foul play."

Hadley couldn't help but wonder about Lord Stuart's death as well. Accounts had it that he'd been shot by highwaymen. He wondered if that was also a bit too convenient. If Victoria had learned of Lord Stuart's investigation, she would not have hesitated to kill the man.

Next they discussed the information they found in Lord Stuart's journal. Victoria had used her ill-gotten gains to build herself a small army, men who owed her in one way or another. Men like Angelo, who had kept Victoria's secrets right up until she killed him. The men she currently had in her employ were loyal, well paid, and ruthless.

"I have no idea where to start to look for Arend. I know he's been spending time with Isobel, but I'm not sure we can trust her," said Christian.

The woman all looked at one another. At last Portia spoke. "It's true I haven't known Isobel for long, but she came out at the same time as I did. I don't believe she was old enough to be involved in planning the Libertine Scholars' downfall. I'm sure she wasn't even in London when Christian was set up for the rape of that young woman and then shanghaied to Canada."

Grayson threw up his hands. "I feel so bloody impotent. There is nothing we can do to find Arend until he either escapes, is able to send us a message, or the Runners find a clue to his whereabouts."

His wife, Portia, patted his hand. "We can continue to go through the journals to see if we can find where Lord Stuart might have documented evidence of Victoria's crimes. Although I suspect he didn't have any solid proof, given that he never confronted her or reported her to the magistrates."

"I think we're past the point of needing evidence. We simply have to stop her before she hurts anyone else. If we could get her to confess in front of someone reputable, we would not need further proof. Besides, if she has caught Arend, she must have some plan for him . . . if he's not dead already."

Hadley nodded at Christian's words. "If we could catch Victoria in the act, then we would have our proof."

Sebastian voiced their frustration. "Right now, we'll just have to wait for some lead as to Arend's whereabouts. Hopefully the Runners will pick up his trail. If I know Arend, he won't stay silent for long."

Hadley sat contemplating the situation. He knew there was no point racing off around the country, for they had no idea which direction Victoria had gone, or whether she even had Arend with her. Instead, his thoughts turned to Augustus and the problem of the Marquis of Corby.

Having had one night with Evangeline, he knew one thing for certain: he had to find a way to save Augustus without marrying Lady Claire.

He wished Arend were here so he could talk with him about the situation. If anyone could get the Marquis of Corby to change his mind, it was Arend. He could scare a ghost into fleeing.

It took him a moment to realize Marisa was standing by his chair.

"Is there somewhere we could have a private word?" Marisa asked.

Hadley looked over toward her husband, but Maitland was busy talking with Grayson. "Is something wrong?"

"I'm not sure."

He noticed Portia looking at her and shaking her head. How odd. "Of course. Let's use Christian's study."

Marisa flashed a defiant look at Portia before walking from the room. Hadley looked at Portia and merely shrugged. Neither of them said anything until they reached Christian's study.

As Hadley closed the door he noted that Marisa was very nervous. She kept fidgeting with the ring on her finger as she paced in front of the fireplace.

"What is it? Your pacing is making me very nervous. Has

something happened?" His heart sped up. "Have you heard something terrible about Evangeline?"

"No. Sorry to upset you like that. No, Evangeline is safe as far as I know." She sat on the chair next to the fire but didn't face him. "Are you going to marry Lady Claire?"

He wasn't offended; he knew Marisa was probably just looking out for Evangeline. "I'm not sure that is any of your business. I don't mean to be cruel, but my private life is my private life, and there are a lot of things going on that you don't understand."

"I understand that Evangeline is in love with you, and I think you are in love with her."

Hadley rubbed the back of his neck. "It's not quite as simple as that. There are other considerations. I have other obligations."

Marisa sat staring at him for quite a period of time, raising the tension in the room. Her fixed gaze made Hadley want to squirm.

At last she said, her voice soft, "You are going to hate me, but I can't stay silent. I can't let you make a mistake you will regret for the rest of your life, simply because you don't have all the facts."

There was a commotion in the corridor, and Beatrice all but flew into the room.

"Don't, Marisa. Please don't interfere. It's not our place."

Hadley looked between the two women. Marisa obviously wanted to tell him something, but Beatrice ran across the room to clap her hand across Marisa's mouth.

Hadley couldn't hide his shock at her behavior. "For goodness' sake, Beatrice. What on earth is going on?"

Beatrice ignored him. "We promised Evangeline that we would give her time. The time she requested is not yet up." At Beatrice's words, Marisa slowly nodded, and Beatrice removed her hand from Marisa's mouth.

Marisa gave him an apologetic yet sad look, and the ladies rose to leave the study. But Hadley blocked their departure.

"What was that about? You can't drag me in here and then be so cryptic. I demand an answer, ladies."

Marisa halted at the door.

"I think you should meet Evangeline's son. It's important."

Beatrice tugged Marisa from the room, saying, "Come on."

As she left, Marisa's face was filled with such sorrow that it tore at Hadley's heart. Since learning that she would be unable to have children of her own, Marisa had redoubled her devotion to children's causes. She was the patron of an orphanage, making sure the children were treated well and educated to a high standard. So it didn't surprise him that she was concerned for Evangeline's son.

However, he wasn't sure what the boy had to do with him. Perhaps she was worried that Hadley would be unable to accept the boy, but that wasn't true. Yes, he was nervous about meeting the lad, and he did hope the boy looked more like Evangeline than Viscount Stuart, but he was sure he would love any child of hers.

He was just about to step out of the study when Sebastian appeared. "I know it must be a terrible shock, but I can understand her not telling you."

"Not telling me what? Who? What the bloody hell is everyone talking about?"

"Oh," Sebastian said slowly. "I thought Marisa told you about Sealey."

"Has something happened to him? I promised Evangeline we would protect her son," and he made to push past his friend.

Sebastian halted him with his arm. "He's fine. I swear."

"Then what are the women going on about?"

"Are you going to marry Lady Claire?" Sebastian asked.

Hadley wanted to shout and stamp his feet like a child. "Why is everyone so concerned with my marital status?"

"I see. So that is a yes." He gave Hadley a sympathetic look.

"It's not what I want, but I have someone else to think of, someone to protect."

Sebastian nodded. "Of course you do. To the rescue, as usual. I think it's time you thought about what *you* want for a change. Your brother is old enough to look after himself. Before you make your decision, I feel it might be prudent to meet the young Lord Stuart. The little viscount might just change your mind."

"Funny, Marisa said the same thing. Why don't you tell me what is so unusual about the boy?"

He laughed and shook his head. "I can't. I made a promise to Beatrice, and I'm not stupid enough to upset my wife. Why don't you come home with me? I'd love to see the look on your face when you meet Sealey."

Chapter Eleven

Augustus was the perfect traveling companion—his stories of Hadley as a young boy kept Evangeline in fits of laughter. But eventually the tales became more sober, and Augustus explained what living with their father had been like.

A shudder ran through her after he'd told her some of what they'd had to endure. "Both of you should be proud of how you survived your father."

"Hadley made sure I never gave up." Augustus paused thoughtfully. "One time, my father took us out into the paddock to teach us how to box. I'm sure he did it on purpose. Father knew I hated violence of any kind. He made Hadley square up against me. I was no match for him, and Hadley knew it. After a few fun punches, Father told him to box with me as if it were a proper match, or he'd be birched. Hadley didn't even look at me; he simply took off his boxing gloves, turned back toward the house, entered Father's study, and assumed the position."

"He loves you."

Augustus looked out the window. "I don't think it's only love. The need to protect is strong in him."

She tried to still her jangling nerves. "I can't wait to tell him we've freed him. I'm pleased to have protected him for a change."

Hadley accompanied Beatrice and Sebastian home. Beatrice excused herself as soon as they walked in the door. She had a young babe, having just given birth a month ago, and all the strain of the search for Victoria was beginning to wear her down.

Having ascertained that Henry and Sealey were out with Sealey's nanny and the Runners, the men settled down to play some billiards.

They had just finished playing one game when they heard visitors arrive. After several minutes, Sebastian's butler, Roberts, knocked and said, "Lady Evangeline and the Duke of Claymore are asking if you are at home."

"Of course, Roberts. Show them in, and please bring some tea for Lady Evangeline."

"Very good, my lord."

Hadley knew from Beatrice's note that Evangeline had gone to Hardstone, but he was surprised that she and his brother had arrived in town together. What on earth was she planning?

"Hadley, I didn't know you'd be here," she said, a look of shock on her face, when she came into the room. "What a surprise," she added haltingly.

Sebastian looked very amused. "This should be interesting."

"I'm so pleased you find my relationships amusing," Hadley hissed under his breath. To Evangeline he said, "You look worried. Has something happened?"

She glanced at Sebastian before looking back at Hadley and shaking her head. Before she could reply, Augustus stepped forward with a very broad smile. Hadley wasn't sure what he had to smile about.

"Lady Evangeline is quite a woman, and I can see no reason why you wouldn't be rushing her to the altar."

Now Hadley was really confused. Had his brother had a change of heart?

Evangeline's smile was back. "We have much to tell you.

Augustus told me about your little problem, and between us we have come up with a solution. Let's just say you no longer have to marry Lady Claire."

"Thank Christ for that," said Sebastian. Then he fixed his eyes on Evangeline, a slightly wicked expression on his face. "Lady Evangeline, I assume you are here to collect your son. Shall I call him for you?"

Evangeline became flustered, a delightful shade of pink invading her cheeks.

Sebastian appeared quite amused as he said to Augustus, "Come, Your Grace, let us leave these two alone for a moment. I'm sure they've got a about." With that, Sebastian led Augustus from the room, leaving Hadley and Evangeline staring at each other.

"Would you care to explain that cryptic message?"

"I'd prefer a kiss first." She walked slowly toward him, not stopping until her breasts brushed his chest. She rose on tiptoe and pressed her lips to his. It was a demanding kiss, a kiss that stirred the desire that had been swimming in his blood from the moment she walked into the room. His heart was still guarded, but the fortress began to crumble with Augustus's implication that Hadley was now free to follow his heart's desire.

He wanted answers. However, unable to deny his need, he opened for her, shuddering beneath the raw force of his passion, the kiss shatteringly familiar and one that he longed to experience for the rest of his life. Was that now possible?

Urgent need gripped him, and he slanted his mouth to deepen the kiss further, his tongue sliding in heated, graceful rhythm across her lips and tongue. How had he lived without her for so long?

He desperately wanted to know if what she had said earlier about having found a solution was true. He regretfully broke the kiss, but still holding her tightly in his arms, he whispered, "Is it true? Please don't fill me with false hope."

"I believe I have found a way to stop Lord Corby." She

wrapped her arms around his neck, burrowing deeper against his chest. "You are free."

"Tell me how."

"It's simple, really. I will tell Lord Corby that the 'man' he witnessed performing certain acts with your brother was actually me. I was having a torrid affair with your brother and did not wish my husband to know, so as a disguise, I dressed as a man." She drew back to look at his face. At his look of horror she added, "It will be the servants' word against that of a duke and a lady. No one will dare dispute our version."

"Brilliant—apart from the fact that your reputation will be ruined."

"Rather ruined than having to watch you marry a woman you don't love. Besides, I've never had a season. Society really doesn't know much about me. The scandal will be quickly forgotten."

"Not if you then marry me."

A flash of annoyance crossed her beautiful face. "Are you saying you're worried about scandal? I thought you'd be happy."

He was being a fool. Why should it matter if society believed he had married Evangeline after his brother no longer wanted her? That he was her second choice? It was just that she deserved better.

"You have already suffered so much. I don't want to see you the target of salacious gossip."

"Words can never hurt me. I've known true hurt and I survived. I shall certainly survive a little bit of gossip."

Having uttered that statement, Evangeline laughed inwardly. Hadley had no idea the gossip that was about to start. Once society clapped their eyes on Sealey, she and Hadley would most certainly be the center of gossip.

She needed to tell him, and tell him now. At any moment their son could walk in through those doors. It was time to inform Hadley that he had a son.

She would just have to trust in his heart and hope that he loved her enough to forgive the fact she'd hid this from him. She knew learning about Sealey would bring him both great joy and also pain. He had missed the first five years of his son's life, years that he could never get them back.

In addition, his son would never carry his name. Her mother and Viscount Stuart had stolen that from him. A part of her worried what Hadley would do to her mother for this injustice. She suspected his vengeance would be harsh, but she really couldn't bring herself to care. Her mother had made her bed, and now she must lie in it.

She stepped out of Hadley's arms saying, "Please sit for a moment. There is something I must tell you," and she indicated that he take a seat on the settee.

Hadley obliged. "I do not know what this can be about, however. I cannot think of anything more serious at the moment than Augustus's problem."

She opened her mouth, praying for the right words. But at that very moment the door burst open and Sebastian said, "You should come downstairs. And prepare yourself—the news is very bad."

Hadley was already at the door before Sebastian had turned away, and she followed quickly behind.

The scene greeting them at the bottom of the stairs was chaos. It took but a moment for Evangeline to recognize Wendy. A cry left her lips as she took in the state of Sealey's nanny. She was being carried by someone who Evangeline supposed was one of the Bow Street Runners sent to guard Wendy and her son, and it was obvious that Sealey's nanny was unconscious. A nasty head wound was evident, as was the blood covering her clothing.

Two other men were also being carried into the house, also covered in blood. One had been shot.

It took her only a moment more to realize that Sealey was not with them. Panic seized her throat and she found it difficult to breathe. "Where is Sealey?" No one heard her. *"Where is Sealey?"* she screamed.

Beatrice arrived at her side and grabbed for her hand. "Isobel is missing too," Beatrice said to Sebastian.

"Oh, God." Evangeline sank onto the bottom step of the stairs, her arms wrapped around herself, rocking slowly. "She has my son."

Hadley grabbed one of the Bow Street Runners. "What happened? Where are the boy and Lady Isobel?"

The Runner looked briefly at Evangeline before pulling Hadley to one side. She couldn't hear what they were saying, but from the look on Hadley's face she knew it was bad.

Hadley moved slowly toward her, his eyes never leaving her face. He crouched down before her and took both of her hands in his.

"It looks as though Isobel led the men into a trap. I believe Victoria has your son, but I swear to you now, on my life, I will get him back."

She could not speak through her grief. All she could do was nod and let Beatrice comfort her.

Hadley immediately turned to find out more information from the Runners, while she could hear Sebastian telling Roberts to send word for the other men to meet them here immediately.

This was her fault. She'd left her son to have a tryst with Hadley when she knew the danger they faced. How selfish could she have been? If anything happened to Sealey, she would never forgive herself. Never.

She looked across at Hadley, and her heart stilled. She gave a wail, burying her face in Beatrice's warm embrace. If something happened to Sealey, Hadley would never get the chance to know his son.

Hadley would never forgive her either.

Hadley's body trembled. He had to save the boy. Evangeline had trusted him and his friends with the most precious thing in the world to her—her son. He'd promised her the boy would be safe. He meant to make good on that promise.

If the boy was injured or, God forbid, died, how could she forgive him a second time?

Evangeline had lost so much already, and if she lost her son . . . He couldn't begin to think of the devastation. Anger built, and he wanted to smash something, preferably Victoria's face—and perhaps Isobel's too. Did they now know the color of Isobel? Had she lured Sealey to his fate? Was she was a party to Victoria's villainy?

Arend was proving right at every turn.

Sealey was in danger because of him. If Isobel hadn't learned of Evangeline's husband's journals, perhaps Victoria would have left her and Sealey alone. Deep down, however, he did not believe that. Evangeline and Sealey had become a target the minute he showed interest in the pair.

Thank goodness the Libertine Scholars all lived close by. Within quarter of an hour Grayson, Christian, Maitland, and Lord Philip, Portia's brother, had arrived with wives in tow. The women took one look at the weeping Evangeline and gathered round her like protective mother hens.

Sebastian took aside one of the Runners who was not as badly injured and suggested they move into the study to plan their next move. Hadley watched Evangeline as the women drew her up the stairs toward the drawing room. He briefly met her eyes and tried to convey a message: *Be strong.* She gave a nod in reply, but her eyes were glazed with fear.

Once in the study, with only the men in attendance, George, a Bow Street Runner, brought them up to date with details of the attack.

"We tried our best to hold them off, but there were at least twenty men. As the bullets were flying, I saw Lady Isobel willingly go with the men, dragging the boy with her."

Grayson slammed his fist on the desk. "You talk as though Lady Isobel was involved. She may have thought she had no other option."

Hadley knew what the other men were thinking: that Arend was right, and she *was* in league with Victoria.

"Can't rightly say. I was too busy fighting them off. She didn't seem to be putting up too much of a struggle, but she did seem to be protecting the boy. It all happened so fast."

"Do you have any idea where they were heading?"

To Hadley's amazement and joy George answered in the affirmative.

"I heard one of the men call out to another 'Head for Angleton.' Unfortunately, I had to take care of the injured. There was only me left, and I couldn't go after them on my own. I wanted to get back to let you know what I had learned. I hope I made the right decision, as I have no idea where Angleton is. I was hoping one of you would."

"I've never heard of such a village," Grayson said.

The men stared at each other silently. Hadley ran a hand through his hair and shook his head. A voice from the corner of the room spoke up.

"It's not a village. It's a house. I know where it is."

Hadley hadn't noticed that Clarence had entered the room.

Clarence, now eighteen, had been one of Angelo's boys when Angelo was operating the Top Hat. Maitland's wife, Marisa, had rescued Clarence and his younger brother, Simon, from the sordid life at the Top Hat, and now Clarence oversaw the many orphanages Marisa was associated with. He kept the orphanages honest, ensuring that young boys and girls did not end up in one of the many, many clubs peddling flesh, but rather were educated with useful skills so they could go into service in respectable houses where they could be safe and earn a living.

Hadley nodded to the lad, indicating that he should continue.

Clarence cleared his throat. "Angleton was one of the houses Angelo used to train new boys. If I remember correctly, it's a large house near Kensington-upon-Thames, less than an hour's ride from here."

Hadley patted the young man on the back. "Thank goodness you were here, Clarence."

Grayson stepped forward. "Clarence, have you been to the house?" At Clarence's nod Grayson called for some paper. "I hope you have a good memory. Can you draw a detailed plan of the house and the outbuildings surrounding it?"

Grayson had had a distinguished military career, as did Christian. Both had fought at Waterloo. The two men were brilliant strategists.

Clarence's memory was outstanding. It turned out he'd spent considerable time at Angleton. He knew the exact location of the stable and the layout of the main house and the servants' quarters. "I'm pretty sure I know where they will be keeping the boy. All new boys are kept in the attic. They think it is escape-proof." Clarence pointed to the rough plan he'd drawn. "Most people think the only way into the attic is through the door at the top of the stairs. There are no windows. But I know another way in— through the roof. When Simon and I were originally at the house we tried to escape one night. With a knife I'd stolen, I managed to pry loose four planks. They were loose enough that with one good kick they would fall open, but not loose enough for anyone to notice. We never used it to escape because Simon fell ill and I couldn't move him. I bet they are still loose."

Hadley wanted to hug the boy. "I'll take the roof."

Grayson nodded and began to outline a plan. The men would split into two groups. One would attack the front of the house, and the other the back. It was unlikely they would think of the roof because, as Clarence said, there were no windows.

Clarence would stay with the horses, and once they'd rescued the boy, Clarence could get Sealey away as fast as possible while the men remained to capture Victoria and Isobel and find Arend if at all possible.

Chapter Twelve

Evangeline sat on a chair in Sebastian's drawing room, a cup of tea in her hand. She didn't notice the liquid splashing into the saucer as her hand shook. She didn't pay any attention to the worried glances from the other women, and whatever they were saying was simply background noise. All she could hear hammering in her head were the words *It isn't fair,* over and over and over.

She'd suffered. She'd had her fair share of heartache. She'd lost five years of her life to a man whom she despised. Yes, there were many women in this situation, married off to men they held no affection for, or indeed downright hated. But it wasn't fair that she lose her son too.

Her beautiful, innocent son.

She couldn't help but feel there would never be a happily-ever-after for her. She was so stupid to have thought she could return to London and everything would fall perfectly into place. That Hadley and she could simply pick up from where they'd left off.

Fate obviously didn't want that for them.

Tears trickled down her cheeks.

"Don't cry, sweetheart. I promise I'll get Sealey back for you."

She looked into Hadley's face. She'd not even heard him enter the room.

Would Sealey get a chance to know his real father? Would he get the chance to grow up to be like Hadley? Would he become a man whom women hungered after, a man with loyal and much-loved friends, a man who wanted to protect those most precious to him? She sucked in a breath.

Hadley would make a wonderful father. He deserved a chance, and she might have taken that from him.

She gripped Hadley's hands. "There is something I need to tell you. I should have told you when I first returned to London."

He pressed a kiss to her forehead. "I'm sure it can wait. We have to leave. We have a lead on where Victoria has taken your son. Every minute counts."

"Please, listen. I just need to tell you—"

Grayson called from the open door. "Are you coming, Hadley? Clarence has given us the directions to Angleton. They're on the table in the entrance hall."

She continued to grip Hadley's hands as if her life depended on it. "Please—"

Hadley stopped her words with a passionate kiss. Finally he broke the kiss and pulled her into his arms, whispering in her ear, "I will bring him home to you. Have faith." And with that he was gone.

She looked up beseechingly at Beatrice, who quietly said, "Perhaps it's better he not know until Sealey is rescued. He needs a clear head."

The women all began talking at once, arguing about what she needed most at the moment. Beatrice suggested a small sherry with a dose of laudanum for her nerves. Evangeline shook her head; merely the idea of eating or drinking anything gave her nausea.

Just then Augustus appeared, sorrow clouding his features. He took the seat across from her and said, "I'm sure my brother will save your boy." She knew what he didn't add: *Or die trying.*

God, she could lose both of them. The thought pulled her out of her self-pity. She'd said she wasn't going to ever be a victim again, yet here she was once again doing nothing.

Well, not this time.

A plan flickered in her head. She couldn't continue to sit here waiting. She wanted to be there when Hadley rescued Sealey. Her son would be so afraid. He would need her.

Without alerting the other ladies to her true intention, she rose to her feet and said, "If you'll excuse me, I need . . ." She spread her hands wide, and they nodded. Yes, the retiring room.

As she made her way toward the door she stopped and whispered to Augustus, "Please meet me at the bottom of the stairs in five minutes."

He frowned at her but nodded.

Once out of the room Evangeline made for the dresser in the entrance hall. Sure enough, there were the directions to Angleton Manor that Clarence had written up. Her eyes swept the house. No one was watching. She grabbed the directions and shoved them into the pocket of her traveling gown.

She paced the floor until Augustus finally appeared. She grabbed his arm and pulled him to one side, out of the view from the upstairs landing.

"I want to go after Sealey. I want to be there when they free him. He'll be so scared. He'll—"

Augustus took a step away. "Oh, no. Absolutely not. Hadley has entrusted me with your safety. I will not let him down."

"Then you'll have to come too, because no one is going to stop me," she quietly insisted. "I shall go with your help or without it."

"I shall stop you. I'll alert—"

"You owe me. I'm going to help you with Lord Corby. You could at least help me. Help my son. Help your nephew."

"He is family, isn't he? My turn to become the protector."

"Sealey is Hadley's son. He doesn't know. I—I need to be there when they rescue him. He looks exactly like Hadley."

Augustus put his hands on his hips. "I understand why you did not tell him at first. But once we'd returned . . ."

"I didn't have time before all this happened. Please, help me."

He opened and closed his mouth several times, without any words coming out. Finally he said, "I'm sorry. If he hadn't felt obligated to help me, perhaps none of this would have happened. You would not have needed to go off to Lathero."

"We have all made mistakes. I should have told him immediately. If anything happens to Hadley or Sealey . . . They don't even know each other." She gave a small sob.

"Even if we could help, we have no idea where they have gone," he finally said, with a touch of despair.

She smiled and pulled the directions from her pocket. "Oh, yes, we do."

Chapter Thirteen

T he men made the outskirts of Kensington-upon-Thames in less than an hour. Luckily the night sky was full of clouds. Under the cover of darkness they rendezvoused at a copse about half a mile from the house.

There were twenty men in total: the four Libertine Scholars, plus Philip and Clarence, and ten Bow Street Runners, as well as several of the servants.

"I'll take half the men to the back of the house. Christian, you'll attack the front with the rest of the men." Grayson turned to two of the servants. "One of you will come with me; the other will go with Christian. Your task is to ensure the guns are reloaded promptly so that we do not run out of shots." He turned to Hadley. "You'll only have your two pistols. You'll more than likely need both your hands to help the boy off the roof. So watch yourself."

The men patted Hadley on the back and wished him luck. One group went to the north and the other to the south. Hadley was to wait five minutes to ensure that the men took care of any guards Victoria might have placed in the grounds.

He drew a few deep breaths, willing his nerves to settle. This was one of the most important tasks he had ever undertaken. He had to bring Sealey home safe and sound. Evangeline loved her son, and the idea of her losing him, of her being in such pain, was unconscionable. This rescue was about his future.

He checked his pocket watch, saw that five minutes had passed, and, remembering the route that Clarence had drawn for him, made his way stealthily to the back of the house. He reached without incident the side of the house where part of the kitchen jutted out. It was only one story high at this point, giving easy access to the roof.

He had to put his pistols away in the pockets of the greatcoat. It was dangerous because he would not be able to get them out quickly should he encounter any trouble. He hoped the men at the front and back of the house did their job and kept the enemy engaged and out of his way.

He took a running jump and managed to grasp the overhang of the roof's eaves. His greatcoat, loaded with pistols, made pulling himself onto the roof difficult. He lay there for a moment, gaining his breath. The next part of the climb would be tricky. The sloping roof made it too difficult to run and jump for the second story, and the attic was yet another story higher. Instead, he gravitated toward the cast-iron downpipe. He gave it a good shake and a tug. It seemed solid enough, and he hoped it would hold his weight.

He was thankful that the cool night was not wet, for it would've made climbing slippery. Within ten minutes he'd made it to the spot where the planks were supposedly loose. He pulled out his dagger and pried up one of the planks. To his relief it popped open with virtually no noise.

Just then he heard gunshots from below. Victoria and her men must have realized they were here. He had to hurry. His pulse raced and he immediately set about removing the other three planks.

The attic was in complete darkness. He prayed that Sealey was here. The poor little boy must be frightened out of his wits. As he stepped quietly into the room he heard little scurrying feet—*rats*. Anger bloomed, and he cursed softly. To leave a child in the dark with rats . . . He couldn't wait to get his hands on Victoria and throttle her.

In a whisper he called for Sealey, but only silence greeted him.

He moved away from his entry hole boards, hoping the limited light from the crescent moon would let him see further than his nose. He waited a moment, letting his eyes adjust to the dimness. He still could see nothing. However, over the scratching of the rats he heard a small snuffle coming from the left—a child weeping. He moved forward cautiously, and almost tripped over a soft bundle huddled on the floor.

He bent down and whispered, "Don't be afraid, Sealey. Your mother has sent me to rescue you." The boy gave a startled cry, and Hadley quickly shushed him. "We have to be quiet. Can you do that for me?"

There was a slight hesitation before Sealey whispered, "Have you really come to rescue me?"

"Absolutely. I promised your mother, and I don't want to disappoint her. So we'd best be moving. We don't want to keep her waiting, do we?"

Hadley scooped the boy into his arms. He was shaking, and his clothes were wet, the smell of urine overpowering.

"I have been very brave. I only cried once, when they took Lady Isobel away."

"Good boy. You only have to be brave a little while longer."

He put Sealey down and climbed through the exit hole, then turned to help Sealey through. Once they were both out he pushed the planks back into place; he hoped they would not check the attic room, but if they did and saw that the boy was no longer there, he did not want them to realize how the boy had escaped. It might buy Hadley some time.

"Can you hop onto my back and lock your arms tight around

my neck? I'm going to have to climb down from the roof. If it's too scary, close your eyes and think about how nice it will be to see your mother."

Sealey scampered onto Hadley's back and held on so tightly that he almost cut Hadley's air supply off. He moved the boy's arms down so they weren't crushing his Adam's apple, and pulled the boy's legs round his torso.

Hadley then proceeded to climb down the way he'd come up. It was easier than going up, as he could virtually slide down the drainpipe. Sealey clung to him and didn't emit even a whimper.

Once on the ground Hadley didn't hesitate. With Sealey still on his back, he ran to the agreed meeting point. His relief at spying Clarence ready and waiting with the horse almost caused him to stumble.

Without hesitating he swung the lad up to sit in front of Clarence. "To London. Take him to his mother. I'm going back to help the men." Before he'd even finished talking, Clarence was off.

Hadley bent over, hands on his knees, drawing deep breaths. He'd saved the boy. His body flushed with triumph. Whatever happened during the rest of the night, the boy was safe. He hadn't let her down.

Pistol shots rang out in the darkness. He stood and had just begun making his way back to the front of the house when he saw a figure moving swiftly and stealthily toward a group of outbuildings—the stable, he figured.

He quickly altered his route and followed the fleeing figure. Probably heading for the horses. He began to run, not caring who might hear him.

As he arrived at the stable he could hear voices. There was more than one person inside. Creeping closer, he heard female and male voices. Was this Victoria trying to escape?

He slid past the stable door, which was slightly ajar, not making a sound. What he saw in front of him made his blood run cold.

Shrouded in a cape, Victoria stood pointing a pistol at his brother, who was standing in front of Evangeline, obviously trying to protect her. How the hell had they gotten here?

Not wishing to alert Victoria to his presence, he moved slowly and carefully, concealing himself behind a post.

"Please don't harm my son. He's innocent in all of this," he heard Evangeline plead.

Victoria laughed coarsely. "Everyone is innocent at some stage in their lives—until they're not. I was an innocent child once." Her voice hardened. "Until men, men who included His Grace's father, ripped that away from me."

Evangeline cleared her throat. "I'm sorry for whatever they did to you. I can't imagine what you have gone through. But think of my son. He's like you were, innocent—"

"No one came to help me. My life was torn from me. I was left in the gutter, left to bleed and heal alone. But I swore I'd survive—swore I'd seek revenge. And I have. I've climbed higher than any of those men dreamed, clawing my way back to respectability."

Augustus spoke up. "Then why start down this road of revenge against men who have done you no harm? Your abusers are dead and likely in hell for what they did to you. You have a good life."

"Those men died before I could get my revenge. No wicked deed should go unpunished." She laughed. "It's rather ironic, no? *I* don't expect to go unpunished for what I am doing now, but I've almost finished with my revenge. All but one Libertine Scholar may still be alive, but one dead will hurt them all. The guilt and pain of Lord Labourd's death will live with them for the rest of their sorry lives. I know that if I hurt one, I hurt them all."

Hadley's throat constricted. Was Victoria confirming that Arend was dead? Rage roared deep within him, but he couldn't react, not yet. Not until Evangeline and Augustus were safe.

Victoria seemed in no dire hurry. She said, "I hadn't planned on the Duke of Lyttleton's wife sustaining such an injury. That was just as good as if I'd killed him. No child for His Grace—his line will die out. I count it as a just reward. However, my biggest success was Lord Fullerton."

At his name Hadley moved closer, and he saw Evangeline's eyes begin to widen as she saw him over Victoria's shoulder. He quickly shook his head, and saw that she immediately understood —it was imperative not to alert Victoria with any reaction.

"I don't understand," Evangeline said, clearly trying to distract Victoria. "Hadley is alive and well, isn't he?"

Victoria sighed. "Unfortunately, yes." She eyed the pair. "I'd love to stay and talk, but my men can only hold the Libertine Scholars at bay for so long. Lady Evangeline, come to me."

"She's not going anywhere with you," Augustus replied.

Her pistol cocked. "Then I'll simply shoot you and take her with me." With that, she drew out another pistol. "I need extra bargaining power should we encounter any of your friends."

Augustus hesitated, clearly not knowing what to do.

Hadley had to act. Perhaps if he kept Victoria here talking, the others might find them and aid in her capture. He stepped away from the beam, pistol in hand.

"I can't let you do that, Lady Victoria."

She moved sideways, keeping the smaller pistol trained on Augustus and Evangeline and pointing the other in his direction. "Oh, what a surprise. The father is here to rescue his son. Or is it the lady he's here for?"

Victoria's words taunted Hadley. "You know very well I'm not the boy's father."

Her smiled widened mockingly. "Well, well, well. I may be a lot of things, but I never lie. Ask her."

His blood stilled and his gaze sought out Evangeline. Her guilty face told the tale. He had a son! A son he'd just put on a horse and sent off to safety.

Why hadn't she told him?

Victoria laughed. "She didn't tell you, and you obviously have not met the boy. He's your exact image. I knew as soon as I saw him. That's when I decided I no longer wanted you dead. I'd rather have you alive, understanding that your son is the next Viscount Stuart and you will never be able to acknowledge him." She aimed the pistol at Evangeline. "Especially if she is dead."

His finger tightened on the pistol's trigger. He'd never wanted to kill someone so much in his life.

She continued her taunts. "I never dreamed my plan would be so successful. Did you know you were the first Libertine Scholar I targeted?"

"I hardly think so. Christian—"

"No, not Christian. This was five years ago." As he cast a glance at Evangeline, Victoria followed his gaze and said, "Who do you think put the idea into your mother's head to trade your beauty for money? Who do you think introduced your mother to Viscount Stuart? I wanted to destroy Hadley's happiness. It worked perfectly. I just didn't understand you were with child." She sent a gloating smile toward Hadley. "And while Lady Marisa cannot have children, this is the ultimate triumph—your firstborn son is denied your name."

"You bitch." Hadley could barely form coherent words.

"Most definitely. Now, Evangeline, be a good girl and come to me."

"Don't move, Evangeline," he countered.

"If you do not come to me, girl, I'll kill him."

He heard Evangeline gasp, but his eyes never left Victoria. "You shoot me, I shoot you. We both might die."

"I'm not afraid of death. I've caused enough of it. I knew you might learn of my identity once Evangeline arrived in London with her husband's journals." She shook her head. "Viscount Stuart was a greedy man—greedy and stupid. He tried to black-mail me about my past. It cost him his life."

"You killed him?" Hadley had suspected as much.

Victoria grinned like a madwoman. "Yes. He underestimated

me. I wouldn't make the same mistake if I were you. Lady Evangeline, over here if you will."

"Stay, Evangeline," he ordered. Instead of showing how fearful he really was, he goaded Victoria instead. "You killing Stuart did me a huge favor. It saved me the task of killing him myself, and leaves Evangeline free to marry me. We'll have another son."

Victoria's smile vanished, and her face grew tight with hatred. She swiveled her arm to point the second gun at his chest as well. He was afraid for himself, yes, but as long as Evangeline was safely out of the pistol's aim, that was all that mattered.

Victoria watched him intently for a few moments, and then a smile of pure evil broke on her lips. She turned one of the pistols back toward Evangeline again.

"You've just told me how I can hurt you. I wasn't sure what your feelings were for Evangeline, but now I know. You love her. You'd give your life for her, that's why you're here. If I kill her now . . . you'll be thwarted once again."

To Hadley's consternation—and admiration—Augustus stepped in front of Evangeline.

"You will have to shoot me first," he said, his voice calm, "and then my brother will kill you."

"I don't think so. I know where Lord Labourd is. He needs me alive."

Augustus looked at him, evidently weighing the options. Hadley nodded at him. None of them looked good.

Hadley took a step forward, and Victoria re-aimed the pistol in her other hand squarely at him. Trying to reason with her, he said, "Why not simply ride off now while you can, before the other Libertine Scholars turn their attention to finding out where I am and search this stable? Look, Evangeline's horse is still saddled—take the mare."

Victoria looked toward the stall, and before Hadley could stop him, Augustus launched himself at the bitch. But His Grace wasn't fast enough. She whipped round like a snake and fired the pistol.

Hadley leaped forward and tackled Victoria to the ground. She was no match for his size and strength, and with one punch he knocked her senseless. He turned from her, his breath ragged, only to see Evangeline kneeling in the straw at Augustus's side, tears streaming down her face.

With a heavy heart he knew his brother was dead even before he reached Augustus's side. He dropped to his knees. It was a small hole with only a trickle of blood, but it was right between his eyes. Augustus had died before he hit the floor of the stable. Grief, guilt, and anger roiled in his stomach. His heart burned in his chest.

"Goddamn it to hell," he cried. "It should have been me. This was not his fight. Why was he even here?"

"It's my fault," Evangeline sobbed. "I forced him to come. I was worried about you rescuing Sealey and learning you are his father." She gripped his arm. "God forgive me, but is Sealey safe? I know it's selfish, but please tell me he's safe."

"He's safe. Clarence has taken him back to London. Supposedly to your waiting arms."

His mind kept trying to deny what he knew to be true: his brother was dead. He barely heard Evangeline's sobs over the anger roaring in his ears. If they hadn't needed Victoria alive in order to find Arend, he didn't know what he'd do to her right now.

"I'm so sorry. I'm so very sorry. Can you ever forgive me?"

Hadley didn't even look at her. Turning his attention to Victoria, he asked Evangeline, "Can you find something to tie her up with?"

She looked at the reins hanging on the wall. "We could use those," and she pointed.

He strode over to the wall and used his dagger to cut a length of leather. His face was closed off, and his body trembled with what she guessed was suppressed sorrow and anger. He roughly turned the still-unconscious Victoria onto her stomach and bound her hands tightly behind her back.

He handed Evangeline both pistols. "Watch her. I'm going to try to find Grayson and the others. We need her alive. She knows where Arend is."

"You're leaving me here? With her?"

"I won't be long, and I won't need to go far. We arranged a signal to use if anyone captured Victoria." With that, he turned abruptly and walked out of the stable.

She looked round her. She could hear the horses stamping, her mare's bridle jingling. She kept flitting glances round, scared of every shadow. Mainly she was trying to ignore the fact that Augustus lay dead not far from her, Hadley's greatcoat over him. She couldn't stop herself from looking at him. For him to die just as he was getting his life together was beyond cruel.

If she hadn't talked him into coming . . . A shudder ran through her body. Perhaps it would have been Hadley lying dead instead. Her hands were blocks of ice and she knew shock was setting in. Her stomach still churned. Until she saw with her own eyes that Sealey was safe and well, she couldn't relax. What if some of Victoria's men had followed Clarence?

Anger grew as she thought through all the things that could happen to Sealey before he reached the safety of London. She also thought of Marisa and all she'd lost. It was all the fault of one person: Victoria.

Her gaze swung back to the unconscious woman who had caused so much heartache and pain. She aimed the pistol at Victoria's head. She could squeeze the trigger. No one would blame her.

She couldn't bring herself to have any pity for Victoria. She knew the Libertine Scholars' fathers had done something terrible to her, and she dreaded to think what that was. Unlike her, Victoria had not been left with money or position to survive the aftermath of her ordeal. She had to thank Dougal for that small mercy at least.

How was it that Victoria had no one to turn to? Evangeline knew nothing of her enemy's background.

Two abused women, each with a different road to survival.

Evangeline had been torn from her life, forced into the bed of a man she did not know or love, and kept there against her will. Yet, once freed, she hadn't set out for revenge; she'd sought out the one person who would make her life happy, the one man who might just love her enough to erase the pain of the past.

Hadley had asked her to forgive him for not rescuing her, for not believing in their love. Would he now forgive her for her foolishness, for demanding Augustus bring her into danger? She had altered his world, and maybe her own. She swallowed her fear.

Hadley was now the Duke of Claymore.

Nothing would really change. His family would still turn to him as they did now. Only now society would recognize his status. They would welcome the handsome, intelligent, honorable man with open arms.

He would also have more options as far as marriageable young ladies were concerned. Every mother in England would be seeking a match with him for their daughters. A wave of unease spread through her. If he couldn't forgive her . . .

Just then the woman at her feet stirred and tried to roll onto her back.

Victoria spat straw from her mouth. When she looked up and saw Evangeline, she croaked, "Go on, gloat. The wicked witch has been caught."

"I don't think I can feel sorry for you after all the evil you have done to those innocent of any crime."

"I don't want your pity." She paused, then added, "Unless, of course, it would make you untie me and let me slip away."

"There is no way I would let you leave. Arend and Isobel are still missing."

"Who do you think brought your son to me? I wouldn't be worrying about Isobel."

Victoria's smile made Evangeline's insides clench in rage.

"Isobel would not hurt a hair on Sealey's head. I don't believe you. You have taken Isobel as well as Arend. Where are they?"

She did not want to believe her friend would be in league with this evil woman. But then a thought came to her, and she bit her lip. It had been Isobel who originally put the idea of visiting the deer in Richmond Park into her son's head.

"That is for me to know and you to ascertain. Maybe Isobel is sympathetic and wants me to win my revenge."

Isobel had never seemed particularly fond of her stepmother. "I don't think so." She stepped closer to really look at Victoria. "What I can't understand is how you can let the innocent suffer for a crime that is not of their doing."

To Evangeline's amazement, Victoria had the gall to say, "I thought you of all people might have some understanding of why I set off down this path."

"I must admit, the temptation to fire this pistol is rather strong," Evangeline told her. "But to do so would make me no better than you. I want justice for my friends, and for the five years of misery you put me through, but everyone deserves a fair trial."

Victoria laughed at that. "Do you really think ten years ago I would have received a fair trial? Those men were rich and powerful, and I was a nobody. Who would've believed my word against a duke, let alone two dukes and a handful of powerful lords?"

Evangeline remained silent but she had to agree. It was unlikely that those men would ever have been brought to trial. What would she have done in Victoria's place?

"Was there no one back then who could have helped you?"

"I was fifteen. My mother was dead. I was an only child, and it was my father who sold me to the Duke of Lyttleton to pay off his gambling debts."

"I can see where you got the idea for your revenge against Hadley. Only it wasn't my father who had the gambling debts but my mother. Surely you felt a twinge of guilt forcing your fate on another. On me."

"Your situation was nothing like mine. You married a wealthy viscount, what did you have to complain about?"

Anger erupted inside Evangeline, and she took a step closer to Victoria, the pistol shaking in her hand. "What did I have to complain about? How about the fact I had to share the bed of a man I loathed? How about the fact you took away my chance to marry the man I loved, the father of my child, a child who will now never carry his name?"

Her chest was heaving.

"The child is alive and a viscount. Count yourself lucky," Victoria retorted. "My child died three weeks after she was born. Given my circumstances and the life I've led, it was probably a blessing."

Victoria's voice had softened, and Evangeline's anger dispersed somewhat. Any woman could empathize with a mother who'd lost her child. The idea of losing Sealey was so horrible she couldn't face it. She lowered the pistol.

"When Emily died—her name was Emily—I swore I would get my revenge. What would you do if Sealey was killed? You have no idea what it's like to see your child die of disease and starvation." Victoria's voice, shrill and distraught, moved Evangeline.

She swallowed back her pity. "You are right. I have no idea what that is like. I'm so sorry for what happened to you." She drew in a deep breath and focused on the truth. "However, you have gone too far. You talk about losing your child—Lady Marisa faces never having a child of her own."

Victoria sighed and tried to sit up but rolled onto her back again. "That was unfortunate. I had no idea the carriage would crash. The drivers did not go unpunished."

That didn't make Evangeline feel any better, and she was sure Marisa would find no peace in that thought either.

"Why hurt the sons? They too have been hurt by their fathers. Do you really feel no remorse for the misery you have caused us all?"

"No."

"Then I will leave it to God to decide your punishment. You do know you'll likely hang for this?"

Victoria's smile made Evangeline's hand grip the pistol harder. "I still have Arend," she said softly. "The threat of hanging is no incentive for me to reveal where he is. The men will want their friend back alive and well. I might do so in exchange for my freedom. I hear the Americas are a land of opportunity."

"If I were you, I'd be more worried about what the men are going to do to you. They want to know where Arend is. They will want to know soon." This time it was her chance to gloat. "Get ready for a world of pain."

A scowl appeared on Victoria's face, and her eyes flashed with anger.

"You are the one who should get ready for a world of pain. Isobel is still out there, and if anything happens to me, her sole goal will be to go after Sealey."

Before Evangeline could respond, the door to the stable scraped open, and Hadley and Grayson entered.

Grayson's gaze momentarily flickered to Augustus's body before he rounded on Victoria, eyes blazing with anger and hatred.

"Your sick game is over, my lady. Your men are either dead or captured. I swear, if anything has happened to Arend I will personally kill you myself, and I promise you it won't be quick."

Grayson's threats made Evangeline shudder. But Victoria didn't seem bothered at all.

"I've been threatened by far scarier men than you. I should also warn you that pain is a welcome friend. If you want Arend back alive, I'd choose another path for negotiation."

She heard Hadley expostulate, "I don't want to negotiate with the bitch!"

Grayson threw him a look but said only, "I don't want to take any chances. Let's find something to bind her feet as well."

Silence reigned as Hadley did Grayson's bidding. Victoria was soon trussed up like a fat turkey ready to be roasted at Christmas.

By then the rest of the Libertine Scholars had entered the stable. The threat of violence hung naked in the air. Evangeline watched Maitland flex his fists, his shoulders taut and his face filled with hatred. She made her way to his side, used her fingers to unfurl one of his fists, and slipped her hand in his. He looked down at their joined hands and gave her a weak smile.

"Think of Arend," she whispered, and he nodded.

Then Hadley said, "I have to take my brother home to Hardstone Hall."

Maitland stepped toward Victoria. "I'll take *Lady* Victoria back to London. I have a windowless and lockable cellar. I'm also sure it's soundproof." Victoria's smirk seemed to egg him on. "I will get the truth from her. I want to know if Arend is still alive."

Evangeline gasped, not even having considered that Arend might already be dead. She looked from face to face and saw that all the men were of the opinion that they could take nothing for granted where Victoria was concerned.

Christian stepped in front of Maitland. "I don't think that's a good idea. Think of your wife."

"I am bloody well thinking of Marisa. She deserves her revenge."

The tension rose until Evangeline quietly said, "Let us not forget that revenge is the reason we find ourselves here. Yes, Victoria will be punished, but it should be through the appropriate channels, or else we are no better than she."

Silence greeted her statement, but she noted Maitland stepping back and turning away. His shoulders shook as he struggled to bring his emotions under control.

"I don't believe we should take her to London," Christian said. "I shall take her to my estate, Henslowe Court. Until we find Arend, the smaller the number of people who know we are holding her, the better. We don't know whom she has working for her, or how long finding Arend will take."

There was no argument from the others.

Evangeline felt superfluous as the men began organizing the horses and dealing with the dead.

Hadley led her toward her mare. "Grayson will see you safely home. To your son." He stopped for a moment, then resumed walking. "*Our* son. Sealey will need you."

He was right—her boy would need her. "Will you be all right? We can come to Hardstone."

He shook his head and returned to help her mount. "No. I'll organize a quiet family funeral and then head to Henslowe Court. I want to help find Arend."

"Of course." She gripped the reins in two hands. "When will I —*we*—see you?" This was so awkward. She really needed a chance to sit with Hadley and talk about Sealey, and about Augustus. As Hadley was now the Duke of Claymore, where would Sealey fit into his life?

He gave the first tentative smile she'd seen tonight. "I know we have a lot to discuss, but Arend's life could be under threat."

"Of course." Hesitantly she volunteered, "I could bring Sealey down to Henslowe Court. The journals might contain more information, such as places she may have a house to hide Arend in. They might also mention more about Isobel and whether she has had any involvement in Victoria's evil plans."

By then Grayson arrived on his stallion, and he had overheard the last part of their conversation. "That's a cracking idea, Lady Evangeline. Portia and I will be traveling down; you should come with us."

Hadley appeared to want to say something but held back.

"Thank you, Grayson. I would feel safer if we were all traveling together. Even though Victoria has been captured, there is still the question of Isobel." She looked at Hadley. "Take care."

He merely nodded and said, "You'll likely get to Henslowe before me. The magistrate will need to be informed about Augustus, and a small private funeral will need to be held as soon as possible. He will be buried in the family chapel at Hardstone."

"If you need me to be there, you only have to say."

"Thank you." He took her hand and pressed a kiss to her palm. "No need. I'll see you at Henslowe."

With that he , to deal with his brother. She watched him kneel beside Augustus's body, his head bowed. He placed a hand on his brother's chest and was still kneeling there as she and Grayson rode off down the drive.

Chapter Fourteen

F ireworks were going off in his head, thoughts ricocheting so fast he couldn't sort them. Two truths were screaming the loudest: his brother was dead, and he had a son with Evangeline.

All his life he'd been protecting Augustus, first from their father and then from life in general. More often than not, he'd resented it. He'd resented the fact that he'd been the person shouldering the burden of the estates. A second son was supposed to be carefree, yet he'd had to take on the responsibility of the dukedom without the title or position that came with it.

If truth be told, he'd not wanted the title. He'd seen how society had kowtowed to Maitland. All that sycophantic behavior could turn a man's head. Would he be the same man he was today if he'd been the recipient of such lavish attention?

Still, it hurt sometimes to hear from others how Augustus had been brilliant at running his estate, how successful the estate was, and on and on, when in fact it was Hadley who kept the estate in such good financial position. No one ever thanked him, or even really noticed him. He'd sacrificed a lot for his brother.

But it was his brother who had made the ultimate sacrifice of all—his life. Why? Why had Augustus tried to tackle Victoria?

His hand lay on his brother's chest, but there was no answering heartbeat. Emotions swamped him, tears welled, and he wished he could howl, scream, rail against the world. More than anything, he wanted to kill Victoria.

A hand landed on his shoulder. "I'll accompany you home to corroborate your story for the magistrate," Maitland said.

He blinked back his tears and cleared his throat. "Thank you. Probably not a good idea for a second son to bring the heir home shot dead, with no witnesses. A duke's word will be more than enough."

"I also want to be there for you. It's not every day a man becomes a duke in such terrible circumstances."

"A duke," Hadley said as he rose to his feet to fetch a horse blanket to wrap his brother in. "Life is ironic, is it not? My father must be celebrating. He always wanted me to be the heir. He tried several times to make that happen, but to no avail. Now the woman set on avenging one of Father's deeds does the job for him."

Maitland sighed. "You'll make a fine duke. You are already a duke in duty and manner; now you are one in name too. You'll receive the recognition you deserve. Although we all know you'd never have wanted the title like this."

"Why didn't he wait? I would have found a way to protect us all."

"He died a hero. He died protecting the ones he loved. Don't diminish his sacrifice by berating it."

Hadley was awash with shame. "Why did Evangeline bring him?"

"She was frightened. For both you and her son. This is not her fault."

"You're right. It *was* Victoria who fired the pistol."

He knew why Evangeline had come. She had been right to worry about him learning he had a son. If the moon had been fuller and in its light he'd recognized himself in the boy, there was no telling what he would have done to Victoria, and Arend might stay lost to them forever.

As he laid his brother's body across his horse, Hadley's heart wept for his own loss, but more for Sealey's. The boy, his firstborn son, would never be the Duke of Claymore. Victoria had stolen not only Hadley's first five years with his son but Sealey's birthright. Sealey would forever bear the name of a man his mother and father hated.

What a mess.

"Let's get moving. I want this over with so we can find Arend. Then I want to see that bitch hang."

The small but distinguished funeral was held three days later. The cold autumn would help, but it was best to bury Augustus quickly.

According to Augustus's will, he did not wish to be placed in the family crypt with their father. Instead, he'd asked to be buried on a small island in the middle of the family's lake at the back of the estate. It had been his hiding place. A place he'd escaped to when their father's bullying had become too much for him to bear.

Later that afternoon Hadley sat in the study at Hardstone, a glass of whiskey in hand, finding some peace. He didn't think he'd ever get used to being called His Grace. The servants, who had always been more informal with him, now treated him with reverence. His life had changed.

The door opened and a young man stepped in. His eyes opened wide when he spotted Hadley, and he stammered, "Oh—I —I'm sorry, Your Grace. I did not know you would be in here."

Hadley took one look at the red eyes, at the sorrow and loss etched on the man's face, and he instinctively knew this was the man with whom Augustus had found love and contentment. He motioned with his hand. "Please, sit."

The man, who looked to be slightly younger than Evangeline, was evidently fearful. Hadley could see his body tremble as he sank into the chair.

It was uncomfortable coming face-to-face with his brother's lover. It wasn't that he found their relationship disgusting or repulsive; Hadley knew better than anyone that the heart wants what the heart wants. It was more that he couldn't understand finding any man sexually attractive. He studied his brother's lover thoroughly.

The man was of medium height and medium build, dark-haired yet angelic-looking. In fact, the word that might best describe him was "medium." There was nothing outstanding about the man at all.

Hadley looked closely. In truth, the young man had lovely eyes. They were the deepest green he'd ever seen on a man, and were surrounded by thick black lashes. Very feminine in nature. Right now those green eyes were bloodshot and puffy from crying. Augustus's death was causing the young man great sorrow. Hadley's heart squeezed tight in his chest. Sorrow was such a personal thing.

"Thank you for bringing my brother such joy and peace. He spoke of you but didn't tell me your name."

"I'm known as Mr. Vickers, Your Grace."

"Well, Vickers. You were Augustus's man of business?"

The young man nodded.

"And much more, I believe. It must be hard to hide your grief."

"I'm not sure what you mean."

"There is no need to be afraid. I know everything there is to know about my brother and his romantic life."

His words did not alleviate Vickers's fear; in fact, he looked about ready to jump up and flee.

"I want you to know that there will always be a position for you here at Hardstone. I have my own man of business, of course, but he is based at my hunting lodge, Lathero, and travels with me to London as well. I will need someone here at Hardstone to oversee matters when I'm not here. The position is yours if you'd like it."

Vickers's mouth gaped open, and Hadley watched him struggle to find words. At last he said, "Thank you, Your Grace. You do me a very great honor, and I gladly accept."

Hadley nodded. "Good. That's sorted. I'll be leaving for Henslowe Court, Lord Markham's estate, first thing tomorrow morning. I expect you to keep an eye on not only the estates but also my mother and sisters. If there are any problems, please send word to Lord Markham. I shall ensure the correspondence is up to date before I leave."

"Very good, Your Grace. I have been in your brother's service for two years. I am well versed on how the estate should run. If I do have any concerns, I could perhaps notify your man of business first, and therefore not bother you unless absolutely necessary."

Hadley studied the young man. "That is an excellent idea. Mr. Burroughs would indeed be an excellent first point of call, especially as I have some urgent business that needs addressing."

Vickers stood to take his leave. He hesitated when he reached the door. He quietly asked, his voice quaking, "Did he suffer?"

"No. It was over very quickly. I promise you, as I promised my family, the perpetrator will be brought to justice. I will not rest until I see her swing at the end of a rope."

"Thank you, Your Grace."

"I shall ensure you're kept informed. We have both lost a good man."

Tears began to well in Vickers's eyes once more, and he quickly took his leave, closing the door softly behind him.

Hadley tipped the rest of his whiskey down his throat, then poured more into his glass before standing and walking to the windows at the other end of the study. He looked out over the garden. "Here's to you, Augustus. I shall miss you." He raised his glass in salute to a brother he hadn't realized he would miss so much.

He stood there for several minutes staring across the manicured lawns, remembering all the good times he'd had with

Augustus as a young boy. Though they'd been few, there *had* been good times, usually when their father was away.

What did he do now? He laughed inwardly, admitting to himself he'd loved secretly running the estate, looking after the family. It had fed his ego to know he was playing a role no one knew about. As his friends said, he was the brother who should have been the duke. It made the nausea rise in his throat. All the time he'd been helping Augustus, protecting him from their father, deep down inside he'd been thinking the same thing: that it was Hadley who'd have made a better duke.

Yet in the very way his life had ended, Augustus had proved just what a good, honorable, and brave man he was. He'd died to protect those he loved. For once Hadley hoped he could live up to the man his brother had been.

Now that he was the Duke of Claymore, he was scared witless. When he'd been the pretend duke it didn't matter if he failed. He was only helping. Augustus would face the music if anything fell to pieces. Now he really was responsible for everything and everyone. He finally understood how Augustus felt and why he'd needed help.

He'd have to step into the light, and he'd be more restricted in his behavior. He'd have to start behaving like a duke.

On a sigh he turned and was surprised to see his mother enter the study, closing the door firmly behind her.

He moved forward quickly and pulled a chair out for her. "How are you?"

His mother's eyes briefly betrayed her loss before she plastered on the public face she'd been showing the staff and neighbors ever since he'd arrived home with her elder son slung over his horse.

"As well as any mother can be when she loses her elder son and the head of the household. It's you I'm worried about. A lot of responsibility has suddenly landed on your shoulders."

How could he tell his mother that he had been running the estate for years and that Augustus was simply the man with the title, a man who had chosen not to learn or to take on the responsibilities of the estate?

"I have Mr. Vickers. He will help me work out what needs to be done. There is no need for you to worry, Mother—I'm quite capable of running the estate as well as Augustus did."

The least he could do for Augustus was to maintain the illusion that he had been the best duke he possibly could be.

"You're lucky that Augustus has such good friends. Lord Corby is downstairs waiting to see you. He came by to offer his condolences. He's been a good friend to Augustus. A *very* good friend. I am sure he'll offer you advice should you require it."

Hadley's hands curled into fists at his sides. He knew why Corby was here. It would be about Claire.

"Mother, I know exactly what sort of friend Lord Corby is to our family, and why he is here. Perhaps you could ask Clinton to show him to Aug—to my study as you leave."

"I'm not finished."

He raised an eyebrow.

"I know you've always had a way with women. You're as handsome as your father. Thank goodness that is where the resemblance ends. Women have always sought you out for company. You should be aware that you will be inundated with women who now see a handsome duke and would love the title of duchess. Don't let the adoration go to your head as your father did."

"There is no need to worry, Mother. I will never become like my father."

She studied him for a moment before finally nodding. "It's just you look so much like him that I worry. When he came into the title he changed. It changed him. He wasn't the same man I'd married."

She rose to leave, but he couldn't help asking, "Is that why you loved Augustus more?"

She didn't pretend not to know what he was talking about. "Augustus was a gentle soul. He needed protecting from your father. You were stronger. I didn't love Augustus more, but I worried about him more. That is why I so wished he'd marry, but he never seemed to find the right woman."

Hadley would never tell his mother the truth. She probably would not care, but it might alter her view of her favorite son.

"I've found the right woman, so you need not worry. I plan to be wed very soon."

"Is it Lady Evangeline?"

"How on earth . . . ?"

"She came here a few days ago to speak with Augustus. I knew there was more to it than simply passing by. She obviously wanted Augustus's support and was worried he would not support your marriage. He hated how she broke your heart all those years ago." The first smile he'd seen in several days lit up his mother's still beautiful face. "Oh, to think I might finally have a grandson."

Hadley stiffened. "Actually, Mother, you already have a grandson." As her smile dimmed he rushed on. "It's a long story and one that I will fully reveal later. All I can say is that five years ago, a woman whom Father and some other men hurt years earlier decided to seek revenge on the sons because the fathers were already dead. She took Evangeline from me. Evangeline did not marry of her own free will. I did not know anything about it at the time, or that she was pregnant with my child. You have a grandson."

His mother looked stunned, but gamely she composed herself. "Well, that is a lot to take in all at once. I want to hear more, but I gather you have more pressing issues, like capturing your brother's killer. All I know is that Lady Evangeline is a beautiful woman, and you have a son. You must invite her to stay immediately. The house is in mourning, obviously, but I want to meet my grandson."

"I can't until we find Lord Labourd."

"You think the woman who killed Augustus has him?"

He nodded. "That's why I must leave tomorrow. I have unfinished business."

She reached out and squeezed his arm. "I would expect nothing less from you. But tell me, what is my grandson's name?"

"Lord Sealey Hadley Masters, Viscount Stuart."

"So he was accepted by Lord Stuart. Good—there should be no odious scandal. It sounds dreadfully snobbish, doesn't it, but it's your sisters I am concerned for. Scandal could hurt their chances of a good match."

He tried to hide his smile. "Mother, they are daughters of a duke, and they have very large dowries. Many sins will be overlooked."

"But I want the right match for them, not just someone who needs their dowry. I hope they will make a love match, not a business arrangement like my marriage."

"I will help you in that regard. Neither of them will ever be forced to marry anyone they don't wish. But knowing them both, I suspect they will find their perfect matches and give you many grandchildren."

"Speaking of grandchildren, how do you know Sealey is yours?"

"Apparently he looks like me."

"Hm. So there will be some scandal after all." His mother stood and cupped his cheek. "You said 'apparently.' You have not met him yet?"

"Not formally. He has no idea that I'm his father. I rescued him in the dead of night. The woman who killed Augustus had taken him. Augustus died a hero protecting Sealey's mother as well as me."

Tears welled again. "Augustus knew you loved her?"

Hadley nodded. He did love Evangeline—always had. That's why it had hurt so much, for far too long, when he'd thought she'd abandoned him.

His mother must have seen the pain of his loss, because she straightened her shoulders and said, "This evil woman, Victoria, has taken much from this family. Please ensure she receives the punishment she deserves."

He took his mother's hand and kissed it. "I swear it on Augustus's grave."

Her mother let her hand slip from his, and she patted him on the arm. "You'll make a fine Duke of Claymore. Now go bring my grandson home."

"I just have to speak to Lord Corby first."

"I'll send him up." With that, she left in a swirl of satin.

Hadley called after her, "Tell Clinton to have my horse readied, and inform Harper that he should pack my bags. He can follow in the family coach."

That conversation had gone better than he'd hoped, he thought with relief. His mother must have liked Evangeline.

Soon there was a knock, and Clinton announced Lord Corby.

Corby entered as if he owned the world. He appeared to be full of confidence, and the smile on his face made Hadley's insides recoil.

"Your Grace," he uttered, "my condolences on your brother's untimely death. Such a tragedy."

"Thank you."

Hadley sat and waited. There was no way he was bringing up the subject of Claire. How desperate was Corby?

The smile on the marquis's face began to fade.

"Was that all? I have many things to oversee, as you can imagine," Hadley said, standing.

"I thought after offering my condolences, I'd just remind you of our arrangement regarding Claire. It was your brother's fondest wish that our families be aligned, and as he is now deceased, and you had agreed to the arrangement . . ."

"Obviously that arrangement is void. My new position means that I cannot possibly marry Lady Claire. Augustus pointed out that she would be lost as a duchess, and that is why he suggested me as an alternative husband." Having said that, Hadley expected he would soon see Corby's true colors.

"I'm sure that since you do not have a younger brother, Augustus would wish you to honor the agreement."

"I'm sure he wouldn't. He actually advised me just recently that perhaps the marriage was not a good idea. You see, I'm in love with another."

Corby's smile was gone. "I know for a fact that he could not possibly have offered you such advice."

"Are you insinuating I'm a liar?"

Corby sat studying him, no doubt wondering how far to push him.

"Shall we lay all the cards on the table? Your brother had a secret I'm sure you'd not wish the world to know."

Hadley rose to his feet. "I wondered when you'd show your true colors. If it were not for my sisters I'd call you out, you sorry excuse for a man."

He could see sweat appear on Corby's forehead.

"If you wish your family not to suffer, I think it would be best if you agree to wed Claire." He drew out a sheet of paper. "I have the contract here."

Hadley slammed his hand on the table before grasping the document and ripping it in two. "I think that says it all."

Corby was visibly shaking now. "I will expose your brother as the sodomite he was."

Hadley moved round the desk to stand over the marquis. "You have no proof."

"My servants saw him with a man."

"No. They saw him with a woman dressed as a man."

Corby's face paled. "You expect everyone to believe that? Why on earth—"

"She was married and therefore slipped out in disguise to meet her lover. I have spoken to the lady concerned, and she is willing to testify to that fact."

Corby didn't know where to look. Hadley leaned over him. "My good friend Lord Labourd found some interesting information about you, Lord Corby. He has several witnesses who swear you like a certain type of, shall we say, sensual experience . . . one that involves bridles and saddles and being ridden like a horse."

Sweat was now dripping down Corby's face, and he seemed suddenly to have shrunk in stature.

Hadley leaned closer. "If I ever hear any rumors about my brother, any bit of gossip at all, I shall expose your perversion to the world, and then I shall beat you to within an inch of your life. Are we clear?"

There was no response.

"Are we clear?" Hadley repeated.

"Absolutely."

Hadley moved back to sit on the edge of his desk. "Now that we have left the unpleasantness behind us, let me say that I will do all that I can to find Lady Claire a suitable husband."

Corby's eyes opened wide.

"She should not have to suffer because her brother is an imbecile. Now get out—I have other business to attend to. Contact me at the start of next season and I will have a list of suitable candidates."

With that, Corby left, though without the swagger he'd entered with.

One problem was solved, Hadley thought. But now he had another one: how to save Arend when all he wanted to do was kill Victoria.

Chapter Fifteen

Evangeline knew she was a coward. As she waited for Hadley to arrive, she walked in Christian's rose gardens, watching Sealey play with Henry. She'd desperately wanted to go to Hardstone to support him, to help him deal with his brother's death, but he hadn't seemed to want her there.

He had every right to loathe her presence. If she had not insisted on dragging Augustus with her to find her son, he might still be alive. On top of that, Hadley had learned from the woman he hated most in this world that he had a son. The look he'd sent Evangeline as Victoria revealed Sealey's parentage—it could have frozen steaming lava.

She decided to put off talking to her son until after Hadley had arrived. She still didn't know if she should tell Sealey who his real father was, but Portia pointed out how cruel other children could be, and soon his parentage would be obvious to all who saw him and knew Hadley.

What had her stomach in a knot, her heart clenching in her chest, and her knees trembling was having to face Hadley. She'd gotten his brother killed.

"He has Hadley's laugh."

The sound of Marisa's voice temporarily pulled her out of her stew of guilt. Kissing her on both cheeks, she asked, "When did you arrive?"

"An hour ago. We overnighted at Hardstone, and Hadley traveled with us."

She peered over Marisa's shoulder. "Hadley is here?"

"I believe he is interrogating our prisoner. Oh, I'd love to go down there and . . . But Maitland won't allow me near her. He thinks it will upset me. Upset me? I don't think I could get more upset than knowing she's in that house!"

Evangeline's courage deserted her. Hadley would rather talk to Victoria than talk with her, and before meeting his son.

Marisa must have seen her face, for she quickly added, "He asked me to find you and see if you'd meet him in Christian's study in an hour." She reached for Evangeline's hand and squeezed. "Don't look so worried. He is nervous but excited to meet Sealey."

Was he excited to see her? That's what she longed to know. Had the events of the other day destroyed any chance of their having a happily-ever-after? Would guilt over his brother's death make a life together impossible? He could never claim Sealey as his heir, so there was no need to marry her.

She had an hour to wait before she would find out her fate. It felt like forever.

Hadley walked down the steps of Christian's dungeon-like cellar, anger rising, pain slicing, the blood boiling in his veins. If it weren't for the burning need to find Arend, he'd have already strangled Victoria.

With one flick of his hand he dismissed the guards standing outside the locked and fortified door. He stood for several moments trying to get his temper under control.

The woman on the other side of the door had stolen much of his life, taken love and happiness and turned it into regret, sorrow, and wrongs that could never be righted. All he wanted to know was why.

At least they had caught her before any of them were mortally injured. That is, if Arend was still alive. He didn't know what game she was about to play with him, but this time he intended to make the rules.

He slowly pushed open the steel door and stepped inside. Her cell was furnished more nicely than it would have been had he been in charge. He would've liked to see her sleeping on the floor, but Christian had furnished the room with a sturdy cot, warm blankets, a table with a lantern on it, and two comfy chairs. He even spied books on the table. However, what annoyed him the most was the sanctimonious smile upon her face.

"Well, if it isn't the new Duke of Claymore. Come to thank me?"

He ignored her taunt, not giving her the satisfaction of knowing how ill it made him just to be in the same room as her.

Instead he spoke calmly. "I came because I want to understand. We all knew what our fathers were like. They were monsters. If only you had come to me, I could have—"

The smile left her face. "Could have done what? Given me a father who cared more for his daughter than money? Or given me my innocence back? My life back? My child back?" She looked at him with the most emotion Hadley had ever seen in her cold, dead eyes. "Some things can never be given back no matter how hard you try."

"You've taught me that lesson. The one person who is the most affected by your evil is my son. You've robbed him of his true heritage, his family name, and nothing I can do will ever fix that."

"Now you understand how powerless you feel when others destroy your life. Perhaps that is better than seeing you in a grave."

"I want to know what happened to you to make you so filled with hate and vengeance against those who played no part in your abuse."

"I thought Evangeline would have given you a hint." At his silence she gave a cackle of a laugh. "You have not talked to her. Do I detect a romance strangled by guilt? It was her fault your brother was there. Really, I think you should thank her. You were running the family estates anyway; now you're truly the duke."

He carefully crossed his legs and pulled at his cuffs. "I hate to disappoint you again, but I do not blame her. I blame *you*. You were the one who chose to pull the trigger." It was unsettling to see how easily she had learned about his family. About him, given how carefully they had hidden his part in the running of the estates.

"That's a pity. It would have been my final curtain call to have destroyed your poignant reunion."

Hadley struggled to maintain his calm. Victoria was such a bitch.

"Maitland arrived with me; his wife is accompanying him. Speaking of vengeance, Marisa has a very large score to settle with you. Tell me something that will make me want to convey to her that perhaps we should have sympathy for you."

She stood up from where she had been sitting on the cot and walked to the other side of the cell. Directly above her, near the roof, was the bottom two inches of the window on the stairwell outside. It let in the briefest amount of natural light, and for one moment a spot of sunlight settled on her face. Hadley thought it ironic that the hard life she must have lived was not reflected there. Her skin was flawless, her beauty undiminished. She really did look the part of the perfect lady. He found it hard to believe that this woman so small in stature had brought so many people to their knees.

"The women will be the hardest to face." When she turned, the truth of her words showed. "However, you won't allow Marisa or any of the other wives to touch me until you have Arend back."

"That would depend on whether we thought he was still alive. You've played us for so long that we grow weary. I think it's time to change the rules. If Arend is alive, I have great faith in his abilities to extract himself from any situation. Why should any of us care whether you even leave this cell alive?"

This time she took the chair opposite him. Being so close to her made his skin crawl, but he gave no outward sign of it.

"I wondered when I'd get to play my ace. If I do not meet Isobel at a certain time and at a predetermined place, she will kill Arend. Isobel is well trained. She'd do anything for me. I'm the mother she's missed all these years. Do you really think that after all my planning, all the years I've put into this revenge, I would not have a plan for what to do if I should be caught?"

For one moment Hadley thought of calling her bluff. Yet he had to admit that she made sense. Victoria's planning, down to the very last detail, had been immaculate. What upset him was that he had not listened to, or acted upon, Arend's suspicions about Isobel sooner.

"It appears we are at a stalemate. For I can tell you now, there is no way that any of us will let you leave this cell unless it is to go to the gallows."

Victoria gave an exaggerated sigh. "Then it would appear you are signing your friend's death warrant. In fact, I'd be quite content either way. It will give me some satisfaction to know, as I go to my death, that I'll likely meet Arend in hell."

They sat staring at each other, Hadley trying to see if Victoria was bluffing. It was obvious that she was deranged, but she was also extremely clever. He would not put anything past her, or underestimate her.

"There is one thing you are overlooking. If I do not meet Isobel, not only will she kill Arend, but she has agreed to continue to avenge the wrongs done to me by your fathers."

Hadley uncrossed his legs and sat up straight in the chair. "We captured you. We can capture her."

"True. But I taught Isobel well. How much damage can she inflict before you do catch her? Look how much damage I caused. You didn't even realize how long ago I started to put this plan together. What could I already have put into play that Isobel is going to finish?" He could not stop the flash of rage that raced across his features. Before he could conceal his emotions, she drove the dagger home. "I suggest you go and talk to the others. Persuade them that it is in everyone's best interest to release me."

He shook his head. "That will never happen. You can't expect us to let you go free. How are we to know that you won't continue to seek revenge upon us?" Before she could speak, he added, "However, I may be able to sway them into letting you go to meet Isobel, if I accompany you. Your freedom in exchange for Arend's safe return." She looked at him in disbelief, her eyebrows raised. "We would also require your word that you and Isobel will leave England's shores, never to return. I would insist on one of my men accompanying you to your final destination. The Americas, perhaps?"

"This plan requires a lot of trust on the part of both parties. I'm not sure our relationship is at that level."

"Are you questioning my honor?"

"Your fathers had no honor."

He could not refute her statement. "I was hoping you would begin to understand the sons are nothing like the fathers."

She shrugged her delicate shoulders. "Perhaps." She studied him for what seemed a long time before finally saying, "Let me think on your suggestion. And I propose that you work hard on persuading the others. I'm not sure they will be happy with this plan."

"I think all of us, including yourself, have suffered enough, don't you? What our fathers started, I want to finish. I've come to realize that an eye for an eye leads to blindness for all. I just want this to end before anyone else gets hurt."

"Perhaps the sons do have more honor."

"Perhaps if you had gotten to know us before you instigated this plan you would already have known that. I know what my father was, and I can quite imagine what he and the others did to you. And having seen what you've done to Evangeline, Sealey, and myself, I understand the driving need for revenge. However, I've also seen what revenge does. It doesn't heal. It doesn't correct mistakes. It doesn't ease the pain."

To his amazement he saw Victoria's eyes fill with tears. "What does ease the pain?"

"Something you have never experienced, and I feel sorry for you because of it."

She looked at him quizzically.

He whispered, "Love. Loving someone, having someone love you back, that's what eases the pain. I have that with Evangeline, and I will have that with Sealey. I doubt you have let anyone close enough to be able to love you, or if you are even capable of love, or if there is anything in you to love."

"I did love once. I loved a little girl who, because I was her mother, starved to death before she was three weeks of age."

"Tell me. Make me understand."

She looked away, and her voice held no emotion as she began her tale.

"My father was Sir Reginald Rathbourne. I was his only child. My mother could not have more children after my birth. We lived a quiet life in a small village near St. Ives. Life was good, we were happy, until my father invested in a South American mining company. We lost everything. Father turned to drink, and soon anything of value in our house had been sold. One drunken night at the gaming table my father lost huge to the Duke of Lyttleton. I was given to him as payment. After the night I was raped by your fathers, except for Lord Labourd, your father kept me as his personal sex slave. I was so traumatized I didn't even try to escape. Then, when I was large and round with child, he took me to London and threw me on the streets."

Hadley could not stop a curse pouring from his mouth. "Christ almighty."

"Christ was certainly not around. I gave birth in a doorway, living off scraps of food I could scrounge. I was so undernourished I had little to no milk for my babe. She literally starved to death. I would have too if one of the local madams hadn't taken me in."

"I'm so sorry. But again, I stress, I and my friends were not the culprits here."

Victoria ignored his remark. "Of course, once I was stronger, the madam put me to work. We all had to earn our keep. When I was gritting my teeth under my first 'customer,' I vowed I'd wreak revenge on those who had forsaken me. I saved hard and hired a man to kill my father. It took me three months to save the amount needed. Such a small amount for a man's life. However, I found the victory hollow, as I was not there to see it. That's when I decided my vengeance had to be more personal. I wanted to look into your father's eyes when he died. When all of them died. Once again the devil spat in my face. They all died before I could seek my revenge. I deserved to be avenged but there was no one to help me. It took me years to rise to a position high enough to instigate payback. Unfortunately, the sons were all that was left of my defilers' bloodline."

"How did you end up married to the Earl of Northumberland?"

"Pah." She waved a hand. "That was easy. He frequented the brothel I owned in Paris. But I run ahead of myself. Let's go back. After I had my father killed, I saved again, took more clients. I became sought after because of my ability to be a lady everywhere but in the bedroom. Lord Sutcliffe took a shine to me, and I became his mistress. He set me up in a lovely house; he bought me jewels and other luxury items. Again I saved, my sole goal being to own a brothel so that I would no longer have to open my legs for degenerate men. I decided on Paris so that I could reinvent myself. Hide my identity and plan a comeback of epic proportions."

"Find a man to blackmail into marriage?"

The wicked smile was back. "Of course. The Earl of Northumberland was just the weak-willed sap I needed. I set him up. I rigged the gaming tables at my establishment until he owed me so much money he'd never be able to repay me. He had no choice but to agree to my plan. The Fleur de Lily was no more, and I became Victoria, Countess of Northumberland. It was such a pity that all your fathers were dead; I would love to have seen their faces when I walked into a London ball on his arm."

"How did you come to fixate on the sons?"

She laughed. "By accident. I was in London with Isobel's father, and I literally bumped into you coming out of Garrard's with Lord Labourd. I heard you mention a ring and I saw how happy you were, and I could not bear that."

"It was a consequence of fate?"

"You were in the wrong place at the wrong time. Arend by your side made it worse. His father knew that what they were going to do that night was wrong, but he walked away and left me there. That to me was unforgivable. That was the moment I hatched my plan. You would be destroyed first, and Arend would be last."

He shook his head on a long sigh. "So much pain, and for what? Where has it got you? I don't think it's healed your soul nor made you happy. Love is the only thing worth a damn, and you've never experienced it."

"I loved once. I loved my mother and father, yet that did not stop my father from betraying me. I loved my little girl. After her death, I dared not love. Love is far too painful. Bitterness and revenge were so much easier."

Hadley couldn't help himself. He reached out and took one of her delicate hands in his. "I'm truly sorry for your loss. I'm also truly sorry for the part my father played in your gruesome tale. But I refuse to be held accountable for something my father did. Neither I nor any of the other Libertine Scholars committed this offense. And we should not have had to pay the price."

Tears trickled down her face. "There was no one else to blame. Revenge was all that had kept me going, and suddenly there was no one to take my revenge upon, to slake my thirst."

He squeezed her hand. "Coming after the sons is the reason I cannot forgive you. What you did to all of us is unforgivable. Yet part of me understands the burning need to seek vengeance, for I feel it. I'd like nothing better than to strangle you with my own two hands."

She pulled her hand from his, any emotional weakness gone. "I don't want your forgiveness, and I don't need it."

"Then what is it you do need?"

She briefly closed her eyes. "I don't know. I don't know what I want anymore. You are right when you say revenge is empty. It doesn't bring my little girl back." She stood and made her way back over to the cot. She lay down and closed her eyes. "Go to your friends. See if they will agree to your plan. I'm tired and will be content to leave this country and all the bad memories behind. England has never done right by me."

He moved to the door and stood looking at her slight form. Such a waste of so many lives. He could not help but feel sorry for all of them.

As Hadley made his way back upstairs and into the light, his anger and hatred still burned, just not as bright. He knew what he had suggested was not going to be easy to get the others to agree to, but what he did know was that it was time to face facts. Someone had to end the cycle of vengeance. He didn't want Sealey or any of his future children born into a world filled with hate. It was time to turn the other cheek.

If only he could trust Victoria.

Somehow he doubted it.

Chapter Sixteen

Hadley rose to greet her as soon as Evangeline entered the room. He looked so handsome she almost couldn't catch her breath. The first thing she noted was that there was no welcoming smile. His face was drawn tight, his lips were pressed firmly together, and his eyes portrayed such sorrow her heart immediately clenched deep within her chest.

What had Victoria said to him?

She rushed forward, her mouth blabbering. "I'm so sorry. I wish when I had returned to London that I'd done things differently. I wish that I had told you about Sealey sooner, but your reaction to my arrival, and finding out the situation you are in with your brother . . . well, how could I have told you?"

He came around the desk and walked toward her.

She held her palms up. "You would've been torn between helping your brother and wanting to do what was right for Sealey. I couldn't put you—"

Before she could finish the sentence he pulled her roughly into his arms, and his mouth crashed down on hers. The kiss was possessive, hard and wanting. His tongue filled her mouth, stroking her.

Her body responded immediately. She wrapped her arms round his neck and pushed in close. She loved how his hands roamed over her clothes, tracing the curves of her breasts, moving down over her waist, until his large hands cupped the globes of her bottom, lifting her up and pulling her tight against his hardness.

All too soon his demanding lips left hers. He rested his forehead against hers, his breathing ragged.

"I've been dreaming about doing that for days."

"You're not angry with me?"

He shook his head. "How could I be? Nothing that has occurred is your fault. I understand perfectly well why you did not tell me about Sealey sooner. You are too generous, kind, and thoughtful to put me in a position where I would have had to choose between my son and my brother. I love you even more for that."

She physically sagged against him. "Thank you. I couldn't bear it if you were angry with me or blamed me for Augustus's death."

He hugged her back. "We all do what we think is right at the time. Hindsight simply lets us know whether the choice we made was a good one."

"I'm not sure my choices were good."

He ran a finger gently down her face. "All I know is that I appreciate what you tried to do for me—for Augustus. Come. Sit. We have a lot to discuss."

Swallowing her hand in his, he led her to the chair by the roaring fire. He waited for her to sit before slowly withdrawing his hand, his fingers trailing the length of hers, and taking a seat opposite her.

"Tell me about my son."

"I'd love to say that he is like every other boy who is nearly five years old, but that would not be true." Looking at the flames flickering in the grate, she tried to find a way to explain to Hadley what his son's life had been like when Dougal was still alive.

"Dougal suspected the babe I carried was not his, and when I gave birth a little over seven months later, to a big, strong, healthy boy, his doubts deepened." She hurriedly continued. "He never really said anything, but he was never affectionate with the baby.

"I knew as soon as Sealey was born that he was your son. The shape of his eyes and his curly brown hair added certainty to my own instinct." She smiled at the memory.

"I wish I could have been with you. Was it a difficult birth?"

"I suspect no more difficult than for any other woman. Besides, the pain is soon forgotten when you hold your child in your arms. He was a beautiful baby, and I lost my heart to him the moment I saw him."

Hadley cleared his throat. "When did Lord Stuart become certain the boy was not his?"

"It was a gradual process. He refused to have Sealey in his presence. I was to keep the child out of his way at all times. He never said to my face that the boy was not his, but he knew."

"Did he ever hurt the boy?"

She shook her head. "Not physically, but emotionally . . . Sealey tried so hard to do what he thought Dougal wanted. Can you imagine what it must have been like to try to please a father who refused to love you? The poor child was so confused and hurt, and often thought he had done something wrong. It broke my heart."

"Augustus faced that every day of his life. My father hated him, was disgusted by him. I felt so guilty watching my father's treatment of him. I could not understand how a father could act that way to his son. Neither could Augustus. I guess that is why I always tried to protect my brother. It wasn't honorable, the way my father behaved."

"I suppose I should be thankful that Dougal never hit Sealey. I was constantly worried that he would. But other than seeing that Sealey behaved, he left the boy alone."

A frown appeared on Hadley's face. "But by claiming the child as his, the boy is now his heir."

"Lord Stuart's first wife bore him no children, and I never fell with child after Sealey's birth. I think he realized the problem lay with him. He had no male cousin or any other male relatives. Claiming Sealey ensured that the Stuart name would continue."

"How strange. It doesn't continue with his bloodline; therefore it seems pointless."

"For once he was thinking of someone other than himself—his unmarried sisters. If the land and title went back to the crown, what would they live on?"

Hadley nodded. "I suppose I would do that for my family too."

"You'd do anything for your family."

He smiled at her comment, then asked, "Did you try to explain to Sealey why Lord Stuart behaved toward him as he did?"

She swallowed, trying to pick her words carefully. "I couldn't tell him. What if he talked about it and others overheard? I didn't want to give anyone grounds to question his right to be Viscount Stuart. I wanted to protect him."

"Of course you did. You love him. How do you think he will react to the knowledge that I am his father?"

"I don't know. He's still very young, and I'm not sure he will understand it all."

"Are you suggesting we don't tell him? That we wait until he is older?"

She tried to read his face, tried to see what he wanted to do. There was never a good time to try and explain to a young boy that the man he thought was his father wasn't. In a way, she was thankful that Sealey hadn't formed any attachment to Dougal. In fact, he'd seemed happier and more carefree after Dougal's death.

"I think we should tell him now," she finally concluded. "He's already missed five years of knowing his real father—why should he have to wait longer? I actually think it may come as a relief to him to finally understand why Dougal wasn't affectionate with him."

Hadley crossed his legs. "I must confess to some nervousness. What if he doesn't like me either?"

"As with any child, if you love him, he will love you back." She smiled encouragingly. "We could tell him tomorrow and simply let him meet you today. Let him get to know you before we announce you're his father. I'm sure he'll soon love you too. Why don't we go and introduce you to him now? He is on the front lawn. Sebastian is teaching Henry and Sealey how to play pall-mall."

She knew they had more to talk about, more than just Sealey, but like the coward she was, she wanted to face one mountain at a time. The state of their relationship, if there was going to be any relationship—and she hoped that the kiss he'd bestowed not long ago was an indication that there would be—could wait. Hadley had waited five years to meet his son, and he shouldn't have to wait a minute longer.

She walked to where he sat and held out her hand. He took a deep breath and slipped his hand into hers. She realized he was nervous, for his hand was shaking. She reached up and pressed a kiss to his cheek. "Don't worry, he's going to love you as much as I do."

With that they left the study and made their way through the house out to the front lawn. They could hear the boys' laughter before they even reached the bottom step.

Upon sighting them from across the lawn, Sealey called to her. "Look, Mother, I can hit the ball," and he swung the mallet as hard as he could, his tongue poking from the side of his mouth. His face was alight with happiness, and he looked so much like Hadley. She wondered if her son would notice the resemblance when he looked at his father.

Hadley halted and sucked in a breath. His eyes totally focused on the wee boy across the grass. Tears welled in his eyes, and he squeezed her hand tightly.

"Oh my God," he whispered.

Sealey ran across the grass to where the ball rested, not more than five feet from where they both stood. He called, "Watch, Mama," and drew the mallet back. But instead of swinging through and hitting the ball, the mallet stopped midflight. Sealey's smile faltered, and a look of disbelief settled there instead. The mallet slowly dropped to the ground.

Sealey looked at her, and then he looked at Hadley, looked at where their hands were still joined. Sealey took a tentative step toward them, his eyes never leaving Hadley's face.

She would never forget the moment her son finally understood why Dougal never loved him. He turned to her, his face a picture of wonderment, hope, and fear. She nodded, conveyed without words what Sealey intuitively understood. This stranger, this man standing with his hand linked with hers, was his father. The likeness was unmistakable even to Sealey.

It was as if the world stood still. She no longer heard the singing of the birds, the wind seemed to die away, and all she could hear was the rapid beating of her heart.

Tears were flowing down Hadley's face. He dropped to his knees and opened his arms, and without hesitation Sealey ran into them.

Her own tears flowed as she watched Hadley hug Sealey as if he'd never let him go.

Hadley didn't know how he found the strength to release the boy—his son. He drew back and held the boy at arm's length, soaking in how perfect he was. He had his mother's lips and chin, but from there on up he was all Fullerton. It was strange seeing how he himself must have looked as a young boy. Sealey's eyes were the exact same ocean deep blue. Sealey's nose was as defined as his own, and his hair, a mass of dark brown curls, was as wild as his hair had been at this age. That's why, as an adult, he kept it cropped short. He found the curls too feminine.

"You look like me," Sealey said, a quaver in his voice.

"Yes. Yes, I do. My name is Hadley Fullerton, the Duke of Claymore."

"I am Sealey Masters, Viscount Stuart. You were the man who rescued me. I recognize your voice. Thank you, sir."

"You were so brave. I was proud of you."

At Hadley's words, his son seemed to stand taller, his little chest puffed outward.

Evangeline stepped forward. "Why don't we take a stroll to the river?"

He stood and held out his hand to his son. Evangeline took Sealey's other hand, and the three of them began to stroll across the lawn to the path at the far end of the garden.

"Are you a friend of my mother's?"

Evangeline answered. "I knew His Grace many years ago, before I married your—before I married Lord Stuart."

Sealey seemed content with that reply and as they made their way to the river, he chatted about the pony Lord Markham had said he could ride while he was at Henslowe.

Hadley told Sealey the story simply, calmly, and dispassionately. He told it in a way that he hoped Sealey would understand. He wanted the boy to know that this was neither Hadley's fault nor his mother's fault, and never his fault.

The little boy listened solemnly, never interrupting. When the tale was told he turned to his mother and asked, "Does that mean we don't have to go back to Scotland?"

Evangeline looked to Hadley for guidance. They hadn't had time to discuss the status of their relationship.

"I was hoping that you and your mother would come to live with me." His happiness was complete when he saw the effect of his words on Evangeline. Her eyes lit up, and she reached out and took his hand.

"That would be perfect," she said. "What do you think of that idea, Sealey?"

The little boy frowned. "Where do you live?"

"My estate, Hardstone"—he still struggled with the idea that Hardstone was now his—"is near Chiddingstone in Kent. I also have a hunting lodge in Surrey, and of course a townhouse in London."

"Is Kent far from here?"

"It's about a two-to-three-day carriage ride from Dorset."

Upon hearing the news, Sealey's face fell. "So I wouldn't be able to visit Henry every day."

"No. However, there is no reason why he couldn't come and stay at Hardstone or you could stay here for holidays."

"Do you have horses at Hardstone? Would I have my own pony?"

He laughed. Such a typical question from a young boy. "There are many horses, and of course you may have a pony. I will teach you to ride myself."

"Then yes, I would like to live there. We would be like a proper family. Would you play with me the same way that Lord Coldhurst plays with Henry?"

"Absolutely. However, there will be days when I have to attend to business, and I may also have to travel. When you're older, I'll let you come with me so you can learn all you need to know about running your own estate in Scotland." Sealey seemed to consider this before nodding his approval.

Hadley hadn't told his son, his eldest son, that he would never be able to inherit his father's title, nor that he would never be the master at Hardstone. The explanation of why he would only ever be Viscount Stewart could wait until Sealey was older. All that mattered was that his son understood that Hadley was his real father and that he loved him with all his heart.

Evangeline shaded her eyes and looked up at the sun. "Goodness, it's getting late. We should return to the house before they send out a search party to find us."

He walked back to the house hand in hand with his son and Evangeline. A lump formed in his throat; never before had he felt so complete. This was *his* family. Finally he had what he'd wanted the last five years: Evangeline and his child. It was like a dream come true. He would not let the fact that Sealey would never be known as a Fullerton ruin this moment.

What did frighten him was the idea of losing them.

If he was to stop the circle of vengeance and find Arend before it was too late, he was going to have to trust Victoria.

A shiver ran down his spine as he contemplated how dangerous his plan would be. He would need Evangeline's help in convincing the others that this was the only way forward. Victoria had them up against a wall, trapped; any which way they moved, disaster could come calling.

Christian stood at the top of the stairs waiting to greet them, a warm smile upon his face. He didn't say anything to them, but he patted Hadley on the back and ruffled Sealey's curls.

The little boy spied Henry and raced off after him.

"You are going to have your hands full with that one," Christian remarked dryly to Evangeline. "He's very much like his father. Would you mind if I steal Hadley away? I'd like to talk to him before we meet with the others later tonight."

Blast. He would've preferred a quiet moment with Evangeline. They had a lot to settle between them. The special license was burning a hole in his pocket. He wanted to make her his legal wife as soon as possible because he knew the immediate future held danger. More than anyone, he realized that happiness could be snatched from them both in an instant.

"It's all right, you go with Christian. I want to speak to Wendy. I'd like her to know the truth in case Sealey starts to ask her any questions."

He drew Evangeline's hand to his lips and placed a kiss on her palm. "I'll come and find you shortly. There is an important question I really want to ask you."

Her face flushed a pretty pink color. "I shall be waiting with anticipation."

He stood and watched her walk up the stairs, still not believing his luck at having her back in his life. Christian elbowed him in his side.

"Come on. The sooner we have this conversation, the sooner you can get back to your proposal."

"I'm hoping we can marry in your chapel as soon as possible. I even have the special license."

"Of course. It will be nice to celebrate such a joyous occasion, instead of all the doom and gloom that is hanging over us."

Hadley didn't tell his friend that he would really love to wait until Arend could be with them before he married, but he could not wait. Finding Arend would be dangerous. His plan was to leave with Victoria, and if anything should happen to him, he wanted Evangeline to carry his name.

He threw Christian a sideways glance as they made their way to his study. "There is one thing you could do for me. I feel the need to dabble in romance."

"Excellent. Serena would love it if I helped a fellow Libertine Scholar win his bride."

Evangeline felt giddy with excitement for the rest of the afternoon. She barely heard, and didn't participate, as the women sat discussing Victoria. She knew she should take an interest, and that she should care how they were going to find Arend, but Hadley's words rang in her head over and over. She was sure he was going to propose.

She couldn't wait to say yes—to finally put the past five years behind her and be able to spend the rest of her life with the man she loved and with Sealey. A part of her kept thinking something was going to go wrong.

She'd just popped up to say goodnight to Sealey. She'd never seen her son so happy. Apparently Hadley had taken dinner with his son. She didn't know what stories Hadley had filled his son's head with, but it was pretty clear Sealey already worshiped him.

She opened the door to her bedchamber, still shaking her head, remembering Sealey's last comment about how his father could beat Henry's father in a fight. What she saw in the room drew her up short.

A fire was blazing in the grate, with several fur throws placed strategically on the floor in front of it. Many candles were lighted and placed round the room, the soft lighting giving the room an ethereal glow. To one side a table for two had been placed, and it was covered with platters. A large carafe of wine stood at the center of the table, next to the biggest bunch of flowers she had seen in a long time.

What really made her breath catch in her throat was the sight of Hadley leaning against the fireplace.

Chapter Seventeen

"I thought we'd have a private dinner in your room, if that is all right with you."

She closed the door softly behind her. "I think that would be lovely. I feel like it's been a million years since we were together at Lathero."

The seriousness of the occasion made her feel nervous, like a young unmarried virgin. She hungrily drank in his features. She'd always thought of him as a physically perfect specimen. She knew there was not an ounce of fat on his elegant frame. Every one of his muscles was exquisitely defined.

His hair had grown longer over the past few weeks. He'd not had time for a cut, and his lovely curls were forming. Five years ago, when they had been courting, she had begged him to let his hair grow longer. She knew he hated his curls. He considered his curls to be unmanly. She blamed his father for Hadley's obsession with looking masculine. He'd seen the way his father treated Augustus.

As he stood before her, his eyes were filled with naked emotion. She read his love for her, joy in meeting his son, and fear that it could all be taken away as it had been five years ago.

Her eyes ran over his clean-cut jaw, and she noted he'd shaved this evening, for her. There was no denying that he was a very handsome man. Her blood heated just looking at him. The prominence of his cheekbones and the long dark eyelashes framing his deep blue eyes could have made him look feminine if it were not for the hardness of his jaw.

He mistook her hesitation. "Don't be nervous, love." He opened his arms, and she ran to him. He hugged her close, and she felt safe and cherished in his arms.

"I can't believe I'm standing here with you. You've met your son, and we are going to get a chance to be together."

Hadley's voice went hard. "It's not over yet, but it soon will be, and I'm determined that we will win this time."

"You mean, when we get Arend back."

"Yes."

They stood embracing in front of the fire, content to be in each other's arms. Finally he said, "We have to move—my derriere is about to combust from the heat."

Laughing, she stepped out of his embrace only to turn and see Hadley take a deep breath and sink to his knees on the furs.

Her stomach was a mass of butterflies.

"There is something important I would like to ask you, sweetheart."

Evangeline's heart beat swiftly. "I believe that you've asked me this question once before, so you'll know my answer."

His eyes sparkled with humor. "You don't know what I'm going to ask you."

It was difficult to remain calm, to stop herself from joining him on the floor, wrestling him beneath her, and smothering him with love.

"Lady Evangeline." He took her hands in his large ones, still on his knees. "Will you do me the very great honor of becoming my wife? I've arranged for a wedding in Lord Markham's chapel tomorrow morning, in front of all our friends and with our son by our side." He let go of one hand to pat his pocket. "I have the special license, and Christian is arranging for the vicar who married them to perform the ceremony."

She could not stop the tears of joy from rolling down her cheeks. She never thought this day would come, but she'd hoped. She'd clung to that hope through the worst years of her marriage. Her hope and her son were the reasons she had come through her ordeal.

As she stood there too choked with joy to reply, Hadley's smile faltered.

"If you require more time," he said, "I can wait. It's just . . . Haven't we waited long enough?"

She nodded and finally got the words out. "Of course I'll marry you. Yes. Yes. *Yes!*" She flung herself at his crouched figure, toppling him, and they landed on the furs in a tangle of arms and legs.

"I wanted to do this properly this time," he growled as he untangled himself and sat up, holding a folded cloth in his hand. "The last time I asked you to marry me we had to hide our relationship. We were to elope, so I could not give you a ring in case your mother saw it. This time I want to shout to the world that you are finally mine and that I'll let no one take you from me." Hadley opened his hand and flipped back the cloth. Sitting in the middle of the cloth was the most gorgeous diamond and ruby ring. She rose to her knees and shuffled closer to look at the glittering jewels. Tentatively she touched it. It was the most beautiful ring she'd ever seen—the diamond clear, the ruby blood red. It was perfect.

"I bought this ring five years ago for you. I was going to give it to you once we'd reached Gretna Green. I've kept it with me ever since. Somewhere deep down I was always hoping that one day you'd wear it."

She held out a shaking hand and he slid it on her finger. It fit perfectly. She raised her eyes in question.

"Remember when I used to loop daisies round your finger when we sat under our tree? I marked the size and had it made."

She cupped his cheek and whispered, "I love you," her heart in every word.

"This time I'll not let anyone take our happiness from us. I swear on my son's life."

Hadley bent his head and kissed her lips. It was meant to be a light kiss, as they still had much to talk about. He needed to tell her about his plan to save Arend, and how she would have to help them convince the others to let Victoria go free. However, his sangfroid abandoned him.

He knew she would not be happy with the idea. So he did what any red-blooded male would do with his fiancée in his arms: he deepened the kiss and began to undress her.

He felt like an inexperienced schoolboy, his palms sweaty, as he pulled off the bodice he'd unbuttoned. He lifted Evangeline to her feet, spun her round, and unlaced her corset.

"I remember undressing you like this when we met under our tree. I used to ply a kiss to a part of your body for each piece of clothing that fell away."

"Why do you think I wore so many clothes?"

He chuckled. Hadley kissed her neck as the corset came off, then her shoulder as she unfastened her chemise.

Her skin smelled of honeysuckle. He drew in a deep breath, letting her scent fill his lungs. "I could lie in bed all day, with only your scent wrapped round me."

"I'm sure that could be arranged, although Sealey would likely be upset. I will have to learn to share you."

He let his lips smile against her skin. He kissed her glossy hair, running the silken strands through his fingers, before he helped her push her gown over her rounded hips. He loved how her backside curved into his hip.

Evangeline trembled in his arms; evidently she was just as nervous as he. Her skin was flushed where he kissed it, and her bare breasts rose as he slid his hand round her waist.

He swung her up into his arms, and on a light squeal she directed, "I prefer the fur to my bed."

He didn't need convincing. He was hard and ready and could think of nothing else but being inside her. He gently lowered her to the pile of fur throws before the fire, and without taking his eyes from her luscious body, he began to remove his clothing. She lay there watching, her eyes blazing with desire. By the time he was naked, all he wanted to do was ravish her. He drew on his inner strength to get his body under control.

He wanted to make love to her, to prolong her pleasure, to show her how completely he loved her.

"I could stand looking at you like this all day."

She crooked her finger. "How disappointing. I like the way you look at me, but I love it more when you're lying next to me, on top of me, *in* me."

With those words she held up a hand and drew him down to her. He landed heavily. Her breasts were crushed against his bare chest, and his restraint fled as he held her hips and slowly pushed inside her.

"I belong here, with you," he sighed, needing to hold still lest he spend too quickly. He wanted to plunge deeply, over and over, until he exhausted them both and washed away the bad memories of the past.

All the women he'd taken to his bed, trying to rid himself of Evangeline's taste and scent, were forgotten. He wanted to love only her, fall asleep with her and wake up with her, spend the day with her, go to bed with her, make more children with her, for the rest of his life.

Evangeline's sheath closed round him like a tight fist. Their enemy was forgotten. To have her back for good, in his arms, in his life, was a joy worth celebrating.

"It's always been you, only you," she whispered, kissing his lips, the bridge of his nose.

"We have five long years of separation to make up for. Once we have Arend back, you'll be lucky if I let you out of bed for a year."

Her lips curved into the wickedest smile he'd ever seen as she wiggled her hips. "I think I love you even more for that promise."

He began to move slowly, drawing out and sliding once more into her tight heat. He was going to die of restraint. Firelight touched her body, her nipples dark against cream-colored skin. Her auburn hair matched the flames, trailing over her shoulders like a flicker of fiery red.

Her face softened, her eyes darkening with her arousal. Her moist lips parted on a sigh of pleasure. The sight excited him, and he could not hold back. He began to move more forcefully between her thighs.

Her legs rose to wrap round his waist as she opened fully to him. She met him thrust for thrust. This coupling was driving away all the fear, all the anger, and all the grief. Nothing mattered but that they had found each other again.

Evangeline's head lolled back, her eyes closed, as she lost herself in the pleasure. He knew she was forgetting the past and thinking of nothing but how he felt inside her.

Her breathing grew ragged; she was drawing close to her climax. That sent his need spiraling even more. He lost his self-control and began to move forcefully, her breasts bouncing free with each thrust.

Her nails dug into his back, the pain only adding to the pleasure, and soon his cry of joy mingled with hers as they peaked together.

Nothing had ever been as perfect as this.

"You feel so good. I've not felt like this . . . ever. It's so . . ."

"Perfect?" His body shuddered with release, and the word came out on a groan.

They fell silent. The crackle of the fire was the only sound other than their ragged breathing.

A few minutes later she said in a quiet voice, "I hope she rots in hell for what she took from us."

Evangeline's sorrow-filled words tore at his soul. No matter what he did, he could never give her back those five years. He could not ease her pain, and that killed him.

"I thought I'd never see you again," Evangeline whispered, her tears scalding his cheek. "I hoped. Oh, how I hoped, but Dougal was only a tad older than you, and . . . I can't tell you how often I dreamed of ways to kill him. Kill my mother."

"Shh." He kissed her hair. It made him ill, thinking about her life with Lord Stuart. He couldn't go on thinking *what if*. What if he'd searched for her? What if he hadn't let her leave his side once they'd planned their elopement? What if they had simply left that day?

Rage trickled through him again, and he had to uncurl his fist. He needed to let the anger, bitterness, and fury go so that he could use Victoria to find Arend.

"We are together now." She was safe and sound, and soon she'd be his wife. He was not leaving her side until after the wedding tomorrow. He'd take no chances this time. "And I'm not letting you out of my sight until we walk into that chapel tomorrow."

"And *I'm* not letting *you* out of my sight until we walk into that chapel tomorrow. You and Sealey are what matter most to me."

He stroked her hair as they lay on the fur, the warmth of the fire making him drowsy. Then he heard her stomach rumble.

"Sorry. I was so nervous about seeing you today that I barely ate anything."

He immediately rose and gathered the robes he'd instructed her maid to place on the end of the bed. He helped her don her robe, then slipped into his before escorting her to the table covered in cheeses, meats, and sweetmeats. He poured them wine and raised his glass.

"Here's to our happiness. Long may it continue."

"To us and our family. Given that we have Victoria locked up downstairs, the future is looking brighter already."

His hand faltered just as the goblet meet his lips. He lowered his glass. "Ah, we need to discuss the situation regarding Victoria."

He hated how the smile on her face dimmed and her eyes narrowed.

"Why did you go to see her as soon as you arrived? It must have been important if she drew your attention before your son, or me, for that matter."

"I want to rescue Arend."

"If he is alive," she countered.

"She has no use for him dead." He paused. "But I concede he might not be alive." A shiver ran over him. "She tells me that she has not hurt him, but I am not stupid enough to trust anything she says."

"Very wise," she replied as she popped a piece of cheese into her lovely mouth. His concentration faltered as he thought of where he'd like that mouth to be. . . .

He shook his head and pinned her with what he hoped was a convincing smile. "She told me that if we do not release her by a certain date, Isobel will kill Arend."

She made a faint noise of distress. "No. I do not believe it. I do not believe Isobel is a party to this."

"Are you willing to bet Arend's life on it?"

She could not hold his gaze. She hung her head, looking at her plate. After a few moments she murmured a faint "No."

"Neither am I."

Her eyes flashed fire as she turned to look at him. "What are we to do? We can't let her go. . . ." Her mouth dropped open as she realized what he intended to do. "No. You can't."

"I have thought long and hard to find a solution. However, the others will need convincing, and I want your support."

She eyed him warily. "Are you going to be a husband who expects blind obedience? Because let me tell you now, that won't happen. I've had that with one husband, and I won't have it with you."

He grimaced, hating that he'd brought Lord Stuart's memory

into this room on this night. "I don't expect blind obedience, but I would hope you'd listen to me and try to support me."

"That sounds fair. I hope you return the courtesy."

"Naturally." He could do that. "Victoria said she told you a little of her ordeal, that she had a child and it died. Is it any wonder after all she endured that she would be eaten up with thoughts of vengeance?"

Evangeline nodded. "I can't imagine what losing a child in those circumstances must do to a woman. I can certainly understand her driving need for revenge but not against the innocent."

"We are in agreement on that point. If she had taken revenge on those who were guilty of the crime, I'd have said bravo. But I think of Marisa and all she has lost, of the five years she stole from us, of all our son has lost . . . I cannot forgive her, but I want this pattern of perpetual revenge broken. Anyway, she hinted to me that she was tired of her vengeance plan. That it had not given her the peace she needed. I'm not sure I believe her, but I suggested a compromise."

He explained to her what he wanted to do. As he'd thought, her immediate reaction was no, that it was too risky both for Arend and for him. "If anything happened to you, I'd be destroyed. I can't lose you again."

Finally, once he'd pointed out that it was either trust Victoria or risk Arend's life, their lives, and their children's lives should Isobel continue with Victoria's quest, she agreed to back his solution.

Now all they had to do was convince the others. Marisa would be the hardest to convince. He suspected she had no pity for Victoria. She had lost the most, and she was out for blood. He hoped his plan would stop Marisa from spiraling into the same pit of bitterness and vengeance that had set Victoria on this path.

They finished their meal and returned to the furs, glasses of wine in their hands. They talked about where they would live. With so many estates and houses between his title and Sealey's, their time would be in demand. They would have to spend part of the year in Hardstone, Lathero, and Rossack Castle, when not in London. They *would* make this work and try not to be apart for more than a few weeks at a time. They discussed how many other children they hoped to have, how he couldn't spoil Sealey just because he had been wronged. But most of all they lay together, still in awe at the happiness they felt.

"I suppose we should get some sleep." Evangeline's words would have been more convincing if she hadn't just untied his robe and stroked her hand down his chest, all the way down, her finger trailing down his stirring member.

"Something tells me neither of us is sleepy." His thoughts scattered as his pulse quickened. "I don't want to wear you out before our wedding day."

She kissed the tip of his nose. "I only have to walk down the aisle." She giggled. "Of course, if you make love to me all night I might not be able to manage even that."

He grinned. "I don't mind carrying you."

Evangeline straddled him, her long auburn locks trailing over his chest, the sides of her silk robe feathering over his thighs. She leaned down and licked his nipple, her teeth lightly grazing the hardened nub. Every muscle in Hadley's body tightened with pleasure, that instant arousal incredible.

She rose up only to guide him to her wet, tight entrance before sliding slowly down. He loved watching her light blue eyes as they sparkled with passion. He should capture her like this on canvas. A canvas only he would ever see. It struck him instantly. This was the first time he'd wanted to paint anything in a long time.

She smacked his chest lightly. "Hey, you're woolgathering."

"I was thinking how beautiful you looked and that I'd love to capture the essence of you on canvas. To keep it with me forever."

"I will be with you forever, in this life and the next. Always."

With that, she began to move, to ride him slowly, exquisitely, the movement driving him wild. Soon any thoughts of painting her, even thoughts of their wedding tomorrow, fled, and he lay back and watched the most erotic display he'd ever seen.

Evangeline moved with such grace, like a ghostly siren whose shape flowed and morphed into and out of the firelight. Shadows danced on her sheened skin, her nipples hard and begging for his mouth. He rose up to suckle her, and the soft moan from her open lips drove him close to the brink.

Her hands gripped his hair, holding him tight to her breasts; her legs gripped his hips, the ride building toward a gallop. He had to slow her down or this would be over too quickly. He wanted this to last all night if he could. He lay back and grasped her hips with his hands, slowing her movements.

She looked down at him, her face a mirror of frustration, until he angled himself and thrust upward. She groaned and closed her eyes, letting her head loll back, her hair competing with the silk of her robe to caress his legs.

He loved controlling their ride. Deciding how far to take her before pulling back. Increasing both their desires until the room rang with their harsh breaths.

Eventually he could no more hold back his quickening thrusts than he could halt time. Evangeline gave of herself without reservation. He could feel every blissful contraction of her sheath, every quiver of her inner muscles as she rode him, her bountiful breasts bouncing delightedly above his face.

"I love being inside you," he groaned.

He knew she'd heard him, as she began to ride him faster, harder. One of her hands moved to stroke between his legs, gently squeezing the ever tightening sacs.

Their pace quickened, his thrusts deepening. Evangeline's eyes squeezed shut, her mouth issuing tiny cries of passion that made his body quiver and want to explode. But not just yet . . . not until he'd made her scream with pleasure. He wanted her to remember this night forever.

Each sumptuous stroke took them closer to that pinnacle. They moved as one, her legs gripping him tightly. He rose and took her lips, his tongue thrusting in time to his body. She was so close, he could feel her body tremble with her approaching climax. He tore his mouth away with a breathless order. "Look at me, my love. Let me see your love for me."

Her eyes opened at once, holding his storm-tossed stare as he clenched his jaw, fighting back his need to release deep within her. His grip on her hips tightened and he began to buck, thrusting wildly, their eyes locked.

"Oh, God—Evangeline! I love you, sweetheart."

They climaxed together with loud, breathless shouts of joy. Their sweating, straining bodies were slick with sweat. She collapsed in a satisfied heap on his chest, his seed still pumping deep into her womb. He pressed kisses to her hair, thanking God for giving her back to him.

Utterly spent, he fell back on the furs, pulling her into his arms as he slowly slipped from her body.

Her hands caught his shoulders. "Don't you dare leave me again! I've agreed to this plan, but you must swear to me that you'll not do anything heroic if it puts you in danger."

He stroked her hair and sighed. "Do you think I would do anything to lose this? I have you in my life, and I have our son too. I've found happiness. I have my dream. I'll not let anything destroy that."

His words were true. He hoped fate was listening.

Chapter Eighteen

"**Y**ou look beautiful."

Evangeline smiled gratefully at Marisa. Her stomach had been a buzz of nerves ever since she'd woken up and shooed Hadley from her room so she could get ready. "I feel beautiful. I can't believe this day is happening."

Marisa squeezed her hand. "Ready?"

"More than ready," she laughed.

Portia, Beatrice, Serena, and Marisa escorted her across the manicured lawns to the small chapel. Serena stopped them before they entered. She made them all hold hands in a circle.

"We are all very lucky women to have found the men we married. Now we welcome Evangeline to our midst. Hadley is one of the finest men I know. He's a good friend who holds his honor and friendships above all else. I wish you, as I have wished each of you on your wedding days, as much joy and happiness and love as I have found with Christian."

The women all smiled and wiped a few tears from their faces. Then the other four slipped into the darkened chapel, leaving Evangeline standing alone in the sunlight for a moment. She closed her eyes, a smile as wide as the vast oceans upon her lips.

She gave thanks to God for listening to her pleas. For leading her back to Hadley.

Then a small hand slipped into hers. She looked down at her son, who was watching her with curious eyes.

"Father said to come and fetch you. He says I should walk you down the aisle in case you change your mind. You won't change your mind, will you? I like having His Grace as my father."

Sealey looked so grown-up in his specially made long pants and jacket. She pressed a kiss to the top of his head.

"You look very handsome. I most definitely have not changed my mind, and I'd be honored to walk down the aisle with you."

He held out his arm as Hadley must have shown him to do, and with happiness swelling in her breast she began the walk across the stone floor of the chapel toward the altar. In the dim light she could not make out Hadley's features until she was almost beside him. He looked to be the happiest man in the world, his eyes alight with love and pride as he watched his family move toward him. He held out his hand and she took it. Then he held out his hand to Sealey, and the three of them turned to face the vicar.

As the vicar began the service, Hadley squeezed her hand and whispered, "Thank you for coming back to me."

His simple words stole her heart once more, and she could not stop the tears of happiness from welling up. The service passed in a blur of words; the next thing she knew, the grip on her hand tightened and she was turning in to his arms for a kiss as his wife.

The champagne was flowing and the joyous occasion lifted the mood in the house. Much drinking and eating and general tomfoolery occurred. It was as if everyone, including Marisa, had forgotten that Victoria was locked in the cellar below.

Later that afternoon Sealey was taken upstairs for his nap, and the Libertine Scholars and their wives settled into the drawing room.

"I'm proud to share my special day with you all, but I'm sad

Arend was not here with us." Hadley's words echoed in the quiet room.

"I've tried the gentlemanly approach with our prisoner downstairs, but she is holding firm on his whereabouts." Christian's statement brought the mood crashing down.

Marisa fairly bristled. "If you'd let me in there with her for only a minute . . ."

Hadley cleared his throat. "I had quite the conversation with her yesterday, and I believe I have found a way to bring Arend back safe and sound."

Marisa's fingers were drumming on the arm of her chair. He ignored the sound and continued.

"She says Isobel has Arend and that unless she meets Isobel at a predetermined place at a predetermined time, Arend dies." The women gasped. "In addition, she swears Isobel will continue to wreak her vengeance upon us."

Marisa jumped to her feet, her chest heaving. "She is pure evil. We have pure evil living below us. I can't stand it!"

Maitland hurried to her side and pulled her into his arms. "Shh. She can't hurt anyone where she is. Let's not react to her threats. We need clear heads if we are to defeat her." He picked his wife up and settled back onto the settee with Marisa sobbing quietly in his arms.

Hadley flashed a look at Evangeline, and she smiled encouragingly at him. "I think we have one chance at saving Arend and putting a stop to Victoria for good." He cleared his throat. "I'm proposing that we trade Victoria for Arend."

"You must be mad if you think we should let her go now that we have caught her." Maitland's tone was as cold as ice. He hugged Marisa tighter.

"I'm not suggesting we let her go. I'm suggesting we let her *think* we are letting her go."

Grayson spoke calmly. "It's too risky. She's like a slippery snake. If we're not careful, she'll slither away."

"I won't deny that's a possibility."

"Probability," Maitland muttered.

"I know it sounds stupid, but please listen," Evangeline put in. "I think Hadley's plan is very clever."

"It needs to be," Maitland growled, but he nodded to indicate he wanted to hear more.

"I will accompany her. She won't tell me the meeting point in advance, and you can't be seen to follow us. She will watch me like a hawk watches a field mouse."

"So how can we protect you, or even recapture Victoria if we have no idea where she takes you?"

"Christian, you breed homing pigeons, do you not?"

The men sat up straighter at his words.

"Yes. I find it faster to use them to send short notes between here and London." Christian began to smile. "This could work."

"I was thinking that I would put Victoria and a maid in the carriage with a guard. It would look odd if she were traveling without a lady's maid. I will ride behind on my stallion. I thought we could fashion two travel bags with air holes and keep the pigeons on my saddle. We will probably need four, as I suspect she'll zigzag across England to ensure no one is following. It wouldn't surprise me if one or more of her men know she's here and follow us."

"How will you release the pigeons without her men seeing?" Sebastian asked.

"I'll go into copses to relieve myself and let them out then. If they see birds flying out, they will likely think it's because I've frightened them. Who would suspect pigeons?"

Maitland didn't look too enthused by the plan. "How do we get to you quickly if you travel far away?"

"That's why I'll need at least four. I'll send one the second day giving you my direction. Then you all set off following me. Runners will stay here and send word each time a pigeon arrives home."

"That's good. At the most we should be only a day behind,

and on horseback we can travel faster." Maitland was warming to the possibility that this plan might succeed.

They sat in silence, each contemplating how they could protect Arend without releasing Victoria. Even Marisa seemed to know this was the only way.

"I think Hadley's plan is good. Besides, it's the only one we have, and each day that Arend is missing means he could be dead. I don't want my happiness and safety to be at the expense of Arend's life." Evangeline's quiet words had the desired effect.

Marisa gave a weak smile. "You are right, of course. I want to see her hang but I want Arend back more. What I'm struggling to believe is that Isobel is involved in her evil plan. She was genuinely frightened when we were both abducted in that carriage. We both could have been killed. Why would she put herself in that danger? Surely not to appear innocent?"

The women begin to speak at once, all of them vouching for Isobel.

Hadley held up his hands. "Please. I promise I won't form any conclusions about Isobel until I have spoken to Arend. Arend was the only one who seriously thought De Palma was Victoria. He has been pretending to court Isobel in order to ascertain her part in Victoria's plots. He will know more."

The women all looked at one another. "If she is not involved, Arend has a lot of apologizing to do" was all Marisa would say. "She would never have knowingly put Sealey in danger. I just know she wouldn't. No woman would."

"I'm sure he'd be more than happy to apologize if she's innocent, but Victoria is a clever opponent, and I for one am not taking anything about this situation for granted."

After the men all agreed to put Hadley's plan into play, Hadley sat back and smiled at his wife. *His wife.* Warmth flooded him. This was his wedding night. His friends had been there to celebrate in his joy, they had liked his plan, and his son had called him Father for the very first time this morning.

Sealey's little voice calling him Father made him want to drop to his knees, hug the boy close, and never let him go. He'd missed five years of his little boy's life. The anger in the pit of his stomach grew again, but if anything, Victoria's vendetta taught him that revenge was a wasted emotion. It didn't give him the five years back. He vowed he would not miss any more of his son's life.

He looked at his beautiful wife and also knew he wanted more children. A son to carry on the family name, as Augustus deserved, but also a little girl with flowing auburn hair and sparkling blue eyes. As if reading his mind, she smiled and blushed.

Christian noted the look. "I think our newlyweds would like to retire." He rose and shook Hadley's hand. "Thank you. Your plan is sensible and may just work. Now take your beautiful bride upstairs. We will remain and discuss the operational aspects of the plan. Let's aim for you to depart as soon as possible."

"Shall we?" He held out his arm for Evangeline. The blush on her cheeks deepened as they said their goodnights and made their way to his bedroom as husband and wife.

There were no words to describe what that phrase meant to them both.

Several hours later, Evangeline rolled over in their marriage bed. She must have dozed off. To her surprise and disappointment the bed beside her was empty. She ran her hand over the sheet and it was cold. Hadley had been gone for a while.

She sat up and looked round the dimly lit room. The only light was from the fire. A smile replaced her frown. Sitting near the fire was Hadley, naked. She loved his body, and she could look at it all day: strong, sleek, the definition of his muscles all shadowy in the light. She wanted to run her hands all over him. Her eyes finally reached his face, and what she saw there made her heart skip several beats.

"What is it?"

"You are so beautiful. I swear I will protect you this time."

Evangeline held his gaze in aching sweetness, longing to reassure him, but life did not hold any surety. Instead, she decided to take his mind to pleasanter pastimes.

"What are you doing sitting way over there?" She seductively patted the bed next to her. He had made it almost all the way back to the bed before she noted the paper in his hand. She raised an eyebrow.

"I was sketching you in your sleep. You are my sleeping beauty. The dream I never thought would come true. I want to put on canvas exactly how I feel about you because words are inadequate. I wonder how I deserve you after—"

She rose to her knees and pressed her finger to his lips. "Don't. You did not fail me. We were part of a madwoman's plan, and we were younger and oblivious to the menace that snapped at our heels. How could either of us know the depths of evil she would plumb?" She pressed against his naked chest. Her breasts were still sensitive from their bout of lovemaking earlier, and her nipples hardened. "I'm more concerned at not being able to protect you. What happens if her men overpower you? What if she has lied and Arend is already dead, and she kills you too?"

He cupped her cheek. "My love, it's not your place to protect me."

"Of course it is. We protect those we love above all else. You taught me that. How can you expect me to not want to protect my family, especially as I lost you once before?" Suddenly she added, "I want to come with you. I want to be the maid in the carriage. Then I can have a weapon trained on Victoria every step of the way."

She wound her arms round his neck and kissed him, hoping to make him let her go with him.

It only took one of his hands to peel her arms from his neck. "No. I can't risk you. If she got in a position to harm you, she'd have me at her mercy. She knows how much you mean to me. Besides, if something does happen to me, Sealey will need you. You'll need each other."

She shivered, and the reality of him leaving with a killer sunk in. She wrapped her arms round his waist. "Don't go. Send one of the others. I can't lose you a second time."

"Whom would you suggest I send? Christian, a man who almost died for his country, a father of a young baby and ward to a young girl? Or perhaps Sebastian, who is also a father after almost losing both Beatrice and his babe? Grayson, whose wife is with child? Or Maitland, who will never be able to have a child of his own, a son to hold? Having met Sealey, I finally know how that must kill him. To see Marisa hurting so . . . I can't ask him to go; he might kill Victoria before we find Arend. Of course we could simply hang her and let Arend die. Choose which one to send instead of me, Evangeline, because I can't."

She hung her head in shame. Hadley the protector was the man she married, and she loved that quality in him. Here she was making him feel guilty for leaving her when she knew if he had any choice he would choose to stay with her and Sealey.

"I'm sorry. It's just that I'm so happy right now, and I'm frightened that this is all too good to be true."

His finger lifted her chin so she had to look him in the eye. "I'm bloody well coming back to you. You and Sealey. I've only just met my son. What's more, I'll rescue Arend to boot. We will have the life Victoria stole from us. I won't waste Augustus's sacrifice."

The paper in his hand fluttered to the floor as his fingers wound in her hair and tipped her head back. He ran his lips over the soft skin of her neck, nibbling, sucking. He wanted to mark her for all to see, but refrained; instead he would let the ring on her finger do that.

"Just wait here, safe, so I know where to find you. I will be back, I swear."

She sighed, her shoulders slumping in resignation. "Make love to me, please."

"It will be my pleasure," he murmured as he pushed her down on the bed beneath him and slipped between her thighs.

Epilogue

Arend now understood what the word "black" truly meant. He could not see anything. Not his nose, fingers, legs—nothing. It was as if his eyes were blindfolded, yet he knew they were open. He felt himself blink.

He didn't need his eyesight to know where he was, though. The rock digging into his back, the dusty soot that made it difficult to breathe, and the distinctive smell all indicated he was underground. In a coal mine, to be precise.

The back of his skull throbbed like hell. He managed to prop himself upright against the rock, but his head swam and nausea rolled in his stomach. His mouth was so dry he could barely swallow.

Even if he could move, he didn't know where he was or which way to crawl. In the complete blackness he could be moving deeper into the mine; worse still, he might fall down a shaft. Anyway, his legs didn't seem to want to move at the moment.

He had no one to blame for his predicament but himself. He'd let a woman's beauty distract him, and he'd never even heard or seen his attacker coming.

"Fool," he whispered into the stale, dust-laden air.

He had fallen for the charms of a woman once before, years

ago in Africa. He'd stupidly let himself believe she had loved him, when all she'd been after was the location of his diamond mine. It had cost him his best friend's life and his faith in human nature.

It also made him wary of a woman whose beauty could turn a man's head. A beauty that could make a man want to lay down his honor and life.

Beautiful women were not to be trusted. Any woman who wanted him had to have an ulterior motive because . . . well, just because. Why else would she want him? Not for his pleasant disposition.

He tried to laugh, but all he managed was a dry, scratchy croak.

Bloody Isobel had turned his head to the point where the hunter had become the hunted. She'd played him like an expert, but then she'd learned from the best—her stepmother.

All she'd had to do was bare her breasts, and he'd salivated over her like a dog in heat. The desire that had ravaged him at one glimpse of her pert, bountiful bosom had blinded him to his foe.

He closed his eyes and cursed himself to hell.

He was *in* hell.

After a moment of self-pity he pulled himself together. He had no intention of visiting hell until he died, and he wasn't dead yet.

He had no idea how long he'd been lying in this coal mine, but from his thirst and hunger it would seem a couple of days at least.

He hoped that his friends were at this moment looking for him.

However, the past had taught him it was best to rely on no one but himself. With that in mind, he turned toward the wall and, feeling the way with his hands, slowly pulled himself up. To his surprise, he could stand upright. He was in a main shaft, then. He stood waiting for the dizziness to fade and in the silence he heard a sound that was, at this point, worth all his diamond mines combined—a trickle of water.

Want to read Arend's Story?

Read on for an excerpt from the next book in Bronwen Evans's
Disgraced Lords series:
A Night of Forever

Distrust is no match for desire as a proper young miss and a self-
professed rogue hunt down a murderer in this thrilling Disgraced
Lords novel from the USA Today bestselling author of A Kiss of
Lies and A Taste of Seduction.

Arend Aubury trusts no one besides his fellow Libertine
Scholars. After his family escaped from France, penniless and
persecuted, only the Scholars took him in. So when the stepdaughter of the villainess who has been plotting against them
approaches Arend with allegations against their enemy, he
suspects a double-cross. Yet Isobel is a tantalizing prize, with lips
as sweet as champagne and skin as creamy as Camembert. Is she a
feast for the senses—or a bitter trap?

Lady Isobel Thompson dreams of marrying an honorable
gentleman with a spotless reputation, a trait that Arend seems to
lack completely. But Isobel believes that her stepmother is responsible for her father's death, and only Arend has the skills to

uncover the truth. As a cover, Arend suggests a fake betrothal—
and soon Isobel finds herself forgetting that their courtship is a
ploy. He's so different from the man of her fantasies, and yet he's
so terribly handsome, so dangerously intoxicating—and all Isobel
wants is more.

A Night Of Forever - Chapter 1

LONDON, LADY BEAUMONT'S BALL

She wished he didn't affect her so. She couldn't understand why he made her pulse leap, her body heat, and her lips slightly part, as if in anticipation of a smile, a word, a kiss . . .

She disliked him intensely.

Yet, ever since he'd escorted her home just over a month ago, after she'd been abducted and had endured a harrowing carriage ride with Marisa, the Duchess of Claymore, she could not get Arend Aubury, Baron Labourd, out of her head.

Isobel watched him from across the room. He was dancing with Lady Evangeline, his dark head close to hers, his massive frame dominating her small one, his arm wrapped firmly around her waist, drawing her close. Isobel's insides crawled with envy. She longed to be in his arms.

Why could she not find the insipid Lord Sheridan as enticing? Or the rather portly Lord Denning? Both men were what she called nice men. Safe men. Men who would give her a boring and uneventful life. She sighed. A life with the darkly handsome and dangerous-looking Baron Labourd would not be uneventful. It would be exciting, stimulating, passionate . . .

More heat arrowed its way to her core.

She tried to look away. This was her first season, and she'd set herself the goal of finding a suitable husband—"suitable" meaning any man who would marry her by the end of the season. She was desperate to escape the clutches of her stepmother, Victoria. Unfortunately, the word "marriage" did not seem to be part of Lord Labourd's vocabulary.

Right now Victoria was talking with Lord Rotham, yet she too was watching Lord Labourd as if she'd like to gobble him up. Given that Victoria was only a few years older than her, and now widowed, Isobel was not surprised at her interest in a man as exciting as Lord Labourd.

Jealousy bit again.

He was the most virile man in the room. Was it any wonder he'd captured the undivided attention of all the women who were present? No other man stood a chance.

She wet her dry lips.

Before arriving in London for her coming out, she'd never met a man like Lord Labourd. From the moment she saw him at her first ball she was captivated by his physical attributes. Unable to drag her eyes away, Isobel tracked him as he waltzed round the ballroom, as graceful as a large black panther.

The image suited him. He looked almost leonine, except for his dark countenance. His hair was blacker than night, and his skin had an olive complexion, no doubt from his French heritage. He'd been born in France. As a young boy, his family escaped to England during the revolution.

Isobel stood on the edge of the dance floor riveted, fascinated, her lustful thoughts swirling like the dancers. Her heart was beating far too rapidly, and she felt an unmistakable warmth pool between her thighs at the primal sight of him.

"He's the one man I'd consider letting ruin me. It would be so worth it." Lady Cassandra's comment was followed by a wicked giggle.

Isobel felt her face flush with heat. "I don't know whom you are talking about."

"Of course you do. You've been practically salivating over him all evening."

"I assure you I have not."

Cassandra pretended to be shocked. "Then how do you know whom I'm talking about?"

Damn.

Cassandra continued. "He's most charmingly wicked, isn't he? The scandal sheets are always full of his wild and reckless affairs." She sighed. "He's one of England's most ineligible and unattainable catches. My mother would swoon dead away if he came to call, but oh, how I'd like one night in his arms."

He was indeed sinfully beautiful. That's what made him so dangerous. One smile could make you forget yourself.

"You and every woman in this room," she muttered under her breath. She didn't know why she said it, because she wasn't supposed to tell anyone, but jealousy made women's tongues reveal things they shouldn't. "I spent a whole day in his company, unescorted."

Cassandra looked as if she'd faint on the spot. "Never!" she all but squealed. Her voice dropped to a whisper. "Oh, you have to tell me more. What was he like? Was he a gentleman? Scrub that —of course he wasn't. What did he say to you? What did you say to him? Goodness, I need to sit down. This is about the most exciting thing that's ever happened to anyone I know."

Isobel immediately regretted her disclosure. If anyone overheard, she would be thoroughly ruined. But Cassandra was her best friend and would never betray her confidence. They had known each other since the age of thirteen, when she'd been sent to Mrs. Potter's School for Young Ladies. It had been just after her mother died, and Cassandra had shown her nothing but comfort and kindness.

As to her journey with Lord Labourd being exciting, it had in fact been excruciatingly embarrassing. He'd made it very obvious that he thought escorting her home was a total bore. On top of that, he'd interrogated her—that was the only word for it—as if the fact she'd been abducted was her fault.

"My carriage had an accident and Lord Labourd saw me home." The short version; she'd never talk about her abduction. "He was . . . an odious traveling companion. He was beautiful until he opened his mouth, and then he was simply obnoxious."

"Did he try to seduce you?"

"Goodness, no." Much to her disappointment.

"Did he tell you anything private?"

How did she tell her friend that he'd mostly ignored her completely? "That's why I've never mentioned it before. He didn't converse with me at all."

Cassandra looked deflated. "You were obviously too beautiful for him."

Had Cassandra lost her mind?

Cassandra noted her look of disbelief. "If you'd been caught alone with him, he'd have to propose. Several nights ago I overheard him telling Lord Fullerton that the one requirement he had in a wife, when he was ready to take a wife, was that she had to be plain."

Isobel shook her head. "Are you sure he said that, or was it wishful thinking? His paramours are usually the most beautiful women in all England."

"Don't be mean. I know I'm not a stunning beauty like you."

Isobel immediately put her hand on Cassandra's. "I did not mean it like that. You're just as lovely as I. But we cannot hold a candle to the *ton* beauties."

Cassandra's smile returned. "Of course we could. I also thought his comment odd. I could not hear any more of the discussion, so we will never know why."

The one hope Isobel took from this conversation was that Lord Labourd admitted he wanted to marry. She could dream, couldn't she? What would it be like married to a man as virile as he? She wasn't sure being his wife would be that much fun, especially if she lost her heart to him. She was sure he would still keep his many mistresses. How did a man who had so many females vying for his attentions deny them?

Finally the dance came to an end and she watched Lord Labourd lead Lady Evangeline from the dance floor. Disappointment surged through her. He was unlikely to dance again this evening.

She inwardly scolded herself for drooling over a man who obviously found women nothing more than disposable pursuits. No more pining, she told herself. She would find a husband from within the group of men who appeared to enjoy a woman's company, and not just in the boudoir.

She turned her back on the crowd and coaxed Cassandra into a conversation about Lady Tessa's new gown. It was the latest fashion from Paris, the neckline indecently low, but the rich, vibrant emerald silk hugged her curves and sparkled in the candlelight. Neither of them could decide whether they liked it, let alone if they'd be bold enough to wear such a gown.

A servant had just offered them another glass of champagne when Cassandra nudged her arm.

"Oh, I say. Isn't that your stepmother in conversation with Lord Labourd? They look very cozy. Do they know each other?"

Isobel swung round to where Cassandra's fan was pointing. The bones of her corset dug into her as she gasped at the sight of Victoria being very familiar with Lord Labourd. Her stepmother's hand was resting on Lord Labourd's chest, and he was studying Victoria, as Isobel imagined a shark would study its next meal.

Her stepmother, Lady Victoria Northumberland, was an enigma. There was nothing Isobel could pinpoint that set her on edge. In fact, since her father's death eighteen months ago, Victoria had been anything other than the mean stepmother. Perhaps it was the fact she had not seemed particularly sad, or indeed surprised, when her father died. Given that he'd died in a suspicious fire, that fact unsettled Isobel.

There was a disturbing coldness about Victoria. She always appeared to be full of gaiety, but her eyes lacked warmth, and she was impossible to read. Isobel always looked for an ulterior motive whenever Victoria did anything.

She managed to stutter, "I—I didn't think they'd been formally introduced."

"Perhaps their relationship is more informal." Cassandra raised one of her beautifully shaped eyebrows. "She *is* a widow, and I would not blame her for seeking amusements with a man like Lord Labourd. I don't mean to be rude, but your father was rather old."

The idea of Victoria and Lord Labourd being lovers made Isobel want to walk over there and scratch Victoria's eyes out. She had to force her fists to uncurl at her sides. Though she hated to admit it, if Lord Labourd was likely to have an affair with anyone, it would be a merry widow. A young virgin debutante would make him run fast and far.

Just when she thought the night couldn't get any worse, the pair turned and looked her way. Victoria was gesturing with her hand and laughing. It was obvious they were discussing her, and Isobel wished the ballroom floor would suddenly splinter beneath her feet and she'd disappear in a cloud of dust.

Instead, she watched, spellbound, caught in Lord Labourd's hypnotic gaze, as Victoria's hand ran down his chest, lower, lower . . . Isobel gasped, watching her stepmother's fingers brush his groin. Then Victoria moved away from him, leaving him staring straight at Isobel with an intensity that made it seem as if she was some puzzle for him to solve.

She tried to catch her breath and move, because . . .

"Goodness. He's coming this way. He's coming for you."

Isobel both feared and hoped Cassandra's words were true. As Lord Labourd prowled closer, all she could think was *Don't faint. Dear God, don't let me faint.*

Lord Labourd had known someone was watching him as he danced with Evangeline. There was nothing unusual in that.

Women wanted him for his looks, and men wanted him for his money. He'd used his sixth sense and ascertained that his voyeurs were none other than Lady Isobel—and her stepmother, Victoria.

He was sure the villainess who'd been hunting him and his friends was Victoria. He just had to prove it.

Victoria had taunted him this evening, their conversation full of double entendres. She'd snidely played devil's advocate regarding Isobel, almost as if she wanted him to investigate her stepdaughter.

Both of them were engaged in the dance of intrigue. What he didn't know was whether young, virginal-looking Isobel was involved. He hoped to hell she was, because on the dance floor he could feel her eyes upon him as if they were her fingers. And he'd liked it.

If he could seduce her, he might learn the answers he sought. Best of all, he might gain the evidence he needed to stop Victoria before she hurt any more of the people he loved.

From across the room Arend peered through his lowered eyelids at Isobel. She stood next to another of this year's pretty debutantes, deep in conversation, trying to pretend she wasn't watching him. Even now she was still staring at him as if fascinated.

It annoyed him to admit she was a beauty. He'd been trying to ignore the throbbing awareness she caused within his loins whenever he saw her. With her delicate, fine-boned face, flawless ivory skin, and womanly curves, she only had to smile to arouse him. Her blue gown flattered her slender, shapely figure, and he tried not to focus on her firm, high breasts, raising his gaze to her face instead.

She wore her rich dark hair pinned up in an elaborate style, pearls woven into the soft curls. He wondered what the thick tresses would feel like against his naked skin. The thought jarred him out of his sensual haze. She could be the enemy.

She looked so young and innocent, but he knew how deceptive a woman's looks could be.

A beautiful woman had killed his friend, and almost killed him, all for greed. He'd thought she'd loved him, but she'd loved another, a man who almost took everything from him.

The woman had made a mistake. She'd shown her true colors too soon. He'd have quite happily married her, and his diamond mines would have been hers anyway. He was thankful he hadn't. He probably would have been knifed to death in his sleep.

And now, again, he was dealing with another evil bitch. What he wanted to know was, who was aiding Victoria? How did she know their every move?

Ever since he'd accompanied Lady Isobel home after the carriage accident that almost cost Marisa her life, he'd had his suspicions. Why had Isobel been kidnapped too? She had nothing to do with the Libertine Scholars and the enemy vendetta they faced. Was Isobel a spy? Had she been placed in that carriage so they would discount her involvement, and then Isobel could freely feed Victoria information?

His feet moved slowly toward his target, his eyes never leaving her face. When she finally locked gazes with him, the impact made him feel an instantaneous heat—an unwanted physical response, one he thought he'd taught himself to ruth-lessly control. He refused to be hostage to a beautiful woman's charms.

To his satisfaction he wasn't the only one affected. She had stiffened at his approach, looking wary and unsettled, the flush upon her face revealing that all her feminine instincts were on keen alert. He watched her shiver, and damn it to hell he felt a response. He could feel himself hardening, all his male instincts roaring to vibrant life.

As he reached her side he heard her quick, indrawn breath. Oh, yes, she'd be ripe for the plucking. She was already under his spell, and he'd not even turned on the charm.

To seduce her would be easy, enjoyable, and bloody dangerous.

For the first time in a very long time, his body was wound

tighter than a drum for a woman he should not want with such ferocity.

"Good evening, Lady Isobel."

She glanced round, as if looking for someone, anyone, to save her from the big bad wolf, before finally saying, "Good evening, my lord."

Was he mistaken, or had she stepped closer to her friend? Her low, husky voice sent a further charge of heat along his nerve endings.

She pretended to be calm. "May I present my friend Lady Cassandra?"

He took Cassandra's hand in his and in his most seductive French accent said, "*Enchanté*, mademoiselle."

Lady Cassandra stood, blinking, staring at him.

He turned back to Isobel. "May I have the pleasure of this dance, Lady Isobel?"

Her eyes narrowed. "Did my stepmother put you up to this?"

Time to dazzle. He gave her one of his most seductive smiles and took her gloved hand, running his thumb over her palm. "No. I spied you from across the room and did not wish to miss the chance to dance with the most beautiful woman in here."

To his surprise, her prickly demeanor did not melt.

"I'm sorry, but my dance card is full."

She was lying. He knew that, and she knew he knew that, or else her partner would be here asking for his turn on the floor.

Annoyance flickered. She'd expect him to do the polite thing and bow out. Well, she had a lot to learn about him, and she might as well start learning now.

He looked round. "It would appear your partner has been detained," he said, and held out his arm. If she wished not to cause a scene, she could do little but take it.

To his dismay, she bested him. She smiled sweetly and said, "I'm sorry, Lord Labourd, but I'm sure you'll understand that I cannot accept your kind invitation. My feet are sore—new slippers, I'm afraid. However," she said, turning to her friend, "I'm sure Lady Cassandra will be my savior and partner you instead. Since you seem so keen to dance."

The defiance in her gaze, in her stance, was a challenge incarnate. She might have won this battle, but she would not win this war. Too many people's lives depended on his success—lives of people he cared about. And since he had no family left, he would claw through the devil's own flames to protect his friends.

This would be a most challenging seduction, he thought. A jolt of pure desire sizzled through Arend at the prospect of pitting his wits against hers.

He took a step toward her, so their bodies were touching. He felt her tremble. It annoyed him at how just this slight touch aroused him so swiftly.

Isobel pushed Cassandra forward, causing him to step back. Her friend was too thunderstruck to object. And that was how he found himself escorting the wrong debutante onto the dance floor.

Arend bit the inside of his cheek to stop a curse from issuing forth.

He would unearth Isobel's secrets, but more crucially, he would find the evidence they needed to stop Victoria—or he'd die trying.

READ MORE

FREE Novella - A Lady Never Concedes

I 've a FREE short novella to introduce my SISTERHOOD OF SCANDAL series - A LADY NEVER CONCEDES.

I hope you enjoy meeting the ladies.

Lord Julian Montague, the second son of the Marquess of Lorne has been Miss Serena Fancot's best friend since childhood. When Julian starts talking about taking a wife, Serena is very aware they are no longer children.

Why does she suddenly notice just how lovely his dimples are and how tall and handsome he is? His clothes fit him like a tight glove and he has a body to rival Apollo. Suddenly, she can't help but notice how the women in society's ballrooms drool over him.

Worse still, he's not once tried to kiss her, or hold her hand, or whispered words of love in her ear. Does he not see her as the love of his life? Has she left it too late to make Julian realize he is the only man she'd ever wish to marry? Has she left it too late to show him he's the love of her life? That won't do. But how do you make your best friend fall in love with you?

Grab your FREE copy

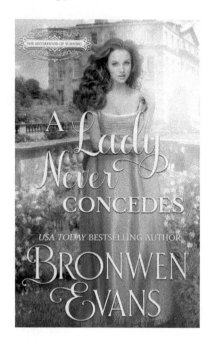

Dedication

For my dear friend, Tim Simpson, who is courageously fighting his personal villain, and I'm praying he kicks arse.

Acknowledgments

People appear genuinely interested when I say I'm a romance author. Usually they talk about what fun that must be, and it is! But it's also hard work. Not just for me, but for everyone who helps a story see the light of day.

I'm one of the fortunate writers who have a lot of support around me. My wonderful agent, Sarah Younger at the Nancy Yost Literary Agency, puts up with my nerves and doubts. I owe Gina Conkle a debt (probably quite a few drinks at the next RWA conference) for the introduction. My fabulous copy-editor Ray Collet, and my talented cover designer Barbara at Forever After Romance Designs.

Then there is my writing support crew: Kendra DeLuga, Jackie Rutherford, Angela Bissell, Rachel Collins and my wonderful sister, Leigh. You guys keep me sane. To my beta readers and fellow historical book lovers who are happy to read and give me feedback, I am always so very grateful.

Of course, I have to thank my family and friends for putting up with me when I'm stressed, either because I'm late with a book or because it's not going well against my plotted-to-the-nth-degree plan. I must be hell to live with. I know you put up with me turning down many invitations because I have to write, yet you still keep inviting me along.

Lastly, I have to thank the most important people in this process, the readers. I am always humbled and grateful that readers want to read my stories, and I hope they love them as much as I do. It's nerve-wracking waiting for feedback, but I learn from all of it, and I think it makes my next story stronger. Without readers I'd have no one to share my stories with, and then I would be sad.

If you would like to keep up with all my releases, sales, and other news, join Bron's Book club. Anyone signing up receives a *free* ebook.

About the Author

USA Today Bestselling author Bronwen Evans is a proud romance writer. She has always indulged her love of storytelling and is constantly gobbling up movies, books, and theatre. Is it any wonder she's a proud romance writer? Evans is a three-time winner of the RomCon Readers' Crown and has been nominated for a RT Reviewers' Choice Award. She lives in the Hawke's Bay, New Zealand with her two Cavoodles, Brandy and Duke.

www.bronwenevans.com

Thank you so much for coming along on this journey. If

you'd like to keep up with my other releases, specials or news, feel free to join my newsletter and receive a FREE book too.

Also by Bronwen Evans

Bron's Book List

Historical Romances

Wicked Wagers

To Dare the Duke of Dangerfield – book #1

To Wager the Marquis of Wolverstone – book #2

To Challenge the Earl of Cravenswood - book #3

Wicked Wagers, The Complete Trilogy Boxed Set

The Disgraced Lords

A Kiss of Lies – Jan 2014

A Promise of More – April 2014

A Touch of Passion – April 2015

A Whisper of Desire – Dec 2015

A Taste of Seduction – August 2016

A Night of Forever – October 2016

A Love To Remember – August 2017

A Dream Of Redemption – February 2018

Imperfect Lords Series

Addicted to the Duke – March 2018

Drawn To the Marquess – September 2018

Attracted To The Earl – February 2019

Taming A Rogue Series

Lord of Wicked (also in a German Translation)

Lord of Danger (also in a German Translation)

Lord of Passion

Lord of Pleasure (Christmas Novella)

The Lady Bachelorette Series

The Awakening of Lady Flora – Novella

The Seduction of Lord Sin

The Allure of Lord Devlin

Sisterhood of Scandal Series

A Lady Never Concedes - FREE short story

A Lady Never Surrenders

Invitation To Series Audio Only (now called Taming A Rogue series)

Invitation to Ruin

(Winner of RomCon Best Historical 2012, RT Best First Historical 2012 Nominee)

Invitation to Scandal

(TRR Best Historical Nominee 2012)

Invitation to Passion

July 2014

(Winner of RomCon Best Historical 2015)

Invitation To Pleasure

Novella February 2020

Contemporaries

The Reluctant Wife

(Winner of RomCon Best Short Contemporary 2014)